In the
Court's Hands

In the
Court's Hands

Fiona Gartland

POOLBEG
CRIMSON

Published 2018 by Crimson
an imprint of Poolbeg Press Ltd
123 Grange Hill, Baldoyle
Dublin 13, Ireland
www.poolbeg.com

1

A catalogue record for this book is available from the British Library.

ISBN 978-1-78199-802-1

f www.facebook.com/poolbegpress
@PoolbegBooks
poolbegbooks

Printed and bound by CPI Group (UK) Ltd, Croydon, CR0 4YY

www.poolbeg.com

About the author

Fiona Gartland has been a journalist with *The Irish Times* for 13 years and has covered many trials at the Criminal Courts of Justice. She was shortlisted for the Francis McManus Short Story competition on half a dozen occasions, has had stories broadcast and has been published in magazines.

She lives in Dublin with her husband and four children.

Acknowledgements

Thank you to everyone at Poolbeg Press, especially Paula and Caroline for their kindness. Thanks to editor Aoife Barrett for her painstaking attention to detail and clarity of mind, and to Gwen Malone Stenography, the unwitting inspiration for this novel.

Thank you to my sisters and brothers for their support, practical help and encouragement, and to my children who sent me off to write when I was procrastinating, made me tea and helped in so many ways. Thanks also to my Dad, who is sorely missed and at whose writing desk I work.

Finally thank you to my husband Paul, for all his love and care over the years, and for believing in me.

To my family, here and no longer here,
for all their encouragement and help

Chapter 1

Friday, 25th April 2014

If it had rained on the 25th of April at least one woman would not have died. Not that I bear any responsibility for that. Nothing I did intentionally caused anyone's death – though the fact remains, people did die.

It began with an innocent change of plan. I'd intended eating at the office, but the sun was so bright by one o'clock, and the Phoenix Park looked so attractive in its spring costume, that I decided to leave the Dublin Criminal Courts of Justice and take my lunch with me.

People have said to me how envious they are of the view from my office window in the glass cylinder that is the country's newest and tallest court building. I can see the Wellington Monument, a nineteenth-century granite obelisk, rising from the park. "Wonderful," they say, "so tranquil, so picture-postcard", and the monument is "powerful" and "inspiring". To me though, that phallic symbol is a reminder of the things I do not have.

I visited the ladies' toilets before I left, to tidy my chignon. As I re-pinned it, I frowned at the roots beginning to show up the red dye; no matter how hard hairdressers try, they can never match my original shade. Still, it's better than conceding to the ribbons of grey.

I reached into my handbag and dabbed a little extra make-up on. Fair skin, prone to freckling, becomes more vulnerable with time and I like to protect my vulnerabilities. I smoothed down my Size 14 pencil skirt and congratulated myself again on the cut of the navy jacket.

I took the glass elevator to the ground floor – some of my colleagues take the stairs, their vertigo a constant torture to them. I like to stand at the back of the transparent lift so that I can watch the cream triangles of the marble foyer rush toward me.

If it weren't for the security checks at the entrance, the Criminal Courts of Justice or CCJ, with its pleasing circular walls, sweeping staircase and neat reception desk, could be confused with a spartan, well-designed hotel. It's won all kinds of architectural awards and yet it is simply a place for processing criminals.

I nodded to Mike the security manager. He had an earpiece in his left ear, index finger pressed against it, making him look like he was communicating about a serious security breach. We both knew he'd actually agreed to take two sugars in his skinny latte.

Outside, I turned right, up toward the gates of the Phoenix Park. I've heard it described as Europe's largest walled park in a city. How we struggle on this little island to have the largest something.

I walked up Chesterfield Avenue in the centre of the park and chose a bench beneath a chestnut tree that was already almost in full leaf. The dappled shadows gave pleasant shade from the sun, yet held its warmth. I unpacked my lunch, of goat's cheese and rocket on focaccia bread, and opened my bottle of sparkling water. I was pleased with my decision to take the air. I find food always tastes better outside. I chewed slowly, relishing the richness of the cheese and the bite of the rocket.

It was then I saw him on the opposite side of the wide road, sitting on a bench the mirror of mine. He had that way some men have of dominating the space, with his arms outstretched along the back of the bench and his legs wide apart. He was wearing the blue-grey suit I had seen on him so many times in court, on this occasion with a pink shirt and dark blue tie. His silver hair, abundant and with a wave, was pushed back from his forehead. It was Stephen O'Farrell – the accused in the high-profile Signal Investment case.

I took another mouthful and wondered if he could see me. I felt that even if he could he would not recognise me. Few people notice the stenographer.

As I watched, from his left, a woman approached. He sat up straight, ran his fingers through his hair, folded his arms and brought his knees together. She sat beside him – a slight woman of indeterminate age, with a sharp nose and a red, A-line skirt, too short for her shapeless legs.

They did not greet each other or even appear to make eye contact, but not long after she sat down, he glanced around him, reached into the inside pocket of his jacket and took something out. It looked to me like an envelope. He passed it to her, and she placed it in her handbag. They made no eye contact, but words were exchanged. She nodded, stood up and walked away.

I watched her as she made her way toward the centre of the park. Before the Phoenix Monument, she got into a car. When I looked back at the bench, its occupant had gone.

I had been the stenographer on Stephen O'Farrell's case for weeks and had become accustomed to the terms used in the world of investments and property – flipping, options and acquisition fees. That's what happens in my business, you learn a new language with each new case. On my next assignment, I could be back to asphyxiation or induced myocardial infarction. There are other things I hear too. The words come out of my fingertips, but I try very hard to ensure that they do not lodge in my brain. Other courtroom participants get counselled when they've had to listen to disturbing experiences, but not stenographers. We are merely the vessels through which experiences flow, to come out on a transcript in 12-point Times New Roman.

When I'd finished my lunch, I packed up the detritus, put a stick of dental chewing gum in my mouth and walked back to the courts. I don't care much for gum, and baulk at the sight of other people masticating like farm animals, but my dentist recommended it post-meal. I chewed rapidly, mouth closed, before depositing it in tissue paper in the bin.

I would be lying if I said I didn't speculate on the encounter I'd witnessed. A romantic meeting? Hardly, unless the lack of physical contact was a disguise for hidden passions. It certainly wasn't his wife. I had seen her sitting at the back of the court, perfectly coiffured and in a beautifully cut dress and jacket, elegant and understated – Louise Kennedy probably. She was at least fifteen years his junior. I supposed it could have been a member of his staff, though the deference I'm sure he would have required seemed absent. I decided it was better to put the meeting out of my mind. It was ten minutes to two, just enough time for me to reapply a layer of lipstick in the bathroom and take up my position in Court 19 on the sixth floor. Judge Reginald Brown was nothing if not punctual. He'd said he would be ready to begin again at exactly ten past two and he would be.

To him, at least, I am not invisible. And he sometimes takes the trouble to stop a barrister in mid-flow to remind him to speak up, so I can hear. He is among the few judges that retain the wig since it became optional. A handful of barristers continue wearing it too. Judge Brown seemed undecided about his wig: wearing it in the morning, taking it off most afternoons and frequently slipping his hand between wig and head to scratch his scalp.

My powers of concentration are immense, but when they wane, my colleague Janine Gracefield takes over. Janine is a reliable sort, despite her youth and relative inexperience. She is in her early thirties, a slight person, with fair hair and the delicacy of a fawn. We have worked together for five years and have become friends.

At five minutes past two, I settled myself in my spot, visible but invisible, from where I could survey the entire courtroom. I find it amusing that, although the new criminal courts were designed for the twenty-first century, they hold on to the eighteenth-century structures of the older Four Courts. The highest bench is reserved for the judge, to the judge's right, one level down is the witness box and, below that, the place where the defendant sits. To the left is the jury. The registrar and assistants sit below the judge on the same level as the witness box. This is where I am, placed discreetly to one side. Solicitors are lower down again and sit facing the body of the court, with a long table between them and Senior Counsel. The next row is for juniors and the benches beyond are for the press and public.

The legal teams get cushions under their rumps, while the rabble must endure the hardwood of bare benches. The privileged must always have their comforts. I cannot complain of course, since I have a decent chair, with a straight, supportive back and comfortable cushion, with space for the stenograph to rest neatly between my knees.

I watched as the different parties made their way into the courtroom.

Leona O'Brien, Senior Counsel for the prosecution, walked calmly in, with her team scurrying around her. I'd worked at her cases many times before and we'd become friends. She'd been the talk of the Law Library when she'd had her baby, Grace, that January, after fifteen years of childless marriage. I'd overheard hushed discussions about how motherhood would spoil Leona's chances of progressing to the judicial appointment she'd looked destined for. I hoped they were wrong.

Her daughter kept her awake at night, she'd told me but, with her blonde bob neatly clipped and curling perfectly just below her ears, she still looked fresher than Raymond Rafferty, Senior Counsel for Stephen O'Farrell. He strolled into court, kicking the ends of his black gown out before him – an old-school, barrel-shaped barrister. His black, slicked-back hair, accentuated an open-pored nose, tinged with the plum colour of a drinker.

The media took up two rows and the public filled out the remaining seats. There was a knot of court watchers, mostly men, retired or unemployed. I had seen them rubbing their chins and nodding to each other in appreciation of a cogent point, occasionally allowing themselves a short laugh at one of Rafferty's witty flourishes.

"All rise," the judge's assistant intoned, and the room got to its feet.

Judge Brown smiled, sat and nodded at the jury minder. The twelve jurors entered, stage left.

I had become fond of this jury. They'd sat through six weeks of evidence already, some of it technical, much of it dull, yet most of them had remained awake. There were two jurors, a man and a woman, who struggled to keep their eyes open in the afternoons, succumbing, no doubt, to the lunchtime meat and two veg; while another two, both men, sat forward in their seats and took copious notes. It is often the way with juries – there are one or two at each end of the enthusiasm spectrum, with the remainder in the middle. They generally reach predictable verdicts, though once in a rare while they go astray in a way that makes me wonder if they've been infected with outside influence.

Leona O'Brien got to her feet.

"The next witness is George Reilly," she said.

"Very good," the judge responded.

A man in a blue double-breasted suit, straining at its buttons, made his way to the witness box and the afternoon's evidence began.

When court is over for the day, I generally go back to the office and work through my transcript for rare, typographical errors. On this occasion, I had an appointment with my hairdresser, so Janine agreed to stay behind and carry out the necessary work.

"Bea," she said, "there's no need to apologise. I owe you one from last Friday."

She did.

"I wouldn't ask, only it's a special occasion," she'd said. "It's Alastair's birthday and I want everything to be just perfect for him."

Alastair was her boyfriend, or perhaps partner is the correct term, since they've moved in together.

"We have a reservation at Chapter One," she'd told me. It was one of the city's few Michelin-starred restaurants. "Alastair likes good food."

I'd met Dr Alastair McAuliffe only once, when I'd called over to Janine's apartment to collect a transcript she'd brought home to work on, after a particularly long day in court. The forty-two-year-old had the excellent bone structure Janine had so enthusiastically described to me, with the chestnut-brown hair of a young Sean Connery, as well as the accent.

"So, this is Beatrice," he'd said, as he shook hands with me. He'd smiled with his head to one side, as though he was viewing a patient or a specimen.

The way he looked at me made me feel foolish. Many medics have a habit of doing that – it's a kind of condescension that I expect is bred into them during training.

Without taking his eyes from me, he said, "You've been a stenographer for some time, I believe." His accent was Edinburgh soft, rolling on his Rs. "Janine says you're the best in the business."

"Janine would say Mass," I responded, joking.

He hesitated before deciding to release a short, dry laugh. Janine squeezed his arm, delighted.

"Well, thanks for this," I'd said, putting the transcript under my arm. "I'll see you at work." I was glad to get away – Dr Alastair McAuliffe made me feel uncomfortable, as though I'd been peered at through a microscope.

The following day, when Janine asked if I liked him, I said he was every bit as handsome as she'd described. She was so pleased, she didn't notice the evasion. I was sorry that I hadn't warmed to him. Janine had a good heart and, if she was fond of him, Alastair had to have something. I promised myself I'd try harder the next time we met.

It was unusual for me to find myself leaving the CCJ just after four o'clock on a weekday, at the same time as the jurors and witnesses.

The forewoman, a twenty-something with a hungry face, exited beside me and I saw, ahead, the heavyset man who sat in the back row of the jury box. We were all making our way toward the Luas tram stop to get into the city centre. The forewoman, a neat, thin person who appeared every morning with her long brown hair firmly controlled in a ponytail, was beside him. They turned at the traffic lights to cross over the Liffey and catch the tram at Heuston Station. I walked further on to the stop outside Collins Barracks, which I preferred.

As I approached the stop, the ding of a bell told me a tram was approaching. I could hear the Luas woman intoning "Museum: Ard-Mhúsaem". I pressed the door button and got on.

I took a seat beside a young man, too skinny for his tracksuit, with the pallor of heroin on him. A few seats up I noticed the jury forewoman, who must have got on at Heuston. She was facing toward me, with her back to the driver. A woman in a red skirt was standing beside her, bent towards her a little as she spoke. I couldn't place her at first, but then I recognised the sharpness of the features, the unattractive legs. She was the woman who'd met O'Farrell in the park. She put her hand on the juror's shoulder.

"Smithfield: Margadh na Feirme," the tram-voice said.

The doors of the carriage opened and the woman in the red skirt got out. I noticed as she passed me outside that she glanced in the window, looked away and looked in again. A line developed between her brows.

At that moment, I believed she recognised me and I felt uneasy and frightened, though I was not sure why. I looked quickly away as the doors of the carriage closed, and the tram slid on.

Chapter 2

Sunday, 18th January 1981

The rain hit the window at an angle, carried on a strong north-westerly wind. It was four o'clock and the bedroom was in semi-darkness. We hadn't got out of bed all day. At least Leo hadn't. I'd been into the kitchen to make us breakfast and then lunch.

The radio was on. 'Woman' was playing and Leo, sitting up in bed, was singing it at me. His two arms were stretched out straight in front, the blankets at his waist.

"I'm sick of that song," I said.

The newspapers had been full of the gunning down of the pacifist musician before Christmas. They'd released 'Woman' after Lennon's death and the stations kept on playing it, over and over again.

I carried two mugs of coffee across the room. Leo took them from me, put them on the bedside locker and pulled me toward him.

"I can't believe you missed Mass, Bea."

It was our first time to spend the entire weekend together. On Saturday, we'd gone to Glendalough and then Leo had got us reservations for dinner at Le Coq Hardi in Ballsbridge.

"Are you trying to impress me?" I'd asked, doing my best not to sound impressed. It was Dublin's most exclusive restaurant, a place my parents had only read about in the newspapers. I'd fussed over what to wear, anxious not to let Leo down. I'd finally settled on a green floral-print dress, tight at my small waist, and piled my red hair up into a soft bun.

"You look sweet," he'd said, and I'd thanked him, though I'd been trying for sophisticated.

The rain on Sunday morning had put an end to any plans for another outing. I wasn't sorry.

Leo kissed me on the mouth, his lips sweet and firm.

"What would your mother say if she found out?" His grin showed the sharp white points of his eye teeth and accentuated his square jaw.

I punched him gently on the shoulder. "You're a bad influence."

My parents wouldn't have approved of my missing Mass or of anything else about that day. Mother would take one look at Leo, with his broad shoulders under his double-breasted suit, and his dark hair pushed back from his forehead, and lecture me about older men. Father might take him aside and ask him, man to man, to leave quietly. And the idea of me taking him into my bed would horrify them. They clung to their 1950s' morality like a sinking ship. But this was 1981 and their rules didn't apply to me anymore.

Neither Mother nor Father had siblings, and their parents had passed away long before my brother and then I arrived. The two of them were late to marriage. When I was growing up, I thought it made them too careful. I used to envy classmates whose packed, busy homes I visited. Their families seemed carefree and filled with fun. I would return to my mother in our neat and quiet living room, with the cushions plumped and perfectly positioned on the settee, and

I'd want to toss them all on the floor. I never did, of course. When other parts of my life were in chaos, I even appreciated the calm sense of order in our house. And the love there too, though it was never spoken. My parents had been baffled by my decision to take a flat in the city centre after I got a job in Melmount Secretarial, instead of remaining with them.

"But why, Beatrice? You're only nineteen and you've only just started that job," was all my mother could say back in March when I'd told her I was moving out and had found a flat. She'd always assumed I'd stay at home until I found a suitable man to marry. My older brother Laurence hadn't moved out and there was no sign of him finding a girl.

"Because it's what women do now."

I was patient with them, explaining how convenient it would be for me and how I'd learn those domestic skills my mother so valued.

"But won't you be lonely?"

"I'll be fine."

What I'd meant was that I longed to be alone, to run my life my own way, without answering to anyone.

"I can't see the wisdom in that at all," was my father's contribution.

"Even so, I'm going." I used my firmest voice and looked directly at him.

He'd stared at me for a few moments, then got up from the table, walked into the sitting room and turned on the television.

They couldn't have stopped me, but a part of me still wanted their approval, so when my father had agreed to drive me and my belongings to the new flat I was pleased and relieved.

It was a small place on the third floor of a Georgian building on Westland Row.

"That's not practical," he'd said, waving in the direction

of the pay phone in the hall. He'd urged me to put my name down for a private telephone. "What if you have to get up late at night and come down to take a call?" He'd almost shuddered at the thought of me creeping downstairs in my nightclothes. "And every dog and divil will be able to hear what you're saying."

I'd promised that I would get on to the phone company, though I knew I'd be waiting for months.

I loved my three-roomed flat, even if it wasn't exactly up to my parents' standards. Father had been shocked when he saw the paper peeling from the walls of the living room. His brow had furrowed at the sight of what passed for my kitchen. He'd switched the cooker on and off again.

"Do you hear that buzzing? That's not safe." As he'd opened the small fridge, its interior light had flickered and gone out and a sour-milk smell had filled the flat.

"It only needs cleaning out," I'd said.

"It needs an electrician. You're not to use any of these until I get Mick to check out the wiring."

I'd nodded.

"He can fit electric heaters while he's here, too. I'm not having you breathing in the gas from that Superser, and where's your dinner table?"

I'd pointed at the red, formica-topped table, folded up and leaning against the wall. There were three folded metal chairs beside it.

He tutted. "It'll do, I suppose, since it's just yourself."

Mick had arrived the day after I'd moved in, fixed the wiring and fit two heaters.

"Just make sure you don't overload the sockets, or you'll blow a fuse," he'd warned.

I'd painted the walls and reglued the peeling paper. I loved the high ceilings, the plaster cornices and ceiling roses that remained from the house's earlier, grander days. Every time I put my hands on the thick window frame, to look out at the busy street below, I imagined the well-to-do Georgian woman who must have been mistress of the house at one time. She'd have stood in my position, her feet on the same floor, her hands touching the same moulded wood. It thrilled me that I was in her place now, mistress of my own home.

My father had raised an eyebrow at the sight of the double bed in the bedroom. Though he passed no comment, I told him it came with the flat and it'd be a waste to throw it out and buy a single one. I was delighted with it – I bought a colourful quilt, pillows and cushions. I immediately started sleeping in the centre of it and discovered the luxury of breakfast in bed with the Sunday newspaper spread out on the quilt all around me. I felt like the queen of my own little castle, with the centre of Dublin on my doorstep.

I'd been living in the flat six months when I met Leo Hackett.

I was at a restaurant with friends from work. We'd had some wine and I was almost overcome with my own sophistication. I told the girls I needed to powder my nose, and they all laughed at me.

On my way back from the ladies' toilets, he bumped into me, his shoulder just grazing my ear. I looked up into his face and saw the most beautiful sky-blue eyes looking down at me.

"I'm so sorry, are you all right?" he asked.

"Fine, really." The words came out in a high pitch and I blushed. He briefly placed his fingers on the top of my arm, and I felt the tingle of an electric shock.

"You're looking a bit flushed Bea," one of my friends said when I got back to the table and the others laughed.

"Shut up."

When we were leaving the restaurant, he reappeared and asked if he could call me. I agreed without hesitation and gave him my number.

On our first date, he came to my apartment with a bunch of freesias. He stood in the doorway, his left shoulder leaning against the frame, with his left foot crossed over his right one, hands in his pockets. He watched as I filled a vase with water and placed the flowers in it. His gaze filled me with embarrassment and excitement.

When I sat into his car, he paused before starting the engine.

"The first thing you need to know about me is that I'm not the marrying kind." He spoke firmly, and I felt he was scanning my face for reaction. "You should leave right now if that matters to you."

"Aren't you taking yourself very seriously for a first date? And anyway, what makes you think I want to be shackled to any man?"

He drove me to the Glenview Hotel in Delgany for lunch. I had vegetable soup and lamb. He ordered egg mayonnaise and pork chops, with apple rings. He was so relaxed being waited on. I wasn't used to it and worried I might fail some test I wasn't even aware of.

"This is a long way to come for lunch. Are you trying to hide me?" I'd been joking but he'd lowered his eyes to the table and it was then I knew there was another woman. I considered making a dramatic exit, snatching my handbag from the back of my chair, turning from him in righteous anger. But then there was the transport problem and my distinct lack of indignation. We were only having a meal, I reasoned, and when it was over I could let him leave me home and then firmly say goodbye. It'd be better than making a scene.

"I'm not married or anything, but it's complicated."

I wondered what complication there might be to prevent a man leaving someone he wasn't married to.

"Have you a child?" That would be appalling, I thought.

"God, no."

I put down my knife and fork, took a sip of the red wine he'd ordered and waited.

"We've, me and Angie, we've been together for a while and she's a really good person, but vulnerable, you know what I mean?"

I said I did, and thought of my mother's friend, Louisa, a wisp of a woman Mother said would blow away in a light breeze.

"Things haven't been right between us for a while. Neither of us is happy. But, well, I'm just waiting for her to realise that . . . I don't think she could take it if it came from me." He spoke in a low voice that threatened to break at any moment.

I imagined a fragile woman, clinging to her own unhappiness and understood why Leo was unwilling to hurt her. I could see the pain in his eyes as he spoke about her and I was filled with pity for him.

"I promise after I leave you home tonight, I won't call you again – unless you want me to."

"Well, let's just enjoy our meal," I said, picking up my cutlery.

Later, when he dropped me home and whispered close to my ear that I was beautiful and made a gentle request to see me again, I said yes.

I let him take me to bed two weeks later. It was the easiest thing in the world. I didn't care that he knew it was my first time or that he'd be getting dressed and going back to another woman afterwards. It was lovely and awkward and tender and passionate. He was gentle with my ignorance.

Afterwards, he talked about Angie and how he had to be patient with her, and how I mustn't expect too much.

"She's the emotionally dependent type," he'd told me with a sigh.

I felt sorry for him and was determined not to be emotionally dependent. I would simply enjoy the fun, I told myself. And I had.

Now, three months later, getting back into bed with Leo, rain splattering the window, I was afraid I was becoming just that – emotionally dependent. I didn't know how to stop myself.

"How's Angie?" I asked, hating myself for bringing her up.

He sighed. "Why now, Bea, when we're having such a nice time?"

He kissed me on the nape of my neck and his lips were warm from the coffee. I knew that it meant nothing had changed and he'd go back to her tonight. I knew he'd promised me nothing and I'd no right to have any expectations, but I couldn't help myself.

"Where will you say you've been all this time?"

He stopped kissing me and sat back against the pillows.

"Come on now, don't do this. You know you don't need to do this."

"You don't understand how I feel." I could hear the pitch in my voice growing shrill and tried to control it. "It gets to me sometimes, to think of you with her. Do you . . . do you do it still?"

He didn't respond. I was ashamed of myself.

"It's just, I really thought . . ."

"What? What did you think?" His brief flash of anger was replaced by exasperation. "I've always been honest with you."

"I know you have. I know you have."

"And haven't we everything we need here?"

I nodded.

"Forget about everything outside this room."

As he dropped his voice to a low purr, I really wanted to forget. He stroked the skin on my shoulders and ran his fingertips along my collarbone. The signet ring on his little finger glinted in the fading light.

"Look at you," he said, kissing me gently where his fingers had been.

I brushed the kisses away.

"But it's torture."

He turned away and stared out at the rain.

"If I could leave her tomorrow I would. She's too fragile – you know that."

I knew it was true. He'd told me many times that she'd threatened suicide if he left her.

"She can't keep you a prisoner forever."

I felt like digging my nails into his lean, bare stomach to communicate my misery.

He looked at me, his eyes filled with sadness and compassion.

"I couldn't live with myself if she . . ." He touched my cheek with the back of his hand. "You – you bring me nothing but happiness. You're my sanctuary."

And just like that, my mood flipped. I brought him happiness and she made him miserable. I provided a bubble of peace and joy. It made me strangely proud to think of me and my little flat doing all that for this special man. I loved that I could do that for him. I reached over and pulled him toward me.

"You're getting very bold," he said.

Chapter 3

Friday, 25ᵗʰ April 2014

Though Marcia was her usual attentive self, I did not enjoy having my hair done. I was too preoccupied to take pleasure in her ministrations. It was just after five when I'd arrived at the salon – a tinted glass and aluminium emporium of beauty. I'd been draped in a nylon cape, seated before one of a dozen mirrors and the pins in my hair had been removed.

Marcia offered me tea or coffee, and a magazine, while she slathered my head with the noxious-smelling dye she was using to try to match my original shade.

"You're Babylon," she smiled.

The name evoked exoticism, burning sun, wantonness – nothing to do with covering grey roots. Ridiculous. Why not just call it Red Number 5?

I opted for a glass of water and turned the pages of the magazine she gave me, barely registering its contents. I am not a magazine reader. They are pitched at other women, women I do not know, who have lots more money and aspire, with all their hearts, to having fit-tastic bodies and multiple orgasms and shoes by Manolo Blahnik.

I turned the pages and tried to picture the woman in the park and then on the Luas. I was sure I had not made a mistake. It was the same woman. The more I thought about it, the clearer it became that I had become involved in something. Could I, in all conscience, pretend that I had seen nothing?

But precisely what was it I had seen? A person who happened to know the defendant, who also happened to know the forewoman. Or perhaps she didn't know her, and what I had witnessed was one stranger simply passing the time of day with another. But no, there had been a degree of familiarity between them. Was it a matter for the gardaí then? Should I have alerted them to what I saw and left it to them? But, perhaps they wouldn't have believed me – I had no proof, no other witness to back me up. Still, any hint of jury contamination could not be ignored.

I looked at myself in the salon mirror, my hair now plastered back from my forehead, the fumes from the treatment making my eyes match my hair colour. Was I prepared to deal with the consequences of telling the authorities?

What might happen? They would, I supposed, pause the trial while they questioned the forewoman. Could they simply remove her and let the trial go on, like cutting the canker from an otherwise perfect apple?

But how would they know the others hadn't already been infected? What I'd witnessed might only have been one in a series of contacts. Perhaps the forewoman had already begun whispering in the jury room. It would be easy enough to spread doubt about some of the evidence or to suggest the gardaí had got something wrong. It was always possible, too, that through his proxy O'Farrell might have made contact with other jurors and managed to gather more support.

While Marcia rinsed away the hair dye and her fingers

massaged my scalp, I realised that if I reported what I'd seen, the trial would collapse. All that work, thousands of pages of transcripts carefully produced, hours of evidence – all for nothing. The cost to the State would be colossal. And worse, O'Farrell might never go to prison. I'd seen the damage people like him could do – the long line of families who'd ended up in the High Court, losing their homes because of the banking collapse in 2008. But there were few convictions among the financiers despite their failings. It made my blood boil.

Marcia snipped at the ends of my shoulder-length hair in what others might have thought a timid fashion, but she knew what I liked. She refixed my hair in its chignon, the grey roots temporarily magicked away.

While she sprayed a fog of droplets to make my hairstyle stay in place, I was picturing Raymond Rafferty, on his feet in court, telling a future judge how his client's reputation had been irreparably damaged by the failed attempt to try him. Rafferty would insist that no jury could have remained uncontaminated by the comprehensive vilification of O'Farrell in the media.

I paid Marcia and tipped her the usual 10 per cent. As I left the salon I was in a state of turmoil. No matter what way I looked at it, no matter what action I took or didn't take, there would be a mistrial or an acquittal.

When I let myself into my terraced house, on the seafront at Clontarf, I couldn't face getting something to eat. I put my handbag down in the hall and went straight upstairs. I hung my suit jacket on the back of my dressing-table chair, slipped out of my skirt, and lay down on the bed. I hoped to clear a pounding headache, born from the combination of fumes in my nostrils, the salon's background music of electro-pop and other people's hairdryers, and the incessant and disturbing thoughts in my head.

I tried to feel comforted by the view through my window of Dublin Bay – Dun Laoghaire glistened on the right, Howth Head shimmered on the left – the two arms of the bay, cradling the capital. Every morning the view was different and every morning it was the same.

Visitors have admired it over the years. One in particular, whom I will not name, liked to stand in the centre of the window, with a towel wrapped round his waist, his Cote D'Azur limbs still damp, and talk about the wonders of Dublin. He'd point out the cranes sprouting from the city's skyline and tell me the name of the consortium that were responsible for them. He once said he could make a million euro for me if I trusted him with the €20,000 I had in my savings account. I'd smiled and shook my head at him.

"Handsome and clever though you are, I won't be investing."

"You'll be left behind in the great advancement of the city and its population, Bea," he'd said, kissing my hand. "I'll miss you then."

He soared for quite a few years after that and I lost track of his progression until, with perfect timing, he sold up everything he owned in Ireland, moved to New York and purchased a well-known Fifth Avenue hotel.

The bed rest was of no value in clearing my head and the view failed to calm my mind. In place of the glistening water, all I could see, as though the trial had already collapsed, was O'Farrell walking through the glass doors of the CCJ to the click of waiting photographers, his face full of smug satisfaction and the inevitable smirk. I knew I could not let that happen.

I got off the bed, put on a dressing gown, and went downstairs – I should have remembered that action was the only cure for destructive thoughts.

I made a pot of tea and sat at my breakfast table with pen

and paper. There had to be some way of dealing with this mess, so that the trial could continue. I wondered if telling Janine might help. Her advice, I knew, could be valuable, but I would be putting her in a position of having to share the responsibility of my burden, and that didn't seem fair.

I wrote '*Options*' at the top of the page. Then I wrote:

1 Tell Leona

2 Tell gardaí

3 Tell the judge

Option 3 wouldn't be done directly of course, but through his judicial assistant, Liam Reidy. Telling Leona might be tricky. Though I knew as a friend she'd be sympathetic, I would be compromising her professionally and she would have to act. I drew a bracket beside 1, 2 and 3 as they all seemed tantamount to the same thing – the trial would collapse. I wrote 'no' beside them.

Then I wrote: *4 Prevent forewoman attending*. I had seen men put away for life on the verdict of 11 jurors, when one juror had become ill near the close of the trial.

I wrote '*Illness*' for option 5, with '*Other diversion*' for option 6.

The coolness of my calculations shocked me, but the more I thought about it, as I sipped my tea, the more I came to believe that the only way to ensure the trial continued, was to prevent the forewoman from going back into the courtroom.

Somehow.

For Option 7 I wrote: *Find her name and address.*

The next day was Saturday, but the CCJ would be open, most likely taken over by teenagers. On the rare and unfortunate occasions when I've had to go there at the weekend, I've seen boys and girls trying to slide down the banister, while other teenagers amused themselves by endlessly travelling up and down in the lifts. The noise they made was shrill and their lack of decorum left me breathless.

There was a time when I might have considered having a child. It never happened for me and, though I've had small regrets after the sensation of a friend's infant warmly sleeping in my arms, when I see those wild hordes, I sigh with relief and thank God for the gifts he has not given.

At the end of the list I wrote: *8 Gabriel Ingram*. It was risky, I knew. I would have to take him into my confidence. But I couldn't do this alone and there was no one else I knew with his particular skills.

I composed a careful text message, asking him to meet me for a drink. He responded instantly – '**Yes**'. It was a start.

By nine, I was sitting at a corner table in Wynn's Hotel, sipping a soda and lime. I admired the polished mahogany and the mock nineteenth-century cornices on the high ceiling. Around me, grey-haired men and women were drinking, the smell of their earlier bacon and roast beef still lingering in the air. It reminded me of a well-to-do nursing home. I felt gratitude for Marcia's 'Babylon'.

I hadn't seen Gabriel in eighteen months and the last encounter had not been pleasant. He'd been going into Ryan's on Parkgate Street when I saw him – trudging, head down, wearing poorly pressed trousers and a clashing jacket that was grubby at the wrists. There was a three-day-old stubble on his chin. He'd always been well groomed and to see him so dishevelled was worrying.

I was coming from work and he remarked that I was looking well.

"Your suit reminds me of Donegal mountain heather."

I was even more concerned.

"Are you getting a drink?" I asked him.

"I am surely."

We'd sat in the tiny snug at the rear of the bar. He talked in a melancholy way about his early retirement from the gardaí, how he'd thought at fifty-five, it was time to put away his notebook and enjoy life a bit more.

He spoke of the shiny young man he'd been when he started, proud of his crisp, blue shirt and tiepin, and how his polished, black brogues were mirrors for his smooth chin. His chin had taken a few knocks in between.

"I had a dislocated jaw once," he said, "and got my nose flattened. They tried to straighten it, but it was never right. I should have taken up boxing. Still, these days the boys are facing the sharp end of a switchblade or the pointy end of a Glock. It's not a game for an old man."

"You're not old, Gabriel. You only have a few years on me, so you couldn't possibly be."

Then he'd told me, with eyes firmly on the pint in his hand, that it was all gone, the lump sum they'd given him for thirty-two years of service in the force.

"I invested it with some private broker recommended by the lads, only the fecker had made a big hole for himself in his investment accounts and used our money to fill it, before he disappeared to Brazil. We've no extradition treaty with Brazil. I'd have been better putting it in a shoebox under the bed."

"I'm so sorry, Gabriel."

I'd done my best to listen to everything he said for the next few hours, while he sobbed and slurped his pints. I commiserated and agreed, while he berated brokers and the "dickwits" in government who let it all happen. He was filled with bitterness and bile, and too emotional to even apologise for his bad language, which he ordinarily would have done. I was tempted to remind him that at least he still had his monthly pension coming in, half his salary, but resisted – it wasn't the time.

When he'd had his fill of pints, and was a drooping, tearful heap, only fit for bed, I brought him home to Clontarf with me in a taxi and got him stretched out in the spare room. I even took his shoes off for him.

When I woke the next day, he'd slipped out without saying goodbye or thank you. Embarrassment, I supposed.

Still, he'd have to get over it – I needed him.

I spotted him as soon as he came in the hotel door. He paused in the entrance, all six foot three inches of him, and looked around the lounge, taking in the details as though he were still on duty. He was neat and clean, in dark trousers, a collared T-shirt and a Harrington jacket. His iron-grey, short back and sides looked newly trimmed. I was relieved.

When he looked in my direction, I raised my hand. He crossed the room in a few long strides.

"Bea, how are you?"

I smiled at the Glenties still in his voice after all the years in Dublin.

"Fine. What will you have?"

"A pint, thanks."

I signalled to the young waiter and the stout was ordered.

"How have you been?" I asked.

"Okay. Doing a bit of private work, keeping my hand in."

"Good."

"You're looking well – I was glad to hear from you."

He took a deep breath and began what must have been the first line of a rehearsed speech.

"Whenever we met the last time – "

I raised my hand to stop him.

"I need your help."

He smiled, in that open, honest way he had that made me wonder how he could ever have been a garda. And his eyes met mine with what looked like relief, at not needing to discuss our last meeting. He rested his elbows on the arms of his chair and laced his fingers across a modest paunch.

"What can I do for you?"

"I need to ask first – do you have any ongoing obligations I should know about? To the force, I mean. Do you have to promise to, I don't know, inform them if you have any concerns about something?"

"What?" he asked, as the Guinness arrived.

He reached for his wallet, but I insisted on paying.

He laughed, shook his head and reached for his pint, its glass clouded and damp on the outside with condensation. He gulped down a third of its contents and wiped his mouth with the back of his hand.

"Okay, good," I said. "Where do I start . . ."

Now that it had come to it, I was uncertain. I knew that if I said nothing, I could pretend nothing had happened, but once I told Gabriel, it would make it real.

"Come on now, Bea, just spit it out."

"All right."

I told him what had happened in as much detail as possible and as calmly as I could. When I'd finished, I ordered another pint for him and a second soda and lime for me.

He quizzed me about the woman's description, tested my certainty, and then accepted it.

"Could you not just pretend you saw nothing?"

"If I do that, he gets what he wants. He'll just be another suit who walks away."

"But Jesus, Bea, are you sure you want to take this on? You don't know what you're dealing with and if it goes wrong – "

"The trial will collapse if I tell anyone. No one wants that to happen except him." I tried not to raise my voice.

"Aye."

He understood. He'd always understood, from the first time I had taken him into my bed. And I'd liked the straightforwardness of him. He had no edges or chips. Our relationship, sweet and clumsy, had not lasted. I'd seen him around the Four Courts for years, but only spoke to him for the first time at a retirement do for Sean O'Toole, a long-serving tipstaff. Gabriel had been standing at the bar in Hughes pub when I went over to order and he'd got the barman's attention for me. By the time the criminal courts moved to the CCJ, four years later in 2010, our relationship was over. His nature had made him want more from me and mine had prevented me from giving it.

He rubbed his chin. "I'll help you on one condition, Bea. If I decide we need to call in the lads, we call in the lads."

His former colleagues were long past being lads, but I knew what he meant and agreed. I hoped it wouldn't be necessary.

"All right then, first thing I need is an address for her. Then we'll see."

I promised him I could get that. "We'll have to be quick – who knows what she'll say in the jury room on Monday."

He rubbed his chin again. I'd forgotten that habit of his. His chin was smooth, with hardly a shadow on it. I pictured him in front of his mirror, stripped to the waist, his face foamed, and he pulling the razor across it. I felt flattered that he'd gone to the trouble. Then I checked myself. It wouldn't be good to start all that again.

"How do we stop her?" I asked.

I tried to draw him out on how we might arrange for her to withdraw. I suggested I could speak to her and tell her I knew everything and that she should stay away from court.

"Can't stop her 'til we know her," Gabriel said, putting an end to my speculation.

"Okay. I'll go and get the address first thing in the morning. I'll call you after."

He drained his glass, thanked me for the pints and stood up to leave.

"The woman you saw, do you think she recognised you?"

I pictured again her furrowed brow, her double take.

"She might have."

"Mind yourself so."

I waited until he left, not wishing to exit the hotel in his company and deal with an awkward moment on the steps outside. Then I gathered my bag and walked out onto Abbey Street.

Mind yourself, he'd said. I stood outside the hotel door and looked up and down. It was shortly after eleven and the streets were busy with young people only beginning their night out. A tram pulled slowly away from its stop, the bell dinging to part the crowds as it crossed the junction with O'Connell Street.

"Any change, missus?"

A gaunt-faced young man appeared suddenly at my elbow and held out a paper cup. He had the look of an addict, from the sagging clothes to the dirty fingernails, yet his eyes looked clearly at me. I threw the few coins I had in my pocket into the cup, tucked my handbag under my arm and walked away. When I turned into O'Connell Street and glanced back over my shoulder, he was still standing in the same spot watching me go.

I took a taxi home.

Chapter 4

Saturday, 14th March 1981

I hadn't intended to introduce Laurence to Leo. Though we'd been together six months, I'd been keeping Leo very much to myself. I suspected my brother had an inkling there was some man on the scene, but he hadn't asked me, and I wasn't ready to volunteer the information.

That changed one Saturday in March. Leo had called me at home, on the communal phone in the hallway. Alex, the young medical student from the flat below, took the call and shouted up the stairs to me.

"Beatrice Barrington! Beatrice! Bea!"

I came running down in slippers and dressing gown, a pillow-crease still on my right cheek, with my hair sleep-tossed. He held out the handset to me and gave me an amused "Good morning".

"Who was that?" Leo asked.

"Just Alex. You met him. He's working over at St James's."

"You really need to get your own phone."

"You sound like my father."

There was a silence then – he didn't like me to say

33

anything that might highlight our age difference, though I'd told him more than once that it didn't bother me. I waited for him to speak for a minute, then lost my patience.

"Did you get me out of bed for no reason?"

He hesitated, then told me Angie had gone away for the weekend.

"There's nothing I'd like better than to take you to Bewley's for breakfast. I'll be by in half an hour," he said, hanging up before I could argue about the timing.

I tore upstairs and got dressed, choosing a pair of high-waisted jeans and a pink blouse with batwing sleeves. I'd planned on washing my hair, but there wasn't time, so I heated up my crimping iron to give it some life.

From my window I saw him arriving at the hall door. He was wearing a blue jumper and he adjusted it at the shoulders before he pressed the doorbell. I thought the gesture so sweet that I ran down the stairs and threw myself into his arms in the hallway.

"Lovely welcome!" he said, breathless from the impact.

"My day is yours."

We strolled slowly through St Stephen's Green and watched people feeding the ducks in the pond and giving their children crumbs to toss into the water.

"I remember being told to do that as a child – hated it," he said.

I tried to imagine him as a little boy, in short trousers and with buckled shoes.

"Did you have a good childhood?"

"Ordinary, just ordinary," he said, as though that was a black mark against him.

We held hands and he made silly jokes, the kind that usually made me cringe when someone else told them, but I laughed at them all. We stopped near Traitor's Gate and he took both my hands.

"You are the most adorable person I've ever met." He leaned down and kissed me lightly and I thought my heart would burst.

"It feels so good to be out in public in the middle of the city," I said.

We had breakfast in Bewley's on Grafton Street. He persuaded me to have coffee instead of tea and it left me thirsty.

"That's easily remedied," he said.

It was shortly after midday when we walked back out onto the street and I spotted Laurence, standing outside Switzer's department store. He was leaning against the window, his lanky right leg bent at the knee, the foot flat against the brickwork below the glass. His hands were dug into the pockets of his leather jacket and his short hair was beginning to sprout over his ears. He looked so handsome I couldn't help but smile at him and call his name.

"So, this is the man," he said, extending a hand.

"Laurence, I'd like you to meet Leo – Leo, my brother Laurence."

"Nice to meet you," Leo shook his hand firmly.

I looked from one to the other, feeling a mixture of delight and anxiety in the pit of my stomach.

Laurence glanced up and down the crowded street, and then at his watch.

"I was waiting for someone, but he looks like a no-show."

"Come for a drink with us, why don't you?" Leo suggested.

Laurence was easily persuaded. I linked them both and we walked into The Duke.

The pub was busy so we sat at the bar, the three of us on high stools in a row. I had vodka with lime and the men had pints of stout. We talked about the band that was beginning to assemble in the corner. Leo said he'd heard them play in the Baggot Inn.

"So did I!" Laurence said.

He enthused about their music and they both agreed the band had something special.

"Do you play a bit of music yourself?" Leo asked.

"A bit of guitar." He took a sup from his glass. "What I'd really like is to travel round the world with it, you know, busking and that."

"He's great – just picks up a tune like that." I clicked my fingers. "And you should see the way the women fall over themselves when he's playing."

"Stop, would you?" Laurence said.

Leo laughed.

"I'm not joking. I had school friends who called to my house just so they could sit and listen to him."

I put one hand under my chin and gazed into Laurence's face, wide-eyed.

"Stop it!" He shoved me gently. "Just busking would be grand, as long as I could pay my way."

"Father would love to hear you saying that, with your permanent and pensionable job in the Civil Service."

He grew serious. "It's my life though, Bea."

"I know that," I said.

I stopped talking and just listened to them both. There was no strain in their conversation and I couldn't decide whether it was Laurence who was working hard or if Leo was skilfully smoothing things along. Whatever it was, an eavesdropping stranger would think they'd known each other a long time. I wanted to hug them and tell them how much I loved them and how great life was.

"There are other routes to making money," Leo said after a while.

He described what he did, how he managed to turn around companies on the verge of collapse.

"It's a matter of trusting your instincts – you get a feel for a business and of course you check the books, then you figure out if it's a flyer. Believe me, there's a lot of money to be made as long as you make the right choices."

"The worst thing about work is the boredom. My boss is a dead-eyed dullard and the work I'm set is mind-numbing," Laurence complained.

I was taken aback by his honesty and the depth of his loathing.

"But when you're there a while, I said, if you get promoted, won't things get more interesting?"

"I look at the older men in the office Bea, the senior executive officers, the ones in their forties with wives and children to support, and their faces are as grey as the pinstripe suits they wear."

I put my hand on Laurence's arm.

"I didn't realise you felt so – "

"Trapped? Yeah well, I try not to go on about it."

Leo signalled for another round.

"It's really hard to save anything when most of my wages are disappearing down the pay-as-you-earn plughole every week," Laurence said.

"That's a mug's game – you need to get yourself out of that," Leo said, pushing a fresh pint in his direction.

I squeezed his knee as I slipped off my stool to go to the ladies' and he caught my eye and smiled at me.

Standing at the mirror in the toilets I noticed the vodka had flushed my cheeks. I put on a little lipstick and pressed my lips together on a tissue. I felt lovely and lucky. 'I Feel Pretty' from the musical *Westside Story* began playing in my brain and I hummed it as I combed my hair. The crimping had worked – instead of flat, shoulder-length red hair in need of a wash, it was full and light. I thought I looked a little like Kate Bush and switched my humming to the chorus of 'Wuthering Heights'.

When I got back to the bar, the two men were leaning

toward each other, talking intensely.

"I'll let you know," I heard Leo say.

"Know what?" I pulled myself back onto the bar stool.

"Just business stuff, honey," Leo responded and winked at Laurence.

For an instant I wanted to kick him in the shins and insist he told me. I wanted to say that he shouldn't patronise me, and especially not in front of my brother, but I didn't. I was too happy.

"I really have to go," Laurence said then.

He put on his leather jacket, kissed me on the cheek and shook hands with Leo.

"He's great, I'm so glad you introduced us," Leo said, when Laurence had left. "I mean it – a really lovely fellow."

I was delighted.

"He's four years older than I am and he's always looked out for me." I told Leo how when I was ten years old I'd been pushed around by an older boy. "He used to wait for me after school and trip me up, grab my schoolbag and empty the books out onto the footpath. I came home crying one day with a scratched knee and Laurence promised me he'd deal with it. He waited for this boy, George was his name, to come out of the school gates and then he picked him up by the collar and pressed him up against the wall and told him he'd burst him if he ever went near me again."

I had a sudden vision of George, his feet dangling an inch off the ground, his cheeks pale, promising he'd leave me alone.

"Laurence was my hero after that."

"He was probably sweet on you."

"What?"

"George, he probably really liked you and that was the only way he could get your attention."

I thought about that for a minute.

"That's a bit sad then, isn't it? I hope he grew out of it."

"Some do, some don't. Would you like another one?"

I said I wouldn't.

"I've enjoyed our day so far and I would like to be escorted back to my flat for a little rest," I smiled.

Leo didn't put up much of a fight.

Chapter 5

Saturday, 26th April 2014

Mike nodded at me on Saturday morning when I passed through the security gate at the Criminal Courts of Justice.

"You're keen."

"Playing catch-up."

I kept walking.

I went into my office first, hung up my coat and turned on the computer on my desk by the window. Once I'd logged on, I located the transcript for the opening day of the trial. I scrolled through the lengthy warnings Judge Brown had given the jury, past the part where the juror numbers were drawn from the drum by the registrar and past the careful rejection and selection of those who were willing to put themselves forward for duty. I found the part where the judge asked the chosen twelve jurors to elect a "foreperson". I smiled when I remembered the way the judge had said it, in his primmest voice, failing to disguise his abhorrence of political correctness.

Then I found the forewoman's name – Rachel Deere.

I used my security swipe key to get into the main Courts

Service office. I supposed my access would be logged somewhere in the system and, if challenged, I'd decided to say my printer had run out of ink and I needed access to the supply cupboard. Strictly speaking, I wasn't supposed to take supplies without authorisation, but I was confident I could talk my way out of it. I'd worked at the CCJ since it opened in 2010 and in the Four Courts before that. I was trusted.

Through a wall of window glass in the main office, the sun cast a dozen desk-shadows on the floor and the air was dusty in the light. I crossed the room to the supply cupboard, took out an ink cartridge and made my way to the filing cabinets in a row at the opposite end of the room. I found the one containing the lists of jurors for ongoing trials, collected by one of the jury clerks. I was grateful that such work was still carried out using paper and ink, and not an encrypted programme that would have been impossible for me to access.

I found the file marked DPP v O'Farrell. The twelve jurors were listed, and Rachel Deere's name was marked with an asterisk. Her number, 247, was written beside it. I moved to another filing cabinet where Sam, a junior member of staff, handled correspondence with prospective jurors. He culled an initial list from the electoral register then wrote to eligible people, 500 at a time, informing them of their duty.

When was the jury sworn in? 11th February. Yes, it was a Tuesday, so the call-up date was the 10th. I began examining the folder for that date, working quickly. Then I stopped. I'd heard something, a noise outside on the corridor.

I closed the drawer as quietly as I could, aware that I was in the wrong place to use the printer-cartridge excuse. I squeezed myself between the wall and the filing cabinet, knowing my shoulder and arm were visible to anyone who looked closely enough. The sound stopped at the door and the door handle began to turn. My palms began to sweat I was so afraid. I hoped whoever it was did not come far enough into the room to notice the folder I'd left on the table.

The door opened, and someone stepped into the room – one, two, three steps. Then whoever it was, stopped. I held my breath and hoped my palpitations were audible only to me. In a moment, the footsteps retreated, and the door was closed.

I waited until I could hear the footsteps going back down the corridor, before coming out of my hiding place. I reminded myself that I was breaking the law. It did not feel good. It was as though I'd caught a glimpse of my naked self in a mirror, at an unflattering angle and I didn't like what I saw.

I resumed my search, hands trembling. I found the address after a few seconds – *Rachel Deere, 95 Botanic Hall, Addison Park, Glasnevin, Dublin 11*. I wrote it on a piece of paper, tidied up the file and closed the cabinet.

I brought the ink cartridge back to my office and changed it. It seemed a shame to bin the half-full one, but I thought it best to follow through on my alibi.

At my desk, I spent a few minutes Googling her name – there was a Facebook entry for her and I could see her photograph. Her glossy brown hair framed a heart-shaped face and she looked like she was in her late twenties or early thirties. She wore a little too much mascara around her green eyes and, despite a soft smile, there was a hardness about her. I could access no more details without signing up to Facebook and there were some things I was just not prepared to do. I erased the search history and switched off the computer.

"All done?" Mike asked me, as I left the building.

"Enough done," I responded.

I sat in my car in the Phoenix Park and called Gabriel to give him the address.

"Okay, I'll phone you when I have news," he said.

There was nothing more I could do until I heard from him. I went grocery shopping and got back home in time to switch on the radio for the one o'clock news. It headlined with a suspicious death. A woman's body had been found at her home in Dublin. The phone rang as the bulletin ended.

"Where are you?" It was Gabriel.

"At home, I just –

"I'm coming over."

He hung up without saying anything else.

I busied myself making a sandwich for him, ham and mustard, and listened to the remainder of the news.

There was a knock at the door then, but it wasn't Gabriel. A man as wide as the doorframe stood there, his tanned, bald head protruding from a black, calf-length Crombie, a clipboard in his hand.

"I've been calling to houses since eleven and it hasn't rained yet," he said.

He flashed an identity card. I couldn't make out his name, but the charity was St Lucian the Evangelist.

"It's a great cause," he said.

He gave me an approximation of a smile, stretching his lips back over nicotine-yellow teeth, and took a step forward, as though hoping to be invited into the hall.

"No, thank you," I said, shutting the door in his face.

I'm not normally rude, but there was something about him that unnerved me.

He stayed outside for a few moments. I could see the shape of his head pressed against the arch of obscure glass. Then I heard him move around the garden. I watched him from the doorway of the living room and caught him peering through the window. Then there were footsteps, a cough and he went away.

There was another knock a few minutes later. This time I called out, "Who is it?"

"It's me," Gabriel said.

I let him in, looking over his shoulder for any sign of the bald man. I stepped outside and looked up and down, expecting to see him knocking on one of my neighbours' doors. But he was gone.

Gabriel said he had passed him in the drive.

"I'm sure I know his face from somewhere."

As I shut the door, I noticed a card on the floor and picked it up. It looked like I'd missed a delivery from a courier company. I dropped it into my handbag, promising myself I'd call them later.

I gave Gabriel his sandwich and tea in the kitchen, before asking him about Rachel Deere.

"I went to the address you gave me. Couldn't get near it – gardaí everywhere."

"What?" I thought of the one o'clock news and told him about it.

"I know. I've put in a couple of calls. We should hear back shortly."

We had more tea and Gabriel used his phone to search St Lucian the Evangelist.

"Mental health charity," he said. "Has a dozen centres in Ireland. Sounds like he was just a pushy salesman."

"Maybe I should complain about him looking in my window."

It hadn't felt like a visit from a pushy salesman. There was something menacing about him, something that made me uneasy.

Gabriel's phone rang then. He answered it and signalled for a pen. I got one from the hall table, took a page from the notepad I always left there, and pushed both across the kitchen table to him.

"Aye, aye, okay, okay . . . listen thanks Bob." He wrote a number on the page and repeated it back. Then he scribbled,

'Bob new mobile' beside it. "I will of course, aye, next week surely, and tell your Ursula I said hello."

"Who's Bob?" I asked when he put his phone down.

"Assistant to the State Pathologist – he does all the cleaning up after, you know?"

I shuddered. "What did he say?"

"It's her."

"No!"

"Nothing sinister, apparently. They think the drink – she was a recovering alcoholic."

I let the news sink in.

"Her boyfriend found her," Gabriel said, "along with a few empty bottles."

"The poor thing, she was so young."

I thought of her Facebook photo and felt a pang of guilt for what I'd been planning, whatever that was.

"Where does that leave us?" I asked. I was already thinking that this would solve my problem. Now I could just forget what I had seen. More guilt followed.

Gabriel could see it in my face. He patted me awkwardly on the arm, but when I looked down at his hand, he removed it.

"Do you think I should tell the gardaí now?" I spoke the words, but more to myself than to Gabriel, who did not respond. "What would be the consequences of that? Probably the same as if she was still alive – the trial would collapse."

I didn't need to remind him that I didn't want that.

"Let's wait and see,"he said. "Bob says he'll let me know when the pathologist has done the post-mortem."

I agreed that was best and, after a few moments of silence, Gabriel stood up to leave.

"You look a bit tired," he said. "Maybe have a rest and try not to think too much."

I nodded.

"And Bea?"

"What?"

"None of this is your fault, you know."

"I know."

When he left, weariness washed over me. I had worried late into the previous night about what I would do and now it seemed I didn't need to do anything.

I lay on the couch and closed my eyes. I dozed or rather hung in that place between sleep and waking, where the conscious and subconscious mix and play tricks of fear and comfort on the weary.

Laurence came into my mind then, as he often did. This time it was when he was in his late teens and threatening our mother that he would emigrate to London if she didn't stop nagging him about his long hair. He had lovely hair, dark and wavy, and he wore it to his shoulders, until he got called for his first job interview in the Civil Service. Father marched him to the barbers the next day.

"Grow up, son," he said.

I'd cried when he came home, shorn like a lamb.

"Ah Bea," he said, and hugged me.

When I awoke, I could still feel his arms around me and, for a moment, the world was a good place.

It was after six o'clock. I sat up quickly, found the remote, and put on the TV.

A reporter was standing outside one of the blocks at Addison Apartments, blue-and-white tape flapping behind him. A young garda near the front door was staring into the camera from below his cap, as though trying to intimidate it.

"The woman has been named locally as Rachel Deere, a thirty-one-year-old unemployed nurse. Sources say her death may have been accidental. They aren't seeking anyone in connection with it at this time." The reporter looked as though he was already bored with the story.

I wondered how long it would be before word got out that

she was a juror in the Stephen O'Farrell trial. I sent Gabriel a text, to which he responded: **'Seen it, early days'.**

It took only until Sunday morning for the additional detail to come out. I bought five newspapers from the corner shop and carried them back home, spreading them out on the table, scanning for any information I could find.

The broadsheets spoke of the legal dilemma facing the judge and the uniqueness of what had happened.

'Never in the history of the State has a juror died while serving,' one report said.

Other trials were recalled, in which jurors lost family members and were excused from duty or in which jurors were taken ill, but no one could remember anything like this.

'It would and should be possible to continue with the trial,' an expert pronounced, **'and given how much it has cost so far, no judge would consider collapsing it.'**

Another expert said the risk of mistrial was great. He speculated about what might happen if another juror was lost and about the moral implications of ploughing on when a juror had died.

'Unconscionable,' he concluded. **'It would be safer, to ensure a sound verdict, to discharge the jury and start again.'**

There was little detail about Rachel, except to label her an alcoholic. A columnist suggested the mental stability of jurors should be examined ahead of a lengthy trial. She found a psychologist who agreed with her and who surmised that the responsibility of being forewoman might have been too much for Rachel, causing her to crack as the trial neared its end. There was even speculation about possible compensation for her family if they chose to take a case against the State.

The tabloids focused on the scene of her death, vivid descriptions of her naked body and what garda sources were saying. Not much, just enough.

Only one article had extra personal detail. The *Irish*

Sunday Express front banner ran: MY HELL WITH RACHEL: DAVE WISEMAN TELLS OF HIS LIFE WITH TRAGIC JUROR

It made me cringe. What sort of a man would spill a story like that when someone he was supposed to have loved lay on the cold slab of a mortuary?

Wiseman recounted how the evening before Rachel died, he'd gone out with a friend. **'She was in good form,'** he said, **'completely sober. She'd been dry since she got treatment. Everything was going so well.'**

He detailed the times when things weren't so good. The article described an out-of-control Rachel, screaming on the street during one nasty bout of all-day drinking.

'It could be hell,' Wiseman said.

The article reported that before she went into rehab 'the bright-eyed brunette' had been a nurse but lost her job when the matron caught her drinking on night duty.

'It got very bad for a while after that – she was drinking vodka for breakfast,' Wiseman said. 'But then when she got help, she became a different person. She was so happy and looking forward to life, making plans, you know? I can't believe she did this to herself again."

The reporter described how Wiseman's voice shook as he spoke and how the tears welled in his eyes. He said when he left her, she was drinking tea, and he'd told her he'd be back in the morning. He was going out with a few mates on a stag night and was staying at a friend's place.

Wiseman got back to the apartment next morning with a friend who wanted to borrow some tools from him. He called her name as he opened the door but there was no response. They saw water flooding the hallway and found her then, slumped in the bathroom, bottles everywhere.

'We were talking about having kids . . . I can't believe she's gone.'

The article finished by explaining how 'broken-hearted Dave' wished he'd stayed in with 'tragic Rachel' that night. It also said the State Pathologist was due to carry out a post-mortem, concluding: 'Gardaí are not looking for anyone else in connection with the death.'

It seemed they'd already decided she drank herself to death. It was sad to imagine her, so committed to staying sober one minute and succumbing to her addiction the next. But the draw of alcohol was strong, and I'd heard of other such cases. Perhaps it was just a coincidence that I'd seen her on the Luas with O'Farrell's woman.

Or maybe it wasn't – had that woman somehow added to the pressure already on Rachel Deere and triggered a drinking binge? I supposed it was possible.

When I'd finished reading the papers, I considered calling Gabriel. But it was gone noon and I thought better of it. I knew him to be a Mass-goer and I believed he liked to attend the midday service at the Holy Family Church on Aughrim Street.

It was a delight I had stopped partaking in. God and I had not seen eye to eye for a long time.

It occurred to me that I could reach the church in time for the end of Mass and catch Gabriel as he left, and before he took up his stool in Walsh's pub. I was anxious to know if he'd learned anything else.

Chapter 6

Sunday, 29th March 1981

I went home for Sunday lunch a couple of weeks after Laurence and Leo first met. My parents had got used to my independence and now and again my mother invited me for meals.

I brought flowers I got from a seller on the street, sunflowers the size of dinner plates, and a bottle of Blue Nun.

"You'd think you were a guest instead of a daughter," Mother laughed, taking them from me. "Are you eating properly? You look like you've lost a little weight?"

I assured her that I was, and I sat down at the table. She moved around the kitchen, opening presses in search of a vase. She was a plump Size 8, her body cinched in the middle by the strings of her lemon-yellow apron, purchased on a rare holiday in Spain. Father examined the flowers as Mother arranged them in her best Aynsley china vase and put them on the centre of the table.

"Hothouse from Holland, no doubt," he said with smile as he picked up the bottle of wine. "I suppose I should open this since you've brought it."

He rummaged in a drawer for a corkscrew. I couldn't help noticing how the hair at his temples had gone from grey to white, and tendrils of white were spread through the darker hair of his crown.

"Ah," he said, when he spotted what he wanted. He twisted it in firmly, pulled, and the cork made a soft pop.

Then I heard Laurence's footsteps on the stairs. He came bounding into the room grinning like a child.

"You look like the Cheshire Cat," Father said.

"Sure, why wouldn't I, about to tuck into a feast and surrounded by my loving family?"

Mother laughed and began laying out dishes of food on the table. The men started talking about the Dublin GAA team and speculating on whether they might do it this year. Father said Kerry was too strong.

"That fecker Pat Spillane – pass the spuds," Laurence said.

I handed him the bowl and he loaded up his plate.

"Gorgeous." He shovelled in a mouthful of roast beef.

"How's work?" Mother asked me.

"It's fine, though my boss, Mrs Carmichael, is an awful moan." I mimicked her voice, the way she said "Miss Barrington" through her nose.

"She is your superior though, she deserves some respect," Mother chided.

Laurence glanced at me and topped up her wineglass.

"Not everyone in authority deserves respect," he said.

"You're right I'm sure," Father said. "But respect should be your basic position. You'll get nowhere otherwise."

"That depends where you want to go. I don't intend to stay in the Civil Service long. I'm going to cut loose and see the world just as soon as I can afford it. I'm thinking of getting involved in business – property investment."

Father put his knife and fork down.

"Sure, what would you know about that?"

"Bea's boyfriend said he'd help me."

Mother looked at me. "Boyfriend?"

"Sorry," Laurence said to me.

"You've nothing to be sorry for!" she said. "How long has this been going on?"

There was a mixture of curiosity and alarm in her voice.

"Not long. His name is Leo. He has his own business. He's a good man."

"Leo? Leo who?"

"Hackett, and he's just a little bit older than me, but great, really, really great."

A crease formed between my father's eyebrows.

"I warned you about older men," Mother said.

"It's not like that, really it's not. I think you'd really like him." I looked at Laurence for help.

He began listing Leo's qualities. It was funny to hear him. His words were a mirror of the things Leo had said to me about Laurence. It was as though they'd joined a mutual admiration society.

"He has real drive and a great head for business, and integrity – you can tell he has a lot of integrity."

"I sincerely hope so," Father said. "How long has this been going on?"

"A couple of months," I muttered.

Mother cast her eyes toward the ceiling. "Months? And you didn't let us know? Well, I don't know what we did to deserve that treatment." She took her napkin from her lap and dabbed at the corner of her eyes, reminding me of similar theatrics when I was still living at home and had come home late from a disco. "I knew things would change when you moved out, but now, well I don't know what to say, Beatrice. I feel like you've really cut us out of your life."

I felt a few pangs of the old familiar guilt, but this time I could see she was being a drama queen.

"I just wanted to be sure of him first, that's all, before I – "

"Before you what? Brought him home for a visit?" The napkin came down and she fixed her gaze on me. "Well I'd very much like to meet this man."

"You really should." Father backed her up as he always did.

I had to promise I'd bring him over.

Before I left, Mother cornered me in the kitchen.

"I hope to God you're being sensible," she said. "If you don't respect yourself, he won't either."

It was the closest she'd ever come to talking to me about sex.

"Of course," I said.

In the hall, when I was leaving, Laurence apologised again, and added.

"It'll be all right."

His attempt at reassurance was unconvincing.

"It better be," I said, "and you better be here when we call."

"I will, I promise."

I fobbed Mother off for a few weeks after that, until she started to drop by the flat unexpectedly, to bring me some "little essentials" – teacloths, a slotted spoon, an oven mitt.

"I thought of you when I saw it. You'll need it if you plan to entertain."

She'd glanced around the room on her most recent visit, as though searching for evidence of Leo's presence. It was only good luck that she hadn't caught us in bed together. I promised again that I'd bring him round for dinner.

"Sunday week."

It was not a question. She put on her coat with an air of finality.

"See you then," I said, letting her out.

I waited until Leo was relaxed and happy in my arms before telling him.

"Please? I won't have another moment's peace unless I bring you around."

"Aren't we a bit grown up for that sort of thing?"

I told him how lovely my parents were really and how they couldn't wait to meet him. And how likely my mother was to keep calling in unannounced if we didn't go to dinner. I said Laurence would be there too.

"Just once, to reassure them, please, Leo?"

"What's it worth?" He gave me a cheeky look and slid down under the blankets.

Sunday came around quickly and I was nervous, waiting for Leo to pick me up. I'd made an effort to wear a dress. I knew Mother liked to see me in one. It was a Laura Ashley print, navy with tiny pink flowers. I wondered what Leo would wear. A suit was respectful, but it might make him look a bit old.

I needn't have worried. He arrived in cream chinos and a brown, V-neck jumper, with a shirt and tie underneath. I thought he'd make just the right impression.

"You're good at this," I said.

Laurence answered the door to us when we arrived. He confided on the way into the living room that Mother had already had a sherry for her nerves.

"They're here," he announced.

Father left his fireside chair and extended a hand to Leo, as Mother came in from the kitchen.

"Excuse the apron," she said, also shaking his hand and primly kissing me on the cheek.

"Thank you so much for having us," Leo said.

He gave my father a bottle of brandy and Mother a box of chocolates. She took them and thanked him, leaving them on the sideboard unopened.

"I'll be with you shortly. Colm, get Leo a drink."

Mother slipped back into the kitchen and I followed her.

"Need any help?"

I could see that she'd made an extra effort with dinner – starters of smoked salmon on brown bread, as well as rack of lamb with all the trimmings for the main course.

"He looks a little older than I'd expected," she said. "He has the look of a man who might rush a girl into something."

"Mother!"

"All right, all right. I'll say no more – just put the salmon out for me, will you? And then call them into the dining room."

I smiled at the effort she'd made. Eating in the dining room meant coaxing Father and Laurence to lift the mahogany table away from the wall and into the centre of the room. It meant polishing it, laying out the best tablecloth and her precious Waterford crystal glasses.

I did what I was told, and we were all soon seated, sipping and chewing, with our best manners. Mother fussed about serving Leo, making sure he was well fed. He accepted the generous portions she gave him and complimented her cooking. He asked her advice about the best variety of potato.

"I'd like to be able to grow them someday when I have a proper home of my own," he smiled.

They talked about gardens and she told him she longed for an old-fashioned herbaceous border, but didn't have the space.

"Perhaps that's a project we could work on together when I have a garden," Leo said.

He flirted with her ever so slightly. It made me smile to see her cheeks flush as she drank her wine.

Laurence made a special effort to highlight Leo's business brain and Father didn't take long to warm to him. Leo flattered him, listening carefully whenever he spoke, nodding as though he was hearing from the oracle.

"I'll certainly bear that in mind the next time, Mr Barrington."

"Less of the mister, call me Colm."

I could see Laurence struggling not to laugh as Father held forth on "the vagaries of the stock markets", as though he'd ever invested a penny in his life.

"You're absolutely right, that's why my primary interests are in property."

"And banks?"

"Of course."

I offered to help Mother with dessert and followed her into the kitchen again.

"He's just a bit older, I think, but . . . " She shrugged and added blobs of cream to slices of apple tart. "Do you think that's enough cream or will I put more into the jug?"

I said I thought there was plenty, but she did it anyway.

When we returned to the dinner table, Leo was describing his latest business venture.

"I'm positive it's a winner and I'm getting in on the ground floor."

"Would you like more cream, Leo?" Mother asked.

When we were leaving, she kissed him on the cheek and she squeezed my arm like she did when I was little and we were about to open the living-room door to see what was under the Christmas tree.

"He's a keeper," she whispered into my ear.

I laughed at him on the way home.

"How did you do that? You had them eating out of your hand."

"They're good people, Bea. It's easy to get along with good people."

His words made fireworks go off inside me – I was so happy I thought I was going to explode.

I didn't even mind when he slipped out from under the covers of my bed an hour later so that he could "show his face" to Angie.

I watched him go out the front door, then wrapped a sheet around me and sat at the window, looking down at my man. He stood for a few moments on the street, searching the traffic, before spotting and hailing a taxi. As he opened the car door, he looked up, waved and disappeared inside. I wondered how he knew I'd be watching.

Chapter 7

Sunday, 27th April 2014

I watched as the thin congregation trickled from the doors of the Holy Family Church on Aughrim Street. The gothic-style, nineteenth-century building made a grey-stone background for the mostly grey crowd, with a few of what the broadsheets like to call the new Irish, peppered among the worshippers. From my position at the church gate, I imagined I could smell the interior – the faint damp of its old walls, the incense-infused pews and the offertory candles before the statue of St Joseph. It was not difficult to spot Gabriel as he emerged from the mahogany-stained doors. He was taller than most of the congregation, with that iron-grey head of hair. He looked at peace with himself.

The priest was standing just outside the door, shaking hands with his parishioners. Gabriel stopped and spoke to him a while, stooping down toward the priest's ear. They began to walk in my direction. Gabriel's words "Yes, Father" were caught by the breeze and floated toward me. When they finished talking, he raised his head, noticed me, said goodbye to the priest and crossed to where I was standing.

"Morning, Beatrice."

"Yes, Father," I mocked him gently, but got a rough response.

"You believe in nothing and you think it makes you superior." His tone was sharp with rebuke.

I hadn't meant or expected to offend him. "I didn't mean . . . "

I rested my arm lightly on his for a moment. "Any news for me?"

"I haven't."

We both walked out of the gates and turned into St Joseph's Road. Gabriel was using those long legs of his to stride quickly, head down. I matched his pace, taking two steps for every one of his, and attempted to restart the conversation.

"Have you seen the papers this morning?"

"Aye. Nothing we didn't know."

I sighed and hoped he wasn't going to sulk for long. I found it a most unattractive attribute in a man and one that was difficult to have patience with.

"What about the *Express*?"

"Surprised at you, reading that rag, Bea." Catching me out seemed to improve his mood.

"Purely research."

He slowed his pace and I told him the details of the newspaper report.

We talked about what might happen the next day.

"You know Brown hates delays," I said.

Gabriel reminded me of a case when Brown told a defence barrister to stop blathering and get on with it. The barrister did what he was told, and his client went to jail. He was released on appeal.

"He hates collapsed trials more than delays, so I think he'll be prepared to wait," Gabriel said. "Bob says they'll have toxicology on Tuesday, maybe Monday evening, even. We'll know then."

"I've never believed in coincidences."

"They do happen, Bea."

We'd reached Walsh's and we stood outside talking for a few moments, but he was like a greyhound with the scent of a rabbit in its nostrils – I couldn't hold him.

"You might have a wee one?" he suggested.

"Thanks, but I won't, Gabriel. Let me know when you hear, will you?"

I left him then and walked back to the church, where I'd parked my car. I could not remember what it was I normally did on a Sunday. It seemed such a long time since lunchtime on Friday. I could read a good book perhaps or take a walk along the Bull Wall. Maybe even get adventurous and drive around to the seafront at Sandymount. The tide would be out and the water's edge would almost be at the horizon, with Howth Head and Dalkey Island appearing equidistant from its strand.

But I knew I needed to feel busier.

I decided to go to Arnotts and check out their new stock. It was about time I bought my summer suit. I am not the sort of woman who buys lots of clothes. Though I do appreciate style, I wouldn't consider myself fashionable. For work, I like to have five good suits – two spring/summer, two autumn/winter and one all-year-rounder. I never wear black. It is the uniform of the legal eagles and they are welcome to it. I like to take my time choosing a suit, maybe visiting a few times to examine the new stock, returning to try some on and then on a third and final visit, making a purchase.

I left the car at home and walked into town, feeling my stresses ease with every step. Wafts of expensive scents and bottles of luxurious make-ups greeted me when I entered Arnotts through the main door on Henry Street. Perfumes and cosmetic concoctions vied for attention, as manicured women held out sprays for me to sample and smiled benignly when I shook my head and walked on.

I took the stairs to ladies' fashion. I made my way to the section featuring Irish designers, past the rails filled with sales items, all last season. I reached the new stock, of soft pastels and that lime green that looks so good on the young. A dusty-pink two-piece caught my eye. The fabric, beautifully cut, had a silken sheen. The price tag of €699 was within my budget. I broke a habit and decided to try it on straight away, searching out a Size 14 and taking it with me to the changing room.

In the cubicle, two-foot square, I slipped out of my jeans and top and put on the skirt, and then the jacket. I would normally have brought nylons and heels – without them it was hard to assess the outfit. In the full-length mirror I critiqued the fit of the skirt, its length, to the knee, and the cut of the material. I was sorry I hadn't taken a blouse in with me, so I could judge how the jacket would sit. I was about to ask for help when the curtain of my cubicle was wrenched to one side and a woman stepped in.

"Hey!" I said, holding the jacket closed to hide the absence of a blouse. "What – "

She pressed a hand firmly over my mouth and pushed me back against the mirror, holding me there. She was about my height, in her early thirties and stronger than I was. Her skin was the colour of a polished chestnut and her brown eyes locked to mine.

"Please don't scream, I only want to warn you. They know who you are. Understand?" Her accent was slightly foreign.

I nodded, though I did not.

"I don't know what you've done, but they are serious. You should take a holiday, a long holiday, far away. They are watching you."

She released her grip and was gone before I could ask a

question. I took some deep breaths. I could feel my heart pounding against my ribcage, as I looked at the prints from her fingers, pressed into my face. What had just happened? Who was she?

I got dressed as quickly as I could, grabbed my bag and returned the suit to the young woman at the exit.

"No good?"

"Not this time. You didn't see where my friend went, did you? She's about your height, dark skin, skinny jeans?"

"She went that way, I think." She gestured toward the back of the store, and the stairs that led to the Liffey Street exit.

I thanked her, hurried downstairs and out onto the street. Sunday shoppers were strolling there. I looked left toward Abbey Street and right, toward Henry Street. I couldn't make her out in the crowd. Then I heard the ding-ding of the Luas, followed by a screech of its brakes as the driver tried to stop. There was a single scream as shoppers turned and began running toward Abbey Street.

I ran too, afraid of what I might find and, at the same time, somehow knowing what was waiting for me. A garda appeared and told the crowd to get back. The driver of the tram came out from his cabin.

"She came out of nowhere," he said.

I saw her then, the woman from my dressing room, lying on the tracks. Her arms were by her sides and her eyes were wide open, a pool of red growing from behind her head.

"Shock," I heard a man say above me, and I found that I was also lying on the ground.

Someone had put a jacket beneath my head. A girl's voice instructed me not to move, that an ambulance was on the way. There was a crowd around me and I thought for a moment I saw a familiar shape, a tanned, bald head looking down, but when I blinked, he was gone.

I tried to get up, but a young garda, who was kneeling

beside me, held me lightly by the shoulder. I told her I didn't want to wait for an ambulance. I insisted I didn't need one.

"Do you know that woman?" she asked.

"No, I don't. It's just the sight of blood makes me woozy."

"If you're sure," she said. She used that tone young people sometimes adopt when speaking to those they consider old or infirm. I felt like telling her I was not ninety-four, but I said instead that I was going to get a taxi home and I would be fine.

As she helped me to my feet, I glanced again toward the woman, splayed on the side of the tracks. A garda had partially covered her with his jacket. Onlookers were standing and watching, hands to mouths, in morbid curiosity. An ambulance turned into the street, its siren sounding to clear the crowd.

I turned away and walked toward O'Connell Street, flagging down the first taxi that I found.

In the back seat of the car, I took out my phone. My hands shook as I rang Gabriel. He answered after seven rings.

"There's been an accident," I said.

"Oh? Are you hurt?" He sounded groggy.

"No, I can't talk. I'm in a taxi on my way home. Can you call by?"

He sighed, and I could picture him, feet up on the couch in his home, a match on the TV. Perhaps he'd been dozing after the morning's pints.

"I'll see you there, give me half an hour," he said at last.

I leaned back against the headrest, closed my eyes and pictured the woman from the dressing room. I tried to remember her words, the inflection and the emphasis in her voice. Her accent was possibly Mauritian, like Angelica in the court canteen, but with something else too, a hint of Wicklow. I thought of the strength in her arms and her smell. What was it? It was not perfume. It was more clinical,

64

antiseptic, like the smell of someone who'd just been in a hospital. I tried to recall every detail of her face, her dark skin and her brown eyes. What was it I'd seen in them? Fear? Anger? Then I realised her photo would probably be all over the media, so I didn't need to worry about giving Gabriel a description.

What had happened after she left me? I tried to picture the scene in my head. How had she somehow managed to walk or run into the path of the tram? Then I saw her again, lying on the tracks, the crowd and the driver's ashen face. I was angry with myself for fainting – there might have been more I could have seen, evidence I could have given to gardaí.

When I got to Clontarf Road I asked the driver to keep the meter running. I suddenly had no desire to go inside. I scanned the three-storey for any sign of interference. But the house's sash windows, set in eggshell-blue render, just stared out onto the seafront as they've always done. The dark-blue front door was intact.

"Do you mind staying a bit longer? I'm just waiting on a friend before I go in," I told the driver.

"No problem," he said. He had the radio tuned to Lyric FM and the theme tune from *Out of Africa* was playing. It conjured up beauty and wide-open spaces. As it came to an end, the taxi driver looked at his watch and then turned around to look at me.

"Are you nervous, is that it? Would you like me to go in with you?"

I was going to say no.

"Would you mind?"

I paid the fare and took the keys from my bag. The driver went ahead of me and looked in the ground-floor windows. Then he stood beside me at the door as I opened it.

When we got inside, he checked each room, upstairs and down, as well as the back garden.

"All right?" he asked.

"Thanks. You're very kind."

"No bother."

I was grateful I hadn't waited. It took Gabriel another hour to call by. He arrived in a taxi, his hair uncombed and his eyelids heavy, as though he'd only just woken from a deep sleep.

"Are you okay?" I asked.

"Never mind me, what happened?" He followed me into the kitchen.

I made him coffee and told him everything I could remember.

"She must have been following you then, all the way from here, probably."

"So she knew where I live?"

"And if she knew, *they* know, whoever they are."

It seemed ridiculous that someone might have been following me. Me. I wondered, not for the first time, how I had got myself into such a mess.

"And you're sure the man in the crowd was the same one who called here?"

"I can't be sure. It happened so quickly – but I feel it was him."

"We'll have to find out more about that charity – St Lucian wasn't it?"

He asked me to repeat the words the woman had spoken. The coffee and the predicament seemed to wake up his brain. I could almost see it working behind his eyes. He rested his left hand under his chin, with his elbow on the table.

"Jesus, Beatrice, what have you stumbled into?"

I did not know. Since Friday, I'd felt like I was working in darkness and, now, it felt like I'd taken a punch to the stomach from an invisible assailant.

"Do you think it's time I told the gardaí?"

He filled his lungs with air and blew it out.

"You know the consequences haven't changed. It'd be a mistrial. Do you want that?"

"You know I don't."

He rubbed his left earlobe and pinched his lower lip between thumb and index finger.

"Okay, let me see what I can find out about this woman."

He looked around the kitchen.

"In the meantime, I don't think you should stay here."

"I have a friend who might put me up for a few days," I said.

"Good. Call her now and I'll go over with you."

I smiled to myself that he assumed it was a woman. He was right.

I called Janine and she answered the phone with her usual efficiency. The sweetness of her tone was a balm. I said my house had an infestation of mice so bad that the exterminators insisted I vacate while they dealt with it. I was amazed at the ease with which I lied.

"You poor thing, of course you can stay here," she said. So trusting.

"You're sure I won't be interrupting anything?" I was thinking of Alastair, with his taste for high cuisine.

"Not at all, I've plenty of space."

I felt guilty for telling her fibs, but consoled myself that I was protecting her and would confess all when the whole business was over. I packed clothes and toiletries for a couple of days, put my suit into a garment bag and locked the door of the house behind me.

I drove with Gabriel to Clifden Heights, a development shoe-horned onto a site that had once housed a flour mill in Phibsboro. Janine had bought a two-bedroom, ground-floor apartment there at the height of the property boom for an outrageous price.

On the car radio, the nine o'clock news detailed the death of an unnamed woman. The reporter said it was a tragic accident.

"Witnesses said the woman darted out onto the road directly into the path of the oncoming tram. The Luas driver had no opportunity to stop. He was taken to Beaumont Hospital where he is currently being treated for shock. The State Pathologist is due to carry out a post-mortem on the woman tomorrow."

Another body to keep her busy.

I parked in a vacant space near Janine's.

"I'm going to walk home to clear my head," Gabriel said.

I suspected he had a detour to the local pub in mind.

"I'll call you tomorrow," he said.

Janine buzzed me into the lobby and then her apartment, to the left of the main door. I realised at once that her pleasantness on the phone had been deceptive. Things were far from okay with her.

She put my belongings in her guest room. I could tell she'd just made up the bed – the floral duvet smelled of fabric conditioner. It was the most colourful thing in the room, which had cream walls and curtains. Cream seemed to be the theme of her apartment. The living area was the same, with splashes of cerise provided by cushions, scattered on the couch, and a rug by the fireplace.

Janine had made me tea by the time I'd unpacked and had poured herself a glass from a half-finished bottle of Merlot. She told me she was glad of the company. She needed a friend – someone to listen.

I nodded and sat down, waiting for the details.

"He says . . . I smother him." There was a break in her voice, as she tried to control her emotions. She recounted how Alastair had phoned her after work and said he wouldn't be home.

"I just asked him if he'd like me to keep him dinner." She furrowed her brow, attempting to understand what had happened next.

"He snapped 'No' at me in the coldest tone and I knew there was something up. I asked him if he was angry with me, though I couldn't imagine why." She sipped again from her glass. "Then he said, 'For God's sake, Janine, just lay off. I can't stand how you smother me.' He said I wasn't to expect him at all tonight and he'd call me." She took a gulp of wine and tears began running down her cheeks. "I think he might be going off me, you know Bea? Even on Saturday, it didn't bother him at all when the hospital called him to come in. I remember in the beginning he hated being on call."

I handed her a tissue.

"I suppose I just try too hard. That's always been my problem."

"You're too good for him."

She looked as though I'd said something utterly preposterous and I regretted my memory lapse. Of course, she thought Alastair was perfection itself. I'd sat through more than one coffee break with her that began "Alastair said" and I'd had to bite hard on my tongue to prevent myself from commenting.

I asked her once, in idle interest, exactly what kind of a doctor he was, and she was delighted to hold forth on his vocation as a psychiatrist with a real heart. He'd told her details about some of his patients and how he'd helped them.

"He goes beyond the pale for them – really, he cares so much about them."

I'd resisted the temptation to mention his obligations to patient confidentiality.

"He worked as a locum for years, but now he has a permanent post at St Jerome's. It's the most prestigious psychiatric hospital in the country – he's very ambitious," she'd told me, as though that could only be a good thing.

I had to remind myself of my own first, blind love that

had allowed me to see only perfection in its object. I remembered doing everything I could to please that man. And Janine was the same with Alastair.

I tried to find some words that might offer her comfort and fished out a time-worn classic.

"If he's for you, Janine, you'll have him."

She nodded and drank more wine.

"Should I text him, do you think?"

"God no!"

I threatened to confiscate her phone if she attempted such a thing.

"Listen to me. You are a fabulous woman – good-looking, hardworking, talented. Any man would be lucky to have you. By tomorrow Alastair will have realised that."

She swirled the wine in the end of her glass and tears plopped into it.

"You have to say that – you're my friend."

I wanted to shake her by the shoulders and shout, "What is wrong with you, woman?", but I swallowed my impatience.

She picked up the wine bottle, tilted it and realised it was empty.

"I think there's another one in the kitchen."

"I think what you need is a good night's sleep. Why don't you head to bed and I'll tidy up?"

She nodded, still sniffling, and finished the dregs of her glass. Then she got up from the couch and dragged herself off to bed.

"Night, Bea."

I put her glass and my mug into the dishwasher and tidied away the snacks she'd laid out on the coffee table.

I checked the locks on the front door and the windows before preparing for bed. When I switched off the light in the guest room, a yellow glow from the street bled through the wooden window blinds, in stripes like tramlines. I saw again the woman lying on the tracks, her wide-open eyes and the blood oozing from her head. I felt sure she'd risked her own safety to warn me – her blood was on my hands.

That old familiar knot twisted my insides and I thought again of my brother Laurence. I had failed him as well. Though it was never said, I knew that. At the time, I considered myself a sort of victim too, but the truth was I could have helped him. I could have done something if I had only managed to see beyond my own limited vision. And if I'd been quicker, I might have been able to help the dead woman too.

Chapter 8

Tuesday, 5ᵗʰ May 1981

Laurence became our frequent companion when Leo and I went out in the city. For Leo, he was a suitable cover story if we happened to bump into Angie's friends. But he liked his company too – he liked the way Laurence admired him. For me, having my brother along was just a pleasure.

He talked often about how restless he felt in the Civil Service, how he needed only one decent break to be able to move on.

One day I came home to the flat after work and found Laurence and Leo already inside. I'd given Leo a key a few weeks before, when I'd found him waiting in the rain outside the flat one evening. He'd hesitated when I put it into his hand.

"I know," I'd said. "It's just to stop you getting wet, that's all."

The two men were sitting at the kitchen counter when I came through the door, with too many bags of shopping. They both got up and took them from me, placing them on the counter top. There were pens there and paper with figures written on them.

"Have you eaten?" I asked. They said they hadn't and I set about making spaghetti bolognese.

Leo picked up the pages and made for the coffee table in the living area – "getting out of my way".

I opened a bottle of wine and filled two glasses, placing them on the little coffee table I'd bought for the room.

"Just give me a chance, will you? I think I can get it for you tomorrow morning as soon as the bank opens."

"If you really want to, Laurence. But I have other investors interested, so you'll have to be quick."

They hardly noticed the wine.

"What's going on?" I asked.

"This could be my chance, Bea." Laurence's eyes were shining. "Leo's giving me a chance."

Leo looked at me briefly and flashed one of his lovely smiles, before turning his focus back on Laurence.

"I'm just a bit concerned we won't be able to pull it all together on time," he said, covering his mouth with his left hand for a moment. "I wish I could stake you, but I'm planning on sinking all of my cash into this."

"No, of course. I wouldn't expect it."

I went back to the kitchenette and began chopping onions, their vapours stinging my eyes a little more than usual. Leo and Laurence had dropped their voices and I couldn't hear what they were saying, but the conversation sounded intense. I felt invisible, inconsequential in either of their lives. Then I scolded myself for childish jealousy and concentrated as hard as I could on cooking the meal.

Just as it was ready, Laurence came and kissed me on the cheek.

"Smells gorgeous, but I have to run, Bea."

He saluted Leo before leaving.

I set up the collapsible table and unfolded two chairs so that we'd be sitting facing each other.

"What was all that?" I asked.

Leo twisted his spaghetti on his fork and, with the aid of a spoon, managed to get it into his mouth without it unravelling. He'd learned that trick on a business trip to Milan.

"It's just business. This is delicious – any Parmesan?"

I got up and found the tub of grated, dried cheese.

"Tell me," I said.

He sighed and then relented.

"I got a tip about a property in London that has just come on the market. It's prime, and they've offered me first rights to it. All I need to do is prove I have the money to pay for it. I have to give them a statement showing that I have the money in the bank. Once they agree to sell it to me, I can line up another buyer and flip it over quickly."

"But – "

"I'll never actually have to spend the money, Bea, because the second sale will come through so quickly I'll be able to use the money from it to make the purchase. What's left over is profit. Understand?"

"Yes, I do, of course I do."

"Well, I happened to bump into Laurence when I was leaving the office and I told him about it. He said he'd like in."

He sat back in his chair and wiped his mouth on a paper napkin.

"I couldn't say no. I hope you don't mind. You know he needs the money."

"How much does he have to give you?"

"£2,000, but it's only for a short while, and I'll be giving him back £2,500."

"That's a lot of money for Laurence."

I thought about the figures.

"£500 profit? If it's so easy why isn't everyone doing it?"

"Because everyone isn't as clever as me, that's why."

"Did he say where he was going to get it?"

Leo shrugged. "He said he had it in savings."

It was possible, I supposed – he led a fairly quiet life really and I knew he'd been saving for his exit from the Civil Service. I thought about all those hours of boring work he'd put into those savings. I hoped he wouldn't regret it.

"Don't look so scared," Leo said. "It's a doddle."

"I'm not scared – it's just, it's such a lot of money and I'm not as brave with money as you."

"But you trust me?" He looked at me as though his whole happiness depended on that.

"Of course I do love. And I'm proud, I really am, that you can do these things."

Laurence called round to the flat the following night. I was alone because Leo was busy on an Angie-related errand. I was glad of the company. He came to the door, dripping with rain. His wavy hair was plastered to his head. I took his jacket from him and hung it close to the fire.

"Honestly, had you no cap or anything?"

I handed him a towel and he rubbed his hair vigorously and then clapped his hands together to get some heat into them. I made hot whiskeys and we sat either side of the fireplace, he cupping his glass in his hands.

"I handed over the money this morning at Leo's office," he said.

"Did you?"

"There was a solicitor there and everything, to witness the agreement."

He got up and put his hand into the inside pocket of his jacket, pulling out a sheet of paper.

"Have a look – it's all very businesslike."

I took it from him and saw that it was a contract, signed

by Laurence and Leo. It said the £2,000 would never leave Leo's bank account.

"But it's such a lot, Laurence, and you've worked so hard for it."

"I'm making €500 – I won't get that in the banks, Bea."

He talked about his great plan. He'd imagined every detail of it already in his head.

"I'll see India first and the great Ganges. I want to see the Forbidden City too, in China."

He talked for a while about a book he was reading on Gandhi and how he'd like to travel on the Pan-American highway.

"I want to make enough to stay away for two years. There's so much I want to see." His eyes were wide and a little shiny from the whiskey as he enthused about Machu Picchu and the Incas.

"Ireland is such a small country, Bea, it's stifling. I can't wait to get out of here."

I was glad for him and said so.

When he was leaving he hugged me ferociously as I handed him an umbrella.

"I'm so grateful to Leo for giving me this chance."

I didn't hear from Leo for a couple of days after that. It wasn't the first time he'd been out of touch so I didn't worry, but I was eager to hear how the investment had gone. After four days he reappeared, bursting into the office where I worked with a huge bouquet of flowers.

Mrs Carmichael scowled at him.

"Five minutes," she said, as I pushed him out into the corridor.

He kissed me and then spoke in a fast, excited patter.

"It's done, Bea! It all worked out beautifully. I've just seen Laurence and given him his money. I've booked the Shelbourne tonight, so hurry home."

He kissed me again and was gone. A wave of relief passed through me. I hadn't realised how anxious I was about the deal.

Back at my desk I'd only started typing when the phone rang. I collected another scowl from Mrs Carmichael.

It was Laurence, so excited about telling me he'd made his profit that I hadn't the heart to say I already knew.

"That's marvellous," I said.

"I know – and it was so easy. Leo says he'll cut me in on the next one."

"Good, that's great."

He said he'd put all of the cash back into his account except €20 which he was going to use to take Mother and Father out for a meal. He asked if I'd like to come along, but I told him I had plans.

I spent two hours getting ready to go out that night, choosing a halter-neck dress in emerald green and putting my hair up. When Leo came to the door I had to push him out to prevent him devouring me on the sofa.

"I worked too hard to look like this. I'm not having you crumple me, not yet anyway."

He kissed me on the neck and took my arm.

At the Shelbourne we ate in the Saddle Room. The lights were soft and the service so quiet that I felt as though the food appeared from nowhere.

"There's something else you need to know," Leo said, after describing in detail how he'd pushed the property deal through.

I took my eyes from my steak and waited for him to speak. He took a deep breath.

"I've told Angie about us."

I was stunned and couldn't think of what to say.

He watched me for a while and took my hand across the table.

"I thought you'd be pleased."

"I am, of course I am. I'm delighted. I just wasn't expecting it. You've always said it wasn't going to happen – "

"I know I have, but when I left your office today I realised I was entitled to be happy. Life is too short for just getting by."

The waiter arrived then to ask if our steaks were all right and Leo ordered a second bottle of champagne.

"Will you stay then, tonight?"

"Every night, if you'll have me."

We walked home from the hotel and the champagne made us both sing. Leo began 'Can't Help Falling in Love' in his best Elvis accent. I told him it showed his age, so he sang 'Let It Be' instead and I harmonised.

We fell into bed when we got back to the flat and I thought I'd never been happier. The people I loved were happy. Leo and I loved each other, and Angie was out of our lives. He was all mine.

Chapter 9

Monday, 28th April 2014

In Court 19, I typed as Judge Brown explained to the jurors what had happened to their forewoman. I had, of course, been in position when Stephen O'Farrell entered. And I'd thought, just before he sat down, that he'd glanced in my direction.

Leona, looking stressed, had nodded at me when she came in and I gave her a small, encouraging smile. I knew how challenging all this must be for her.

"So, we'll see you at half ten tomorrow morning then," Judge Brown concluded.

They stood up in unison and filed through the door into their jury room. One or two of the women had looked upset about Rachel Deere's death, but none showed surprise. It would have been impossible for them to avoid the media reports over the weekend.

When they left, the judge addressed the barristers: "Where does that leave us?"

Leona stood up. She was adamant that the case could continue, must continue.

"The case has come this far, Judge, and there are only two remaining witnesses."

Raymond Rafferty disagreed, of course.

"The wave of publicity at the weekend has ensured my client will not now receive a fair trial. In the interests of justice, Judge, discharge this jury and order a retrial."

Judge Brown smiled with a degree of indulgence at the sentiment.

"I want to hear from the gardaí – have you someone for me, Ms O'Brien?"

Detective Superintendent Rodger Fortune took the stand. I watched him as he took the oath. He had the look of a career garda, with his polished fingernails and perfectly trimmed hair.

"You are the officer in charge of the case?" Leona asked.

"I am."

"And what can you tell us about Ms Deere's untimely death?"

He took out his notebook.

"So, at approximately 12.15 p.m. on Saturday afternoon an emergency call was received from a male caller."

He detailed what the garda saw on his arrival at the apartment and what happened afterward. There was nothing in his evidence that had not already made its way into the media reports.

"A post-mortem has been completed and the pathologist is awaiting toxicology results," he concluded.

"And at this stage, Detective Superintendent Fortune, is there any cause for suspicion?"

"I cannot say for certain at this stage, but it appears to be a case of accidental death due to excessive alcohol."

He paused, and I stretched my fingers before resuming position. I could feel a tremendous headache coming on and wanted to rub my forehead, but I resisted.

"As I've said, there were numerous open bottles and no signs at all of a struggle of any kind," the Detective Superintendent said.

"Unfortunate, and very sad for her family," said the judge. "We extend our condolences." He slipped his hand beneath his wig and scratched. "In terms of toxicology results, what are we talking about timewise?"

"Possibly later today, certainly within 48 hours."

"Thank you. Please sit down."

He looked from one set of counsel to the other.

"One would hope the former rather than the latter in terms of timescale."

There was muttered agreement between the barristers.

"On balance, I think it best to wait for the final pathology results. I want to be informed as soon as those become available, but my thinking at the moment is that we should continue."

When he left the courtroom, there was a flurry of action from the reporters, who between them took up two benches. They were typing rapidly on their various devices to be the first out with news of the day's adjournment.

O'Farrell stood and left the court with Raymond Rafferty, their heads close together.

I searched in my bag for pain relief and swallowed two tablets with some bottled water.

When I got back to the office, I asked Janine to cross-check my brief transcript from the morning. She looked utterly surprised.

"Of course. I'm free until after lunch. Everything okay?"

"Thanks, Janine. Yes, everything's fine. I just need to go home and check on the exterminators. There's some problem," I lied. "How are things with you?" I was thinking of her tears over Alastair.

"Fine now, thanks Bea."

"I'm glad."

I took a tram as far as Jervis Street, crossed the Liffey and walked up to Dublin Castle. The thirteenth-century fortification held the Companies Registration Office in its grounds. I went to reception and asked for information on St Lucian the Evangelist Ltd.

The woman at the counter brought back a folder and fixed me with a quizzical look. She was in her twenties, with long auburn hair either side of a plump, apple-shaped face. Her tiny eyes were sunken, and her complexion was the colour of unbaked dough.

"You know it's a registered charity, right?" she asked, still holding onto the hefty file, as though she wanted to test first that I was a responsible enough person to be given it.

"Yes, I do."

"And you know you can look at all this on our website?"

"I didn't think I could get that much detail online."

"You can, for a small fee."

She nodded at me with the degree of indulgence the computer literate reserve for those less skilled.

"Really, it's much easier. You can do it from your own home, provided you have a computer, of course."

I wondered who it was easier for.

"I'll bear that in mind."

I took the folder from her, thanked her and found a seat in the corner of the reading room.

I balanced the folder on my lap and began examining its contents. There were financial statements and annual reports for five years. I started at 2008. I wasn't sure what I was looking for, so I read the foreword. It detailed the excellent work of the charity and thanked the various corporate sponsors who had helped to fund the growth of its facilities. I glanced over accounts, but the figures meant nothing to me. I looked at the lists of non-executive directors and recognised none of them.

84

As each year passed, the foreword seemed to contain less sponsors and more complaints against unsustainable cuts in State funding. There was nothing enlightening in any of the documents until I got to 2013. There, in the foreword, was his name – Stephen O'Farrell.

'The company is delighted to announce the appointment of Stephen O'Farrell to its Board of Directors. We believe his presence, particularly given his reputation for hard work and his background in pharmaceuticals, will make an excellent addition to the board.'

O'Farrell had a connection with the bald man's charity. And he had a background in pharmaceuticals. I wondered what that meant. What interest would O'Farrell have in a charity? I went back to the woman at reception and asked whether she could search under people's names.

"That's not a service we offer," she said, dropping her voice. "I might be able to carry out a bit of a search unofficially. It will be on my own time, you understand – €50?"

"Okay," I agreed.

She nodded and began speaking loudly as a colleague came into view.

"I'm afraid that's archived but, if you wish, you can request it and I will have it for you in a week."

She pushed a piece of paper across the table to me.

"Put the name there," she said in a low voice, "and the address if you have it, and your phone number."

I wrote *'Stephen O'Farrell, Killiney, Dublin'* and pushed it back across the desk to her. I couldn't remember his exact address, though I knew it was on court documents.

She looked at the page, raised her eyebrows, folded it and put it in the pocket of her jeans.

"I'll do my best," she muttered, then continued loudly, "I'll phone you when I have something for you."

On my way back to Janine's, I called Gabriel and told him

what I'd found. He suggested we meet up at eight. I couldn't very well invite him back to Janine's and expect her to disappear while we talked, so I said I would call to his place.

At Janine's, I changed out of my work suit, into jeans and a white shirt, and then drove to Gabriel's.

He smiled widely when I arrived at his red-brick, two-up two-down on Oxmantown Road, a ten-minute walk from the CCJ. The door of Number 9 looked freshly painted. The black had bubbled in parts and there were hairs on it too from the paintbrush. In some places, the hairs had been removed and furrows were left behind. As he opened the door, he caught me looking at them.

"It looks nice and fresh," I said.

He scowled and ground his teeth. "I'll have to do it again."

He was proud of his house, an early twentieth-century end-of-terrace, with a front door that opened directly onto the street and a foot-scraper built into the wall. He'd told me it was to take the muck off boots when the place was called Cowtown and was a through-road for cattle on the way to market.

There weren't any cows any more and where there used to be a mart, there were red-bricked flats and scrawny cherry blossoms.

Inside, the wall between the two main rooms had been taken down. A round table was positioned on one side and a grey sofa, faced an empty fireplace. A kitchenette had been squeezed into the backyard before Gabriel bought the house. He went into it and picked up a half-empty mug of coffee.

"Would you like one?"

I asked for water and sat at the table. He'd been painting inside too – magnolia on the walls, white on the skirting boards – and the fumes were making me want to sneeze. I could hear the tap running in the kitchen and knew he was chilling the water for me. He came out and handed me the glass. He sat opposite me and I told him about St Lucian's and O'Farrell.

"The directorship isn't even a paid role," Gabriel said. "What's he got to gain? Prestige, is it, a reputation, 'some man for one man' and all that?"

"You'd have to wonder if a man who would do what they say he's done, would have any charitable instincts."

Gabriel swirled the coffee in the end of his cup.

"What have we so? A shifty-looking charity collector who calls to your door and O'Farrell involved in the same charity. It's not much."

"No, but I paid the receptionist €50 to find out more about O'Farrell."

"Bessie?" he smiled. "She usually does it for €30 – she saw you coming."

"I guess so."

"Listen," he said, looking serious. "I'm told they've identified the woman who died on the tram tracks. She was a nurse from Mauritius, Precious Alexander. They've checked CCTV around the area. She was running and looked back over her shoulder just before impact. No sign of anyone making physical contact with her."

"An accident then?"

"It seems so, but it's possible she was running from someone."

I thought of the bald-headed man. If he was chasing her then did he know she'd been speaking to me? I had a picture of myself going about my business on Sunday, with Precious Alexander behind me and the bald man somewhere behind her. It made me nauseous. I realised I'd need to stay with Janine for longer than a couple of days.

"I want to go back to my house and pick up a few more things," I told Gabriel.

"Is that wise? They may be watching it."

I knew Gabriel would go if I asked him, but I wanted to go myself. It wasn't just that I needed more clothes – I wanted to see the house, to check if it was all right, as strange as that sounded.

"Will you come with me?"

"I suppose so, but we'd better be quick and . . . " he paused and looked me up and down "we'll wait until it's dark and you can cover up or something."

He left the room for a while and I could hear him upstairs. He came back with a dark donkey jacket and a baseball cap.

"It wouldn't be any harm to put these on," he said.

We watched the news at nine, waiting to hear something we didn't know already. But there was nothing in the speculation about O'Farrell's trial that we were not aware of and there was only a brief word about the death of Precious Alexander.

I'd scoffed at the idea of the dark clothes at first, but now I put on the jacket. It reached to my knees and I rolled up the sleeves so that my pale, freckled hands poked out. I turned up the collar and pulled the cap down over my eyes.

I looked up at Gabriel from beneath the brim.

"I promise not to laugh," he said.

We took his car and parked on a side street off Clontarf Road. When we got out, we kept close to the wall, walking along, heads down. I hoped no one was paying too much attention. Gabriel walked at my side and I put one hand on his arm.

We turned the corner and paused, both scanning the area for a sign of anyone watching the house. But there was only the traffic, going up and down, and, on the other side of the road, at the water's edge, a handful of late walkers enjoying the seaweed-scented air.

When we reached my house, I noticed the garden gate was open, and the instant I turned the key in the front door, I knew something was wrong.

When we entered the hallway, it all looked normal, but

there was a breeze blowing through that should not have been there. I had been careful to lock the back door and close all the windows. Gabriel shut the front door quietly and pressed a finger to his lips. We stood still, listening.

Above our heads there were the sounds of someone moving around in my bedroom. Gabriel signalled that we should wait in the living room. We made as little noise as we could as we stepped into the room and stood behind the door so that we wouldn't be seen by anyone coming downstairs. There were papers on the floor, books tipped from their shelves, and cushions thrown everywhere.

Gabriel took what looked like a cosh from his pocket. He put the leather strap around his right wrist and held the cosh's lead-weighted end in his left palm. Gardaí were supposed to return their equipment when they retired, but at that moment I was grateful he hadn't followed regulations.

We stood where we were for a couple of tense minutes before the footsteps moved across the landing and began coming downstairs. When the intruder came to the bottom of the stairs and turned into the hall, Gabriel stepped out from the sitting room, ready to strike. I saw a fleeting change in the intruder's expression when he realised what was about to happen, before he turned and darted down the hall, through the kitchen and out the open back door. Gabriel gave chase but went no further when the man easily vaulted the back wall into the lane.

Gabriel came back, out of breath and flushed.

"Know the face?" he asked.

I didn't. I tried to picture the man again – mid-thirties, red-brown hair, freckled skin, long nose, turned at the bridge as though by an old punch. What else was there to notice about him as he'd looked at us?

"Did you see his hands? Like shovels they were," I said.

"We better have a look at the damage. Will we start upstairs?" he asked.

Gabriel led the way and I followed in some trepidation. My bedroom was in chaos – anything that had been upright was turned over, the wardrobe was open, clothes had been pulled from hangers, an old suitcase had been pierced with a blade and every drawer had been pulled out and the contents spilled on the floor. I saw my underwear and night things at Gabriel's feet and I suddenly wished he'd leave the room, but he didn't seem to notice them.

"He was armed," he said, pointing to the slashed suitcase.

I shivered at the thought of what might have happened if I'd returned to the house alone.

"Are they trying to frighten me, is that it?"

"Don't know. I'd say this fella was looking for something."

"A random burglar?" I asked.

He looked sceptical. "Another coincidence to swallow. Think Bea, have you anything they might want?"

If there was something, I must have had it unknown to myself.

We checked the other rooms and they'd been ransacked in the same way. The intruder had even gone through the attic room that I used only for storage and upturned cardboard boxes. Laurence's old record collection was spread out on the bare floorboards.

"Anything from the court case?"

"Not here – that's all in my office and it would only be transcripts anyway. Should we call the guards Gabriel?"

"You'd have to tell them everything." He knew that wasn't what I wanted. "Let's not decide yet. Why don't we start a clean-up first?"

We started with the sitting room and Gabriel made me close my eyes and visualise how it had looked before, in an attempt to recall if there was anything missing.

I had nothing of extravagant value – a nice TV, a three-year-old computer, modest sound equipment, and a couple of pieces of jewellery in an ornate box that I liked to keep on the mantlepiece, beside an antique Ormolu clock. Nothing had been taken. We worked our way through the whole house, cleaning as we went, and when the work was done, I could think of nothing that wasn't still in my possession.

Gabriel found my drinks cabinet, where I kept a small collection of spirits for visitors. He took out the gin and poured some into two tumblers.

"Straight back – for the shock," he said.

I poured my tumbler into his, put the kettle on and found some camomile teabags. We sat at the kitchen table and I sipped at the soothing drink.

"What's going on, Gabriel?"

"I don't know, but I'm worried Bea. I don't like this carry-on at all."

Janine sent me a text message as I emptied my cup, asking if I was okay. It was only then I realised how late it was, gone two. I texted back, "Fine, I'm in good company" and she responded approvingly with a smiley face.

"I'm sorry I brought you into this mess Gabriel, I really am. Maybe it would be better if you just left it."

"And then what? Read about you in the newspaper?"

He sounded exasperated and I realised he felt some responsibility toward me. I wanted to tell him to go home, then and there, and leave me alone.

"Anyway, they know I'm involved now – your man would have told them," he said, gesturing toward the back door. "And after tonight, do you still imagine this is something either of us can walk away from? This isn't a love affair you can opt out of, Beatrice."

My eyes began to burn then, and I put my head in my hands. The cruel opportunism of the remark made me feel like I'd been slapped.

Gabriel stood up and put his hand on my shoulder.

"Look, sorry, that was uncalled for. Come on, we'll fix

this door and we'll get out of here."

I found some short planks of wood in the garden shed, off-cuts from repair work on my dining-room floor. Gabriel hammered them across the back door to secure it.

"You'll have to get someone to replace that tomorrow."

"I will," I nodded.

We drove the long way back, with Gabriel checking his rear-view mirrors and twice pulling down narrow lanes to park and wait.

"I'm seeing nothing," he said, "but it's best to be careful."

It was after three when we reached Janine's.

"You've just been in the wrong place, at the wrong time, with the wrong people, Bea."

"Story of my life," I said, as I got out of the car.

"Right so." He gave me a weary smile and waited until I let myself in before he drove away.

I went straight to the bedroom, got out of my clothes, had a quick wash and slid under the duvet, pulling it up to my chin. I was exhausted and slipped quickly into a deep sleep.

Oblivion lasted for about two hours. I woke with my heart thumping and my palms sweaty. Laurence had been in my dreams, thumping on the door of my childhood bedroom. I answered it and he burst in, shouting and crying with snots running from his nose.

"This place is a kip, Beatrice, do you hear me, get out as soon as you can."

Before I could ask him what he meant, Mother appeared and led him from the room.

"Go back to bed, Beatrice, he's just a bit upset," she said over her shoulder.

He had turned eighteen that morning and I thought maybe he'd been for a few pints and got himself into a state.

When I asked at the breakfast table next day what he meant, he said "Nothing" and wouldn't look at me.

"Guinness gibberish, that's what that was," Mother said.

And then I dreamed of his face, as pale and lifeless as candle wax, his eyes closed and his dark lashes almost touching his cheekbones. They'd twined a rosary through his fingers and in my dream I felt again the urge to rip it away. He would have hated that and the carving of Christ with his crown of thorns on the side of the mahogany box and the silver crucifix on the lid. I looked away when the men came to close it for the last time.

When I awoke, the dream-feeling remained, like a kick in the stomach. I lay on my side for a time with my knees pulled up, waiting for it to pass. I was dreaming more of Laurence now than I had done in a very long time. I wondered if he was trying to tell me something, to reach out of the past and warn me. But I dismissed the notion as fanciful, a result of the nightmare and the strange events of the last few days.

There was no going back to sleep, so I closed my eyes and began mentally visiting each room in my house. I inspected the drawers and the presses, pictured the bookshelves. Was anything missing, anything at all? I opened the hall-table drawer in my mind and rifled through the mix of things it contained: a nail scissors, a set of sewing needles, a pen, a notepad and a button.

It was then I remembered the card from the courier company that I'd found in the hall on Saturday – 'failed delivery of a package', it said, and that it had to be collected at the courier's office. I'd forgotten all about it. Was that what the man was looking for? Where had I put it? Would I have to go back to the house again and search for it?

I turned on the bedside lamp and found my handbag. I upended its contents onto the bed and the card was there from Speedy Delivery, with an address on Westmoreland Street. Could this be what he wanted?

I got up deciding I would make a detour and call into the delivery office on my way to work.

Chapter 10

Tuesday, 25th August 1981

I supposed this was domesticity – the cosy feeling I had when Leo and I came in from work and ate a meal together and then sat on the couch with the TV on. Sometimes I'd burst out laughing at myself because I never imagined a simple life like this could make me happy. I used to look at my parents and want to shake them for being so settled, yet here I was homemaking for Leo.

Mother and Father soon found out that he'd moved in, but they made no comment. And when Leo produced a diamond for my ring finger and I wore it when we visited them, I thought Mother would faint she was so happy. I felt it was conventional, but at the same time I was proud of it – proud that a man like Leo, a brilliant, gorgeous man, could love me and want me for the rest of his life.

He'd proposed during a dinner I'd made him of roast pork and apple sauce. I'd been taking lessons, one evening a week, at the College of Catering on Cathal Brugha Street.

"God, this is the best," he'd said, lifting his glass and toasting the food. "I can't wait a moment longer."

He got up and went to his coat and came back to the table with a little box. Then he got down on one knee, right there beside the formica table in my flat, and asked me to marry him.

"This isn't just because of the roast pork, is it?" I laughed.

"I've been planning it for a while, but, well, let's just say the roast pork tipped me over the edge."

After a few seconds he realised I hadn't answered him. There was an endearing look of uncertainty.

"Well?"

"Of course, yes – of course."

Mother had hugged us both when we told her and cried with what looked like relief. Father shook hands with Leo, pumping his arm up and down. I saw then how worried they'd been about the relationship.

"Are you setting the date?" Mother asked.

I looked at Leo, suddenly feeling shy.

"Perhaps next summer, June or July?" Leo said.

I nodded, and Mother said June had the best chance of good weather.

"Well, Miss, we'll have a lot of planning to do," Mother said.

I'd given it little thought, the actual mechanics of a wedding. I'd only been thinking about the result. I now saw there would be details to be sorted out, decisions to be made about a wedding dress, the venue, guests and food. Mother, it seemed, expected to be a big part of that, and I supposed I'd have to let her. I was, after all, her only opportunity to be the Mother of the bride. She offered to buy some magazines.

"We have to start somewhere," she'd said.

Sitting down beside Leo on the couch, I asked him what type of wedding he wanted.

"I assume you'll want a church wedding," he said. All

your friends and relatives, perhaps the Shelbourne or would you prefer a hotel by the sea?" he said. "I've heard the Marine Hotel at Sutton Cross has lovely views."

I burst out laughing and he looked puzzled.

"I didn't realise you'd given it this much thought," I said.

"There was something else I wanted to say to you, or perhaps I should have said it to your father. I know it's traditional for the father of the bride to pay but I'd prefer it if I paid."

"We can both pay," I said.

He laughed then, but when he saw my face became serious again.

"We should open a joint account and we'll both pay what we can afford into it," he suggested.

I agreed. It'd be foolish, given that we were living together, to expect Father to foot the bill, as though I was a virgin bride.

"We'll have to think about houses," he said. "Which side of the Liffey have you a preference for?"

"I like Westland Row," I said.

"We can't stay in this poky little flat."

I was a little hurt though I tried not to show it. I knew he was right, the flat was tiny. But it was our cosy nest, our love nest, and I was sure no other home would feel the same.

"We should think about viewing properties. I know someone who's selling new homes off the plans out on Howth Head. Imagine that, Bea, opening your bedroom curtains to a sea view."

"It wouldn't be the same as living in the centre of the city, though. Still – it could have its advantages." I imagined us as a married couple, sitting together at a bay window, looking out at the sea.

"I'll make an appointment with the estate agent for us. What about other locations?"

"Now that you've put a sea view into my head, if I have to move from Westland Row, the sea is what I want."

Laurence arrived at the door just as the news came on. He'd brought a bottle of champagne to celebrate our good news.

"You shouldn't be so flaithiúlach," I scolded him.

"It's your man I have to thank for it," he said, popping open the bottle without being asked. He'd made two more investments with Leo, growing his exit money each time.

"Won't be long now till I'm riding off into the sunset."

"Hold your horses – you'll have to wait until after the wedding," I said, looking him in the eye and pressing my lips into a straight line so that he was in no doubt I was serious.

"God, would you make me stay in that place even a minute longer than I have to Bea?" He gave me his best hangdog look.

"Would you have me walk down the aisle without my only brother to see it?"

"I suppose I wouldn't, but maybe you'd think about hurrying it up a bit."

Leo put his hand on my shoulder and said, "We might."

I didn't disagree with him, though in my own mind I was reckoning Laurence had a lot more saving to do before he could say goodbye to the Civil Service.

We clinked our glasses together and I told Laurence we were thinking of moving to Howth or along the seafront at Clontarf.

"It has to be just up from the Bull Wall, with a beautiful view of the bay. I wouldn't like the other end, looking out on the Poolbeg chimneys."

"Isn't it well for you – too good for the chimneys now," he said.

He swallowed the contents of his glass and topped it up before topping up mine and Leo's.

"Might you have something for me again soon, Leo?" he asked.

"I have a whiff of something, all right. Call by in a couple of weeks and I'll let you know."

Laurence did as he was told and came over a few weeks later. It was in mid-September, the day had been fine, but the light was beginning to go. I dawdled at a flower stall on Grafton Street to buy the last of the leggy sunflowers, their brown hearts and yellow petals promising summer would cling on a little longer. When I came home, Laurence was there with Leo, both talking so intently they barely looked up to say hello. I set about finding a vase.

"I don't know, it's a big one," Leo said. "I'm not sure it's right for you to go in this deep."

"Come on, give me a chance. I'll have it in 24 hours."

Laurence's face was golden from the evening light and his eyes were wide.

"I've other investors who are used to dealing in big numbers."

"What is it?" I asked.

Leo took out a brochure of a property in Paris, close to the Ritz Hotel, a block of art-deco apartments.

"They're gorgeous!" I said.

"I know, and I'll have no bother moving them on, but, well, it would be another league."

"Please, Leo, just let me in," Laurence said. "I won't bother you again 'cause I'll have enough to head off with."

I had a look at the brochure – it had a guide price of £250,000 – monopoly money, I thought.

"If I let you in there's others I'm disappointing," Leo said. He looked from me to Laurence and back again. "I can give you 24 hours."

Laurence jumped to his feet.

"Thanks, I won't let you down."

He ran out of the flat with the brochure in his hand.

"How much will he have to raise?"

"Fifty."

"Jesus!"

"Don't worry about it. If he doesn't do it, someone else will."

I realised he thought I was worrying about his business.

"It's not all about you, you know," I said, half joking.

He laughed and pulled me down onto his lap.

"It's all about us. When this deal goes through, you can tell your mother to plan a Christmas wedding."

Though I thought his comment a bit high-handed, I didn't say so. What did it matter anyhow when we made it official, since we were already living as man and wife?

Laurence managed to raise the £50,000. After he handed over the cheque to Leo he told me he'd borrowed some money, sunk all his savings in and persuaded Father to invest as well.

"I'll pay back the loan next week and then Father and I will share the profits, £15,000 or more on this one, Leo says. You won't see me for dust."

He'd brought brochures around with Indian hotels in them and an atlas in which he'd marked out his route.

"I'll have to give two weeks' notice Bea, then I'll be gone."

I asked him again to wait for the wedding and told him it could be as early as Christmas. He agreed, if it was before the New Year.

"I can stick it out until then."

He opened the atlas on the kitchen table. It was an old school one, with pages tatty from use. Inside the front cover his name was written: '*Laurence Barrington, Sandymount Lane, Dublin 4, Ireland, Europe, the World, the Universe.*

Underneath it, in my childish hand, was: *Beatrice Barrington, Class 3K.*

He loved that atlas. I remember finding sheets of Mother's greaseproof paper in it that he'd used to trace the outline of the countries. Mother used to say he knew every capital city and he'd sit at the kitchen table and mark each one with a black pencil dot, concentration scrunching his features. He had that same look of intensity as he showed me the route he'd planned for his trip.

"Every continent, and as many capitals as I can."

"I've heard of people teaching English along the way, so they can keep travelling," I said.

"I could do that, but once this deal comes through I won't have to," Laurence said.

Before I put out our bedside light that night I asked Leo how things were going with the deal.

"Swimmingly," he said.

Chapter 11

I waited twenty minutes at the hatch of Speedy Delivery while a young woman tapped on her computer keyboard and complained that the system was a bit slow. I told her I didn't have much time.

"I have it now," she announced, in a triumphant voice. "Yes, our courier tried to deliver it on Saturday, but he got no response."

"I told you that," I said.

"Just a moment."

She held up a finger at me, got to her feet, and went out a door behind her. I could see a series of cubbyholes with letters of the alphabet above them, each one filled with parcels and envelopes. I wanted to ask her why she didn't just look in the 'B' cubbyhole but decided not to bother. After another few minutes, and having consulted with a colleague, she reached into the cubbyhole and emerged with an A4-sized envelope of stiff card. Do not bend was printed across its front.

"Thank you," I said, reaching for it.

"Sign first please, and could I see some ID or a utility bill?"

I searched my purse and produced my work ID. She squinted at the photo and back at me as though not quite convinced, but then she handed the envelope over.

"Thank you," I said, as I put it in my bag.

I walked quickly back over O'Connell Bridge to catch the tram for work, glancing backward once or twice to check there was no one following me, before telling myself not to be so on edge.

I dared not open the envelope in public and by the time I got to the CCJ it was almost half ten. I got to my office and put it in a folder marked 'Closed cases', locked the filing cabinet and left.

I barely had time to settle myself in Court 19 before the judge made his entrance. He looked over the top of his spectacles at the State's barrister.

"Well, Ms O'Brien?"

Leona got to her feet, looking more tired than usual, I thought.

"Judge, the toxicology results are back – would you like to take evidence?"

"Just tell me."

Leona's solicitor handed a typed sheet to the registrar who passed it to the judge – a time-honoured tradition ensuring that no document passes directly from any hand to a judge's, without an intermediary.

Judge Brown looked at it briefly.

"Ah," he said.

"Yes, Judge, as you can see, toxicology shows Ms Deere's blood alcohol levels. She had 420 mg per 100 ml of blood in her system at the time of death. I understand 350 mg is considered fatal. The toxicologist is available this afternoon if you wish to hear from him."

"I don't think that will be necessary, unless . . ." The judge looked at Mr Rafferty.

"We accept the findings, Judge."

"A tragic accident," the judge said.

"I'd like to address you on discharging the jury at this point," Mr Rafferty said.

The judge sighed, and I thought I heard a muttered, "If you must."

Mr Rafferty spoke for twenty minutes and Leona spoke for fifteen. Then everyone in the court waited while the judge retired briefly to consider what he should do. I scanned the public seats, filled as usual with court-watchers, but avoided looking at O'Farrell.

It was then I noticed a text message from Gabriel: '**Call me as soon as you can.**' It had been sent at 10.25 a.m.

I texted back: '**In court – will call at lunch.**'

"All rise," the judge's assistant said as the judge returned after five minutes.

"Mr Rafferty, I've considered what you've said, but I believe the correct course is to continue."

Counsel got to his feet.

"With all due respect, it is preposterous that the trial should continue. There is no possibility of my client receiving a fair trial now Judge, in the interests of justice – "

Judge Brown held up a hand.

"I heard your submission and I've made my decision Mr Rafferty. It's now a matter for another jurisdiction should you wish to continue to pursue it. Ms O'Brien, do you have your final witnesses for me today?"

Leona got to her feet and had trouble not smiling.

"Yes, Judge."

The judge signalled to the jury minder and moments later the jury filed in and sat down.

The first witness was called – a computer expert who

worked with the gardaí. His role was just procedural. He had to swear to the court that the documents produced were printed out from bank files and that they were not forgeries or misrepresentations.

When Mr Rafferty had no questions at cross-examination, Leona looked a little disappointed.

"My last witness is unavailable until two o'clock," she said.

The judge checked his watch. It was just past noon.

"Apologies, Judge, but he has to travel."

"I see. Jury, please be back in your room by five to two. We will start promptly at two o'clock."

When the court emptied, I gathered up my papers and bag. I went quickly to my office and phoned Gabriel.

"Are you free now?" he asked.

"Yes, I am."

"I'll wait for you in the rose gardens."

I left a note for Janine, saying I'd gone out for lunch, and I made my way to the park.

As I approached the gardens, I could see Gabriel on a bench by the yellow roses.

"Elina," he said, when I sat down beside him. "They're hybrid teas."

"I didn't know you had an interest."

"I did at one time."

He looked around him. "She died of alcohol poisoning."

"I know, they said so in court."

He looked worried and I waited for him to continue.

"Thing is, my friend Bob, he says the pathologist who's now in charge of this case is Ed McGrane, one of the assistants to the State Pathologist. Bob says McGrane had a bad feeling about the whole thing and had another look early this morning."

He sucked on his teeth as though he had something stuck in between them.

"He found an injection site at her groin."

"What does that mean? Was she taking drugs?"

"Toxicology didn't show up any drugs. There's a possibility the alcohol was injected into her system."

"That would be murder then, wouldn't it?"

"He's doing some tissue tests. He'll know for sure after that."

"The poor woman." Her death was sad, but the idea she'd been killed was shocking.

I thought of the courtroom and the judge going on with the case. It would surely collapse when they found out.

"Bob says McGrane's keeping a lid on it for the moment, terrified in case he's wrong. The court won't hear a thing until he's absolutely sure and neither will the guards."

"I'd give this case one more week at the outside – there's only the defence left. Will he know before then?" I asked.

"I imagine he will."

We were both silent, contemplating the implications, the winners and the losers. I imagined O'Farrell swaggering from the court, addressing the media, smiling wide enough to show off his porcelain crowns.

"You need to be careful, Bea. If they'd do that . . . " Gabriel said, after a while.

"Maybe they'll convict him before the news breaks."

"Maybe."

I remembered the envelope then. "I might have found what the intruder was searching for."

I told Gabriel about picking it up.

"I'm not due back in court until two – will you wait, and I'll get it?"

"I'll grab Ryan's snug before the lunchtime crowd get in."

We walked briskly through the park and parted at the CCJ.

I went straight to the office and retrieved the envelope. I was glad not to be opening it alone. As I left, I saw Janine

107

making her way in my direction. I waved, before jumping into a lift.

In Ryan's, I ordered a sandwich and tea, and made my way to Gabriel in the snug at the back of the pub. A small wooden table took up almost the entire space. There was a bench on one side by the wall and on the other side, two wooden half-doors that concealed the seated drinkers. We could just about fit in it together. When I sat down, our knees were too close together beneath the table.

The crusts from a ham sandwich were on Gabriel's plate and his pint glass was three-quarters empty.

"Will I get you another one?" I asked.

"No, I'm grand."

"This is it."

I took the envelope from my bag and was about to run my finger under the flap when Gabriel took it from me.

"Never do that," he said. He made space on the table, lay the envelope flat, ran his fingers over its surface, picked it up again, smelt it all over, squeezed it and shook it. Then he examined the writing on its front.

"Postmark is Dublin anyway."

My name and address, in blue biro, had been printed in capitals.

"Hard to tell if the writer is male or female, written like that," Gabriel said.

The barman arrived with my lunch and Gabriel picked up the envelope to make space for plate, teacup and saucer and the pot of tea.

"Is that everything?" the barman asked.

"Thanks," Gabriel said.

When he'd gone, Gabriel took out a penknife and ran it carefully down one side of the envelope. He sniffed it again.

"What do you expect to smell?" I asked, as I bit into my sandwich.

"Anything."

He opened it carefully. Inside there were photographs and a cardboard file. Gabriel lifted them out and began examining them.

The first photo showed a window through which a man and a woman could be seen embracing. It was taken from some distance and the faces were unclear. They were both naked, a dark-haired woman, with a grey-haired man. The second was closer, but slightly out of focus. It was of the same couple, lying entwined on a bed. A third photo was closer again, showing only the head and bare shoulders of the pair.

"Oh!"

I recognised the faces – Stephen O'Farrell and Rachel Deere.

"They were having an affair Gabriel or, at least, they were having something."

He turned the photos over and examined them for date marks. There were none and no indication of the photographer.

"Bloody hell," he said.

He slipped the photos back into the envelope and began looking at the file. It had Rachel Deere written in marker on the front and an oval stamp beside it.

"See if you can read that stamp."

"Too small." I finished off my sandwich.

"Just a sec."

He put his hand into his pocket and took out his keys. Attached to the bunch was a keyring with a magnifying glass. He passed it to me and I held it over the stamp. I could make out the word 'discharge' and the date, 20 June 2013. Around the edge of the stamp were the words: St Lucian the Evangelist.

Inside the file, there were pages of notes, with dates and comments in various pen-and-ink scrawls.

"It's a medical file from St Lucian's," I said. "Why would someone send me this?"

I noticed the time – the court was due to sit again in fifteen minutes. I drained the last of my tea.

"I'm going to have to go."

I refilled the envelope with all of its contents.

"We really need to find out more about her. I might try to track down the boyfriend," Gabriel said. While I put my coat on he picked up the envelope, "Will you let me hold onto this?"

I was reluctant to let it go, after all it had been sent to me.

"I think I can find out who took the pictures. There aren't that many PIs in Dublin would be able to take these without getting caught."

It was as good a reason as any to give them to him, though I knew he really wanted to take the file to protect me. If I was found with it, by gardaí or by whoever was behind all this, I could be in trouble.

I left it with him and hurried back to court. I imagined a private investigator in a tree somewhere outside a hotel, with a long-lens camera snapping away, maybe getting closer for an intimate shot. Would they have seen him at the window?

I tried to think back to Rachel Deere's face when she was sworn onto the jury. The judge had warned about not serving if you knew anyone involved. But there was nothing in Rachel's expression to betray her friendship, or whatever it was, with Stephen O'Farrell. Not a flicker throughout the trial. No eye contact that I'd noticed between them. I supposed she would have been warned how to behave.

I tried to work out why they had killed her. Had she already served her purpose on the jury and been dumped because of it? Or perhaps she wasn't doing what she was told. I wondered if Gabriel might be able to find out what her boyfriend had said to the guards, or better still, speak to him. He might have some idea why she was killed.

The afternoon session was over quickly. The expert who appeared at two swore the phone calls played in court had been obtained legally. He spent ten minutes explaining how easy it was to record a phone call through unlawful means. I hadn't realised quite how vulnerable the networks were and promised myself I'd keep my phone time with Gabriel to a minimum.

Again, Raymond Rafferty had no questions for the expert.

"In that case, could you indicate how many witnesses you will be calling, Mr Rafferty?" Judge Brown asked.

The barrister paused for a few seconds before answering the question. The courtroom strained to hear his short response.

"None, Judge."

He glanced over his shoulder as he spoke, to see the reaction of the journalists. Their faces registered disappointment – O'Farrell in the stand would have been a big news day.

"The State has singularly failed to prove anything against my client."

"Best to hold your closing speech until after the prosecution's I think Mr Rafferty," the judge said. "Alright ladies and gentlemen, we'll see you back here tomorrow at half ten."

As the court emptied, I noticed a man with his back to me making his way toward the door. The width of his shoulders and his bald head were familiar. As he reached the exit, he turned and looked back into the courtroom, directly at me. He smiled, nodded and then left.

I froze. What was he doing in court? Why had he looked at me that way? I imagined him outside the courtroom, lingering by the lifts. I decided to break court rules and use the jury- room exit.

"I must have a word with Brian," I said for the registrar's benefit. When I caught up with the jury minder, I asked him inanely if he'd enjoyed his holidays with his wife in Morocco. He gave me a puzzled look, but answered politely enough.

"Yes, we had a pleasant break," he said, "but three months ago seems like a lifetime. I need to . . . " he nodded his head toward the jurors.

"Of course, I'll just slip out this way."

I indicated the jury exit and, before he could object, I opened the door and was gone.

I hurried back to the office, unsettled at the sight of the bald man. If he was trying to frighten me, he was succeeding.

Janine was already at her desk when I got back, and I asked her, for the second time, if she'd mind cross-checking my morning's notes.

"I know I'm asking a lot of you recently, but I promise it's not for much longer," I said.

She agreed straight away, as I knew she would.

"But you have to get back early this evening and tell me all about this new man."

"I'll do my very best," I smiled, adding a wink that clearly startled her.

"He must really be something because you're not yourself, Beatrice."

"I suppose I'm not," I said.

Emerging from the office with my coat and bag, I looked up and down, but could see no sign of the bald man. As the glass lift descended, I scoured the lobby. There was the usual cluster of Junior Counsel huddled outside Courtroom One. Defendants stood here and there, some with supporters, some without, awaiting their fate.

I spoke to Mike in security at the entrance, making small talk about the weather and the gaggle of noisy anti-water charges protesters he'd had to deal with earlier. While we

talked, I scanned the area beyond the glass doors. I couldn't
see the bald man.

I phoned Gabriel as soon as I was outside and asked him
to meet me at Janine's. Then I took a taxi straight there. I
was reluctant to get on public transport.

When I got to Janine's apartment, I changed out of my
work clothes into jeans and a pale-pink blouse. I had only
just put the kettle on when Gabriel arrived, a plastic bag in
his hand. I could smell porter off him.

"Busy afternoon?" I asked, as I let him in.

He ignored my reproachful tone.

"As a matter of fact, I have. I managed to meet up with
that boyfriend of Rachel's – Dave Wiseman. Found him
drinking in a pub around the corner from their flat. Barman
said he'd hardly stopped since Sunday."

"Will I make you some coffee?"

"You needn't – tea will be fine. And you needn't be so
sniffy either. I had two pints with him, both in the line of
duty."

He sat down at the table, a little heavily, and opened the
bag, producing the envelope.

"You didn't show that to him, did you?"

I failed not to sound alarmed.

He gave me a 'what do you take me for' look and I didn't
press him any further. I wet the tea and poured out two
mugs.

"So, what happened?" I asked, giving him a mug.

"I bought him a drink. The first thing he said was, 'If
you're a hack you can fuck off!' I told him I wasn't, that I
was in the guards and he said he was sick of talking to
guards."

"Was that not a bit risky?"

"I didn't tell him when I was in the guards. Anyway, I said
we needed to know more about Rachel's background and

could he tell me about the time she was in St Lucian's."

I pushed a plate of buttered scones toward him. He nodded an acknowledgement, pausing in his tale to squash the top and bottom of a scone together and take an enormous bite. He chewed and fine crumbs sprinkled onto Janine's tablecloth, a yellow oilcloth, with little, blue flowers. I made a mental note to clean it before she came home – she'd never liked mess, but since she'd become involved with Alastair, she liked it even less.

"Dave said he truly believed Lucian's had straightened her out. She spent a few weeks there and came back really upbeat." He took a slurp from his tea.

I nodded – it was nothing we didn't know already.

"Did he say if she mentioned anything about Stephen O'Farrell?"

"No, but you wouldn't expect her to, would you? So, then he told me Rachel had trained in England – Leeds, he said. And she'd had trouble before. Spent two weeks in a psychiatric unit after an overdose and a complete breakdown."

"Poor thing."

"He kept on talking about how they were planning a holiday together, said Rachel had booked them on flights to New York and they were going to cross America in a camper van."

He shoved the remainder of the scone into his mouth.

"Doesn't sound like a suicidal woman."

"No. So I said they must have saved hard to afford that and he said they didn't. Rachel had got some money recently, some relation of hers left it to her."

He paused, and I knew he had a nugget to deliver to me.

"One of the lads told me she'd no relatives, none whatsoever. Only child, with parents and grandparents all dead, and one uncle long dead."

"So not even a great-aunt tucked away in some nursing home?"

"No."

"So where did she get the money?"

"Exactly."

I knew we were both thinking the same thing – someone was paying her for something.

"Did you believe him?"

"I think he was too drunk to lie. He kept saying he couldn't understand why she did it."

He looked at the remaining scones, weighing up whether or not to have another, before reaching for one.

"There's a bit too much soda in them, I'll make more tea. Go on, what happened next?"

I refilled the kettle and set it to boil.

"After a while I persuaded him that the answer to why Rachel did it might be in their flat and that if he brought me back there, I could help him search for it."

"Would the gardaí not have searched already?"

"They did, of course, but Dave said it was only a quick look and that they seemed happy enough once they found all the bottles. The curtains were still pulled in the flat when we got there, and the air stank of alcohol. We started looking in drawers and presses and then Dave got fed up and fell asleep on the couch. I had a good look then, eventually found this between the pages of a book."

He handed me a folded sheet of paper. I opened it and saw a table in red ink with dates across the top of each column and writing in two rows down the side. At the top of the page was: 'cont'd'.

"There was just that one page," Gabriel said, anticipating my question.

The dates were the first and fourteenth of each month, stretching from January to the end of the year. Written on the first row was 'Doc €250' and there was a red tick mark under each date up to 14th April. On the second row was: 'Dick €500'. Under the first two dates, there was a horizontal line and then ticks were filled in up to 14th April.

"Blackmail?"

"Looks like it."

"She's very organised, isn't she, keeping track like that?"

He nodded. "Blackmailers need to be."

"Dick looks wealthier than Doc. Did you find anything else, any clue about who they might be?"

"No. Dave woke up, so I didn't do any more searching. Obviously, I didn't tell him what I found. What do you think?"

I studied the dates again.

"The Dick payments don't begin until 14th February. That's a week after the trial started so it's just about right if she was blackmailing O'Farrell and the name's not inappropriate," I smiled.

Gabriel pretended to be shocked. "Are you losing it or what?"

"I forgot to say, when I was leaving court I saw the bald man standing at the back."

"Did he say anything or . . .?"

I told him about my alternative exit route.

"And you didn't notice if he interacted with O'Farrell, no eye contact?"

"I don't know. I only spotted him at the end, but he could have been there for ages."

I thought of the bald man, standing at the back of the court during proceedings, watching me while I was oblivious to his presence. It gave me shivers.

"That reminds me, I checked out the website for St Lucian the Evangelist," Gabriel said. "Have you a computer 'til I show you? Your man might be on it."

I fetched Janine's laptop and we scrolled through images of staff. None of the men were familiar. But just as we were about to switch it off, I recognised one of the women – her sharpness, the hardness in her face, concealed behind a smile. It was the woman in the red skirt that I'd seen talking to O'Farrell and then to Rachel Deere.

"Are you sure?"

I was. The longer I looked, the surer I felt – those were the eyes that had looked at me through the tram window. Her gaze was unmistakable. Now we had a name – Dr Dorothy Whittaker.

"Great, good, I'll see what I can find out about her," Gabriel said.

"Could she be Doc, do you think? It could explain the meet-up with O'Farrell and with Deere?"

"It could, but – "

His phone went off then and he stepped out into the hallway. I could just hear "What have you got for me?", as he closed the door behind him.

When he returned he said he'd asked the lads a few questions about Dave Wiseman's background.

"They've nothing on him and he was definitely out with a friend that night. They have CCTV of him in the pub."

"So, he had nothing to do with it."

I ticked his name off the mental list in my head and, at the same time, wrote Dr Dorothy Whittaker on it, right below Stephen O'Farrell.

"Let's have another look at the envelope."

I spread out the contents on the table. Gabriel opened the medical file. It looked like it had been well-thumbed by him.

"She signed herself into the hospital on 12th March 2013, as a voluntary patient," he said. I didn't find anything unexpected in the notes. Her psychiatrist was a Dr Niall Forester, so that's another 'Doc' she was in contact with.

Some stuff about her childhood, alcoholic father, absentee mother. Nothing in here about O'Farrell."

"I was wondering, if they did inject her, would they have had to hold her down? Was there any sign of a struggle?"

Gabriel moved the pages around on the table to make room for the photos.

"Bob didn't mention it. And Dave might have said it if he saw bruises or anything. He told me how he found her. Terrible. Says he hates going to sleep 'cause he sees her in his dreams."

I picked up one of the pages and turned it over.

"I wonder who sent me this. It couldn't have been her, could it?"

"She'd have had to get access to her own file – not as easy as you'd think. Who else?"

"What about Precious Alexander? Nurses access files all the time."

"True." He didn't sound convinced.

The kettle boiled and I made more tea.

"If it was Rachel, why would she pick on me?"

Gabriel flipped back the lid of the teapot and gave the contents a stir.

"I wonder if she only recognised O'Farrell when she came into court." he said.

I found it hard to imagine that she wouldn't have known him. He was all over the media when he was charged, smiling and declaring his innocence.

"We need a date for these photos. They could be very old," Gabriel said.

We scrutinised them for anything we could recognise.

"The close-up is grainy – means it must have been blown up," Gabriel said.

"Neither of them looks much different. They don't look younger, I mean, and her hair looks about the same," I said.

"This is a sash window."

He tapped another photo with his finger. The window had a granite sill and was set in a red-brick wall.

"It's a ground-floor room anyway, let's suppose a hotel. Not too many hotels in Dublin with bedrooms on the ground floor."

"That's an unusual shape." I pointed out the arch at the top of the window frame. "Georgian is it?"

"Time for Google, I think."

We used Janine's laptop again to search for Georgian hotels in Dublin.

"Of course, we don't know this was taken in Dublin," Gabriel said.

"I know, but we have to start somewhere."

We honed in on eight hotels around the city that might fit.

It was then I heard Janine's key in the door. There was only time to scoop the papers from the kitchen table.

"So, this is who you were rushing off to," Janine smiled, hands on her hips. "How long has it been?"

She bent down and placed a small kiss on Gabriel's cheek.

"Four years – it feels longer," he said.

Gabriel attempted to shut down the laptop.

"I hope you don't mind – we were just searching," I said.

Janine looked over my shoulder and saw the list of hotels.

"Planning a getaway? Good for you, Bea. You know I always thought you made a lovely couple."

There was no right answer to that. We both blushed.

Gabriel took a pen from his pocket and wrote down the names and addresses of the hotels, then switched off the laptop.

"I need to head," he said to me, getting to his feet. "Nice to see you again, Janine."

At the door he said he would visit the hotels.

"Give me a minute and I'll come with you."

He looked puzzled.

"To be honest, I feel safer in your company than anywhere else right now, and anyway, I feel better when I'm doing something useful."

"Right so."

I went back inside for a jacket and my bag. Janine hugged me, briefly and awkwardly, from one side, then pulled away.

"So pleased!" she said.

Chapter 12

Monday, 21ˢᵗ September 1981

When I told Mother we were moving the wedding to December, she panicked. We were in her kitchen together, the day after Laurence gave Leo the money. My fiancé had left for Paris. I'd been rolling the word fiancé around in my mouth and laughing at the pleasure it gave me.

Father was in the living room watching a football match. Mother was making tea and had her back to me. Her shoulders were curled forward, and her spine looked bent at the neck. It was the first time I really noticed age on her.

"But there's so much to do!" she said, putting a china plate onto a patterned tray and carefully arranging Mikado biscuits on it. I smiled to myself at the way she counted them out – two for each of us. After a pause, she looked at me slyly and asked if there was anything hurrying us along.

"Mother!" I'd the good grace to blush.

"Don't 'Mother' me! Do you think I came down with the last shower?"

I didn't want to tell her we were moving the date to suit Laurence.

"It just feels like the right time," I said.

She nodded her head. "We'll have to have a rethink so."

She took down the pile of wedding magazines that had been added to her cookery-bookshelf and began flicking through the pages.

"I saw one in here with sheer lace to the wrist – wouldn't that be lovely for winter?"

She found it and pointed it out to me. The dress was floor length over a dense, silk skirt, with not only full-length lace sleeves, but, over a firm bodice, lace right up to the chin.

"I'd look like Miss Havisham."

"There's nothing wrong with a bit of modesty," she said, putting the magazine to one side. "We'll go into Alexander's. You'll get a better idea there."

Mother wet the pot and made the tea, and though I offered to carry in the tray, she insisted on doing it herself. I'd visions of being bossed around by her in Alexander's, with two matronly shop assistants colluding and cajoling until I agreed to walk down the aisle in whatever monstrosity they chose for me. I remembered a shopping trip when I, on the cusp of puberty, had burst into tears when she insisted on putting me in a hideous gingham skirt when all I wanted was a pair of Levi's.

"Do people still go to Gretna Green?" I asked Father, as I poured milk into my tea.

"Hmm?" He moved his gaze from the television set to me and back again. "I suppose."

Mother looked at me and glanced heavenward.

Father took a cup and saucer from her without looking.

"You may wait until half time if you're looking for conversation."

I thought of Leo and his careful attentiveness. I couldn't imagine him being so engrossed in anything that he wouldn't have time to look at me. If anything, I supposed business could be a strong enough distraction, though, as he'd said himself, it was only a means to an end, a method of achieving the life he wanted, first for himself and then, for both of us.

"When will Leo be back?" Mother asked me.

"I'm not sure. He said at least three days, more if it's tricky, so Thursday maybe, or Friday."

Leo had called me earlier from Dublin Airport, while I was at work. I had to brave scowls from Mrs Carmichael.

"I'm catching an afternoon flight to Paris so I can do the negotiating in person. Sometimes you need to see the whites of their eyes. I'll call you when I get to the hotel. I imagine it will be late, certainly after eight, but don't worry if I don't ring until tomorrow."

He made kissing noises in place of a goodbye.

"Love you!"

"Good luck," I'd said, as he hung up.

I'd gone straight from work to my parents.

"Have you given any thought to a guest list?" Mother asked.

"We were thinking we'd keep it to about thirty guests."

She gulped her tea and coughed.

"Thirty – but that's very small. Who will I leave out?" She looked worried at this fresh challenge. "If you're going to keep it that small, you'd be better going to Rome."

There was firmness in her tone. I wanted to say that it wasn't about her; I wanted to say it was our wedding and we could have as many or as few as we thought was right.

"We'll talk about it more when Leo gets back," I said instead.

"Bring him over and I'll talk some sense into him."

I checked my watch. It was gone seven.

"I'll have to go. I want to be home in case Leo phones."

When I walked through the door of the flat I looked

fondly at the telephone sitting just inside my front door, black and solid on a little table. I was pleased I'd persisted with my Post and Telegraphs application for a private phone. I'd managed to nag them into giving me one by calling into the office on my lunch break every day for two weeks until they were sick of the sight of me. I'd developed the habit of picking up the receiver just to be sure we were still connected.

I hung up my coat and shoulder bag on the stand we'd bought together at an antique shop on Thomas Street. It was a thin pole of mahogany, with three animal-like claws for feet and a head of five branches. Leo had carried it all the way home, resting the central pole on his left shoulder. I'd told him he looked like a rifleman and he'd marched home, left right, left right, to make me laugh.

I noticed that Leo's overcoat was missing from the stand. I supposed, in late September, the evenings could get chilly in Paris. He'd taken his three newest suits from the wardrobe too, and quite a few shirts. He'd only bought two of the suits the fortnight before. I'd gone with him to Kevin & Howlin on Nassau Street. I'd never been to a proper tailor's and outfitter's before, but Leo was perfectly at home.

The shop assistant greeted him like a friend and seemed to know what new items he might like. A classic navy tweed took his attention. When he put it on, he looked so handsome I found it hard to breathe and was tempted to join him in the dressing room. I teased him a little though, as he stood in front of a floor-length mirror, turning one way and then the other to see the cut of the fabric.

A tailor approached him with a tape and chalk and made all the required measurements, marking on the fabric where adjustments should be made. Leo became engrossed in discussion with him about the quality of the material and whether it would be possible to lengthen the sleeve.

I hadn't realised until that moment how important his appearance was to Leo. I felt oddly uncomfortable watching him. He was so self-absorbed. I looked down at my own paisley-patterned day dress and wondered if he judged me by the way I looked. Though if women could take such great care with their appearance, then why not men? And, after all, I appreciated the result of his efforts.

He bought a second suit in a grey herringbone. They were both altered to fit his broader shoulders. I didn't ask how much they cost, but I noticed a shirt with a button-down collar that would have eaten my week's wages. He collected them a few days' later and I made him try them on for me, just in case they'd made a mistake while altering them. They hadn't, and the sight of him almost made me swoon.

I thought how nervous he must have been about doing business in Paris to feel the need to take three suits. I supposed the French had much higher standards when it came to appearance, so he'd need to make a special effort. For a moment, I considered he might have to do business with a woman and jealousy passed through me like an electric current. Then I told myself not to be so foolish; my fiancé had never been anything but trustworthy and he adored me. When I left home, I hadn't set out to seek ownership over Leo, or over any man, and yet here I was laying claim to him with that word – fiancé. It was delicious. I sat on the couch and thought about him. I longed to feel his arms around me and chided myself for wanting him so badly when he'd only just left.

He'd said he would find the perfect hotel for our honeymoon while he was in Paris. It'd not necessarily be the most expensive, but it'd be the most romantic and the chicest.

"I'm not sure I would fit in with chic – I'd be more at home on the Left Bank," I'd told him.

"In that case I'll bring you back a smock and a beret."

I made myself something to eat and watched some TV. The phone didn't ring. I wasn't disappointed, though I had that longing, as those left behind often do, to hear the voice of the traveller simply to be reassured of his safety. It must have been torture when family left behind by emigrants had to wait for the post and read letters from loved ones, but never hear their voices again.

I reasoned that Leo was too tired or that he'd gone straight to a business meeting and didn't want to phone me late at night. I dozed on the couch and dreamed we were both at the top of the Eiffel Tower, looking out over the city. I was in the lace wedding dress that Mother had shown me and he, in top hat and tails, was holding a suitcase. Where the handkerchief should have been in his top pocket, there were 100-franc notes and when I looked down I was holding a bouquet with roses made of pound notes.

When I awoke it was one in the morning. I checked the dial tone on the phone again before going to bed.

I held his pillow close to me, inhaling the smell of him still on it.

Chapter 13

Tuesday, 29ᵗʰ April 2014

When I sat into the car, Gabriel had switched on the CD player – Johnny Cash's 'Folsom Prison Blues'. I've never cared for country.

"The hard man," I couldn't help saying.

"Don't knock it."

Gabriel beat out the rhythm with his thumbs on the steering wheel, singing along. His voice was as gruff as his idol's.

"Cheerful stuff," I said, when the song was over.

"Real, that's what it is," Gabriel responded.

We drove around the city, edging along with the tail-to-tail evening traffic.

We targeted the central hotels first and rapidly crossed them off our list. Then we worked our way to the Southside.

The fifth hotel we reached was in Ballsbridge – Findlater's. It was the first one that looked like it had real possibilities. We parked on the side of the road and walked in the pillared entrance gates and up the path, past clipped lawns and tall trees. The Georgian building, in red and cream brick, was impressive and immaculately restored.

"Townhouse and then old school, I believe," Gabriel said.

I imagined it 100 years ago, filled with boarders. It would have seemed more austere without its welcoming modern entrance and the ankle-level garden lights leading to its front door.

Laurence came suddenly to mind. When he turned twelve, Father was adamant he had to go to a private boarding school in the Midlands.

"It will be to his advantage," he'd insisted.

Mother had agreed, weeping as she packed Laurence's suitcase for him. And when we were alone, I'd asked him if he was frightened. He'd swallowed hard and told me all brave men were frightened, but they faced their fears. I wish I could have comforted him when his greatest fears became real, instead of letting him slip away.

We didn't use the entrance, but walked round the side of the hotel instead. Through the windows, we could see into the foyer, and then two function rooms and a restaurant. Round the back of the hotel there was a row of bedroom windows at ground level, just like the one in the photograph.

Gabriel gave a satisfied nod and pointed out a tree behind us.

"He was probably up there with a zoom."

We walked back toward the door of the hotel.

"I don't want you to say anything – just stand beside me and look like a detective," Gabriel muttered.

I had no idea how I would achieve that, but I tried to arrange my features in an inquisitorial way.

"Stop it!" Gabriel said, laughing at me. He stood still and ran his hand down over his face, switching from smiling to serious instantly.

When we got inside, he seemed to draw himself up a little taller before marching across the foyer and up to the reception desk. I followed, doing my best to imitate his posture and trying to employ a neutral expression.

From his pocket Gabriel took an identity card and flashed it under the nose of the receptionist.

"I'm Detective Sergeant Gabriel Ingram, Ringsend Garda Station. We've had a complaint about your hotel – a complaint of a delicate nature."

He glanced over his shoulder as a guest appeared and then disappeared into a lift.

"Are you in charge, tonight?"

"The manager will be back in twenty minutes if you'll wait."

Gabriel leaned toward the young woman, who looked shocked.

"We have reason to believe there is a prostitution ring being run from this hotel." He paused to allow time for his words to sink in.

The receptionist flushed. "Ah no."

"Don't worry, we'll be discreet. We just need to see your database. There are certain individuals we need to track down."

She hesitated, looking up and down, obviously hoping someone senior would arrive to take over the situation.

"Do you not need a warrant or something?"

"Either you help me now or I go and get a warrant and we're back in an hour with half a dozen uniformed gardaí. How will your manager like that?"

She hesitated and then gestured for us to come behind the reception desk. She let us into a small office where a computer sat on a mahogany desk. She tapped rapidly on it and pulled up the archived reservation files.

"They're all there," she said.

When the door shut behind her I turned on Gabriel.

"What if she calls Ringsend station to check you out?"

"Don't worry, we'll be quick."

He gestured to the seat at the desk.

"You're better at these things than me."

I pressed control F and then typed in Stephen O'Farrell. The egg-timer appeared and twirled and then offered twenty-three bookings. They were all for double rooms and each with the same confirmation address – 67 Buttevant Road, Killiney, Co Dublin. It was familiar to me from court transcripts. The bookings were dated between June and September 2013, almost one a week. There was also one dated 6th February 2014. Gabriel wrote each date down.

"No details of his companion?"

I searched again, this time for Rachel Deere, but found nothing. Then I erased the search history and we left the office.

The receptionist looked at us nervously. Gabriel produced one of the photos from the file.

"This man has been a frequent visitor, how many women did you see him with besides this one?"

The receptionist took the photo in her hand and squinted at it. The bare shoulders and the positions of O'Farrell and Deere seemed to reinforce Gabriel's story and she visibly relaxed.

"That's Stephen O'Farrell. I only ever saw him with her – just her."

"Sure?"

She nodded. "All the times I saw him anyway, the same one every time, dark hair, a good deal younger than him. But she didn't look like a . . . "

She shook her head.

"No wait, there was another woman once, older, a bit . . . I don't know, sharp-looking. But they only had coffee in the lobby."

"Okay. Anything else?"

"She definitely didn't look . . . she looked like a professional.

130

She had one of those voices – full of authority or something. I suppose she could have been the madam." The girl's eyes were beginning to shine, as though she was already formulating the story she would tell her friends.

"When do you think that was?"

"Maybe six weeks ago, a bit more."

On a hunch, I googled Dr Dorothy Whittaker on my phone and held up a photograph.

"Is this her?"

The receptionist took it from me and looked closely at the picture.

"I'm not sure, it could be." She handed it back. "Is this going to be in the papers? Only my boss will need to know."

"Only way it'll get into the papers is if you tell them, okay?" Gabriel said.

She nodded.

"Don't worry about it. Thanks for your help – we'll be in touch."

We left the hotel and walked quickly back to the car. My heartbeat began to return to normal.

"Why did you give her your real name?"

"I can't be done for impersonating myself."

I didn't object when he put Johnny Cash back on.

"How does it help us to know where they . . . did it?" I asked.

"It's all part of the picture. When you're trying to figure things out, you need all the details, even the ones you think don't matter. And now we have dates too."

I thought about that for a while and I watched Gabriel's face as he drove. He seemed content or peaceful or excited maybe. I considered how hard it must have been for him, to be doing this kind of absorbing work, to be deep into it and then to be suddenly retired.

"Do you miss it?"

"What?"

"This, the work."

He glanced sideways at me and then back at the road ahead.

"Sometimes, I suppose, but I don't regret getting out, if that's what you're asking. I couldn't stick the way things were going in there."

I didn't know for sure what that meant, but I could tell he didn't want to say any more about it. I changed the subject.

"So, they were having an affair and it finished in January. They got back together one last time in February. He'd hardly have her killed for ending it, would he?"

"You'd be surprised what people are killed for. I worked on a case in the 1980s where a woman killed her husband with a scissors after he told her he didn't like the shoes she was wearing. When we questioned her, she said he told her the shoes were frumpy and the way she said it – like it was the worst thing in the world he could have said, like it was worse than murder to her. People are strange, Bea, very strange."

The light had almost drained from the sky when we got back to Janine's place. Gabriel wouldn't come in.

"Mind yourself and I'll call you tomorrow," he said as we parted.

The apartment was empty when I opened the door. I could tell by the male musk, fresh in the hall, and the briefcase set down in the middle of the living room, that Alastair had returned. There was a note from Janine saying they'd gone out for a meal and I could join them if I wished.

It was the last thing I wanted. I'd been single a long time and always abhorred being the third. I was too familiar with how it went – couples filled up and spilling over with their own love thought of poor, lonely Beatrice and how they might spread some joy by inviting her out with them. I'd sat through a few of those threesomes, embarrassed by their excruciating generosity. Even worse were the invitations that turned out to be matchmaking attempts, when a surprise single friend of the couple's appeared at the table.

I sent Janine a text message saying I couldn't make it, but I was glad she and Alastair had sorted things out. When my phone beeped again, I thought she might be trying to change my mind but it was a message from Leona.

'Can you talk?'

I texted '**Yes**', wondering if her call would be social or professional. My mobile rang almost immediately.

"I'm really sorry to bother you Bea. Is there any chance you could come over? I need to talk to you, but I've no one to mind Gracie."

I agreed to drive over to her apartment in Ringsend. I ate a sandwich quickly, then, before I left, I decided to make a copy of all the documents I had on O'Farrell, just in case.

I used Janine's scanner to upload them onto her laptop, then I copied them onto a memory stick and erased the laptop files. I put the memory stick into my bag, then took it out and put it into a black vase on the bookshelf.

I gathered up all of the papers and placed them in my work bag. In the morning, I would put them into a file in my office. I'd call it Doc, I decided.

Leona answered the door to her fifth-floor apartment and then rushed back inside.

"Sorry Bea, I'll have to deal with this," she said, over her shoulder.

I could hear a mewing sound coming from a baby monitor on the mantelpiece.

I sat down on her soft beige couch and looked around the room. It was still furnished, with simple colours and well-chosen objects d'art. Tasteful, it would have been called, in one of those interiors magazines, when it was first put together. Except now, scattered amidst the delicate vases and the silver-framed portrait photos, was the paraphernalia of parenthood – the talcum powder, a tub of Sudocrem, an opened packet of baby wipes and a half-empty bottle of formula.

After a few moments I could hear her cooing at her six-month old daughter. I wondered where Michael, her husband, was.

She returned with the baby in her arms. The infant snuffled and turned her head searching for her mother's nipple. She had not yet lost the reflex, though she'd been weaned at two months.

"Sorry, she'll settle in a minute. Michael's not here."

She placed the baby in a bouncing chair and used her foot to move it gently. She looked tired.

"Has he been away long?"

"Three days working on a case in Donegal, but it seems like forever."

Grace cried again, more insistently.

"I'm going to have to make up a feed. Would you mind holding her for a minute?"

Before I could refuse she had thrust the baby into my arms and gone out to the kitchen. The crying started in earnest then and not knowing what else to do, I stood up and jiggled Grace in my arms while walking around the room. She seemed confused by the action and undecided about crying. She whimpered and then gave up.

I stood at the window and, as always, admired the view, continuing the jiggling motion. We were well above the rooftops of the nearby redbrick terraces and I could see the shimmering glass doughnut of Lansdowne Road Stadium and the city sky reflected in it.

I heard the microwave ping and shortly after, Leona came

back, carrying a tray with a pot of coffee, milk, two cups and a baby's bottle. She put the tray down, directed me to help myself and then took the warm infant from my arms and sat on the couch. She tested the milk's temperature on her wrist before placing the teat in her daughter's mouth. The baby suckled hungrily.

I poured out the coffee.

"I see Grace has settled herself in around here," I smiled.

"It used to be so different when it was just mine. Now it mostly smells of nappies and baby sick. It's not ideal for child-rearing but Michael doesn't want to move out to a semi-d in the suburbs. He likes the address, you know, Dublin 4?" Leona said. "And we could never afford a house around here."

I doubted that as they were both very successful in their areas of expertise.

She sat Grace up, supporting the baby's head with one hand, just under her chin, and gently rubbing her back until she burped. I could sense the reason she'd asked me over was about to be revealed.

"It's been a strange few days, you must be exhausted," I said.

She didn't disagree. "You know I've been working on the O'Farrell case for two years – hundreds and thousands of papers, accounts, emails, phone recordings and it all comes down to a few days of hearings, make or break. There were multiple offences the DPP could have opted for, but I honed in on theft and fraud and singled out O'Farrell, the chief executive, the face of Signal Investments. The thinking was if we could get his conviction we'd get others afterwards."

She didn't say it, but I knew she was thinking of the political pressure, the need to provide any white-collar scalp, a salve for public fury over the economic collapse.

"It's the hardest case I've ever worked on. There were

times when I thought we'd lost the jury completely. Do you ever look at their faces, Bea?" She stared at me and I felt there was scrutiny in her gaze.

"Not often – I don't really have time."

"I tried to keep the technicalities to a minimum, but there are things that have to be explained. When the expert gave them two days on balance-sheet manipulation I could see them wilting before my eyes."

She re-arranged the baby in her arms again.

"I know there are always one or two jurors who'll struggle to engage, but when the bright ones started to look like they'd lost the will to live, I knew I was really struggling."

After a few moments, the suckling noises stopped. Grace was lying still, content and sated.

"And then Rafferty with his cross-examination – he really tied our expert up in knots, don't you think? I'm going to have to fix that in closing arguments."

I didn't know why she was telling me this. Her remarks were of a kind she should have been making to another barrister or to Michael, not to me. I changed the subject to deflect her.

"How's Michael doing?"

"Good, really good, I think. He mainly does work for the banks now, chasing mortgage defaulters. It's very well paid."

I tried not to wince as I thought of the human misery of the repossession courts. Leona sensed my unease.

"I remember when I met him first at college. It was at a talk by Albie Sachs on social and economic rights, you know, the South-African judge?" She sighed. "We talked for hours afterwards – we were going to see the world and then change it."

I shrugged and sipped my coffee.

"You do good work, Leona and look at your lovely Grace."

She looked down at the baby sleeping soundly now in her arms, a late and unexpected gift.

"On the day she was born, when the midwife handed her to Michael, he wouldn't stop crying. He said he didn't know he'd feel so much for her."

"That's lovely."

"It took me three weeks to love her. It was so hard at the beginning, then one morning, I went into her room and she was sleeping in her Moses basket, and I thought my heart would burst open."

I didn't know how to respond – motherhood was a mystery to me.

She stood up and carried the baby back into her nursery. When she returned, she sat on an armchair directly opposite me.

"We've been friends a good while, haven't we Bea?"

I said we had, and braced myself.

"I'm in a bit of difficulty – I hear you know things."

I caught my breath and hoped my shock didn't show on my face. This was about me.

"This case matters, Bea. You and I both know O'Farrell is guilty. You know what he did to those people. He's no better than a common criminal."

I nodded.

She was sitting on the edge of her seat now, leaning forward, scanning my face with courtroom-level intensity. I felt like a witness under cross-examination and temporarily empathised with the people I'd seen her grill.

"Where's all this coming from Leona?" I tried to keep my voice steady.

She didn't answer my question. "Whatever you think you know, there is just one thing I need from you – keep it to yourself, please. This man deserves to be behind bars."

I wanted to tell her I couldn't agree with her more, but I feared such a comment would expose me. I didn't want her believing there was any substance to her concerns, whatever they were.

"You're right – he does need to go to prison, Leona," I said. "But I don't know 'things' and I have no intention of interfering in this trial."

She sat back then, looking tired and older than her years.

"Will you tell me what this is all about?" I asked.

She was silent for a while as though weighing up what it was safe to say.

"You know as well as I do, Bea, that we shouldn't even be having this conversation. It's just, I was worried about you, that's all."

I knew very well that she was taking a risk talking to me like this. If the prosecution found out she would be compromised and so would I.

"I'm fine, really I am. Please don't worry," I said.

She gave me a tired smile.

"Time I left, I think," I said, getting up and hugging her briefly.

"Mind yourself," she said, as I closed her hall door behind me.

I didn't know what to make of her remarks. What was it she thought I knew? Could she possibly have an inkling about what I'd seen in the park or on the tram? Did she know I had a file on Rachel Deere?

Driving back to Janine's I wondered where Leona would have got her information from. I could understand why she was being cautious, but we were friends and I wished she'd been clearer. If she knew I had the file and what was in it, surely she would have sought a retrial herself? Thinking about it though, I knew she wouldn't want to do that. O'Farrell's trial marked the peak of her career so far. We'd talked about it over a drink one night, not long after she was given the brief. She'd been enthusiastic and excited about the case and what it could do for her reputation.

"Of course, if anything goes badly wrong, it won't do my career any favours," she'd said.

"You'll be well able for it," I'd told her.

I supposed now, if she had somehow found out about the file, she would want it kept quiet as much as I did.

But what if it wasn't about the file or Rachel Deere? Had I been making too many assumptions? Maybe this was about someone who had a grudge against Leona, instead of someone who wanted to get O'Farrell off. Could someone just want to collapse the trial by any means to get at her?

My head was too full of possibilities and questions and I was too wound up to go back to Janine's. I decided to call by Gabriel's house instead. I needed to talk to him and tell him what had happened.

He was slow coming to the door and quick about suggesting my visit, shortly before midnight, was a bit late, but he let me in anyway. He was wearing an old dressing gown of rough tweed. His bare hairy legs were visible below it and he had nothing on his feet.

I sat on a kitchen chair and watched as he made coffees, dissolving instant granules in boiling water. He added two spoonfuls of sugar to one of the cups.

"Sugar?"

I declined and he put the coffee down in front of me. It spilled a little on his formica-topped table. He handed me a tea towel to mop it up, a look of embarrassment on his face.

It reminded me of the first day I'd seen him working in court, in the early 2000s. He'd been on a case involving one of the boyos from McDavitt Street. The young lad had let out a stream of filthy language when he got into the witness box, so much so that the judge had adjourned the case for an hour and told him he'd add contempt of court to the charges if the defendant didn't return to court a chastened man.

I'd looked over at Gabriel and he had that same look of embarrassment, as though he had been responsible for the bad behaviour. He told me, a few years later, that he and a

139

couple of the other officers helped the young lad's chastening process with a few discreet digs in the ribs before his solicitor came out to speak to him. The defendant hadn't much to say on his return to the witness box.

I'd seen that look of embarrassment too one evening when we were together, and I'd admired the width of his shoulders and his neat hair, prematurely grey. He could never handle a compliment and to divert me he'd told me the greying had been instantaneous.

"I found a missing child lying face down in a puddle. I knew it was her by the description that had been circulated – long brown hair, white dress with pink flowers and short sleeves, the O'Shea child."

He'd expected to see the rest, the brown eyes, the freckles, but when he'd turned the body over her face was an unrecognisable mash of purple and blue.

"The following morning, I woke up to an old man in the mirror," he'd said. "In fairness we got the fucker, sorry, the mother's boyfriend. He was a man who wasn't keen on interruptions and took the child out to teach her a lesson."

Gabriel ran his hand through his hair, greyer now, and rubbed his eyes. He yawned and a wave of stale stout, overlaid with his first few mouthfuls of coffee, wafted toward me. I told him about Leona's request and my new theory.

"But who'd have a grudge against Leona?"

"I don't know. Maybe a professional grudge?"

He raised an eyebrow, unconvinced.

"That's a bit far-fetched now."

"What about the people she's helped to put away?"

He warmed to that idea.

"Could we find out?" he asked. "Could you get a list of her recent cases?"

"I think so. Janine and myself have done stenography at most of them."

"Focus on the convictions, obviously."

"Most of hers have been."

Her conviction rate was the envy of the criminal bar association. I'd heard one barrister suggesting the DPP gave her the cases most likely to succeed because they were both women. I'd been standing outside Court 8 as he'd bemoaned "the sisterhood".

"It's not a level playing pitch," he'd said.

I'd felt like explaining that he wasn't even in the same league as Leona, much less on the same pitch, but I'd held my counsel.

"How did she find out?" I asked Gabriel.

"We don't know that she did. She could mean something else entirely Bea."

He put his hand briefly over mine.

"Try not to worry."

The clock on his mantelpiece struck once. I pulled away my hand.

"I ought to be going."

I could feel a pulse in my temples, a precursor to a headache, as I drove away from Oxmantown Road.

When I reached Clifden Heights, I was conscious of the quietness. The development was set behind pillared gates, off the Phibsborough Road. There was barely any light from the apartment windows, each one with blinds down, like so many closed eyelids.

I walked up the short path to Janine's apartment block and, as I searched in my bag for the key, I heard footsteps in the distance.

"Blast!"

I couldn't see it, and the footsteps were getting louder. Then I felt cool metal in the corner of the bag and pulled it out. My hands shook a little as I put the key in the lock. There were definitely two pairs of feet, and they were coming closer.

The lock was stiff and the harder I tried to turn it, the more it resisted. I wondered if I would have time to take my phone out and call for help.

I remembered a self-defence class I took once, when a lithe young woman told me how to take a man's eye out by inserting a house key between my thumb and index finger. I took a deep breath and pulled the door toward me with one hand, simultaneously turning the key in the lock with the other. The door opened and I stepped gratefully into the lobby. I had almost closed the door behind me when I felt pressure against it and then a firm shove.

"Where were you 'til this hour?" Janine asked, stepping over the threshold, with Alastair close behind.

I must have looked a fright.

"What's the matter?" She stood staring at me, Alastair beside her, all concern.

I shook myself. "Too vivid an imagination," I said.

"Would you like a drink?" Alastair asked. He said the words with a gentleness that surprised me.

"No, but thank you." I was tired and wanted to go straight to bed.

"You'll feel better in the morning," Janine said.

Alastair nodded, and I thought I saw compassion in his gaze. It was comforting and that surprised me as well.

Chapter 14

Wednesday, 30th April 2014

I rose early on Wednesday and left a note propped against the coffee pot at Janine's to let her know I'd see her at work. I needed to search through Leona's cases in peace. I also preferred not to have to see the loving couple as they breakfasted together.

I got to work shortly before eight, hurried to my office and placed the Rachel Deere documents in a new folder. I filed them under D for Doc and locked the filing cabinet.

Then I started searching the database of all of our past cases to find ones Leona had prosecuted to completion in the last three years. Discounting acquittals, there were nine. I transcribed the name, address, date of birth and solicitor for each defendant. Paranoia prevented me from emailing what I'd found to Gabriel. Instead I texted him saying I'd leave a list at reception for him to collect whenever he had the time. I wrote his name on an envelope, put the list inside and taped it shut. Gabriel had told me it was easier to see if an envelope was tampered with if it was taped instead of glued.

Louise at the ground-floor reception didn't ask any questions.

"No bother," she said, with her soft Donegal accent, the sound of rain on the hills in it.

I knew Gabriel would appreciate it, and perhaps he'd even pause a while to chat with her, just so that he could listen to her voice, an echo of his childhood.

In court, Leona nodded and smiled briefly at me when she took her seat. There was no hint of what had passed between us the night before, no concern in her gaze. I knew she was focused on the closing arguments.

In more than a dozen years of working in courtrooms, I've found it is in the closing argument that the techniques of a barrister are fully exposed – the theatrical flourish, the systematic delivery of a methodical mind, the barrister who flirts with the jury or the one who uses risky condescension in the hope the jury will bow to his or her superior intelligence. A case can be won or lost on the turn of a phrase, on the inclination of a head.

Judge Brown took his place and signalled for the jury to be admitted. They sat in their allotted seats looking rested, and as eager as racehorses that have spotted the finish line. It is an eagerness that has always drawn pity from me – they are unaware that closing speeches may last for hours and a judge's directions can sometimes take an entire day. For me too, the closing speeches of a trial present challenges. Barristers sometimes forget me in their rush to convince and I need all my concentration. I knew this morning would be particularly tough as my focus was elsewhere.

At a nod from the judge, Leona got to her feet and began.

"Ladies and gentlemen of the jury do not be fooled by what my colleague will try to tell you later today. This case is simple. It is not about a flawed business plan for Signal Investments or an over-enthusiastic investor or a man who has made human errors. It is about deception and theft, nothing more, nothing less . . . "

The jury asked for a comfort break when Leona had finished with them. Her address was as eloquent as I'd ever heard from her. She appealed implicitly to the jury members' anger at how the economy in Ireland had gone. She didn't try to directly connect O'Farrell with the downturn, of course, but implied his crimes had contributed to it.

Raymond Rafferty took half an hour more to say less. He painted his client as a hapless victim of circumstance, whose business would have continued successfully if it had not been for the economic collapse.

"Mr O'Farrell was just as much a victim of the recession and the collapse of the economy as anybody else. In hindsight, he made mistakes, he's not denying that. But who among us didn't at that time?"

He finished in time for lunch. The judge told the jury he would address them at two o'clock. I hoped he'd be quick – I felt like there was a stopwatch now, counting down to the pathologist's finding of murder, and I needed the jury to return a guilty verdict before that knowledge became public.

When I got back to my office, Janine was already there, and Alastair was with her, a cooler box in his hand and a rug under one arm. She was pink with delight.

"Alastair's brought us a picnic, Bea, we're going to the park."

"That's nice." I smiled as warmly as I could.

"I've brought enough for three. I'd love it if you'd join us," Alastair said. The gesture, like his kindness of the previous night, caught me by surprise.

He just didn't strike me as the kind of man who wanted to ingratiate himself with the friends of his girlfriend, quite the opposite. My instinct was to decline, but Janine gave me an imploring look and I felt I ought to give him a chance. I checked my watch and put the memory key from my stenograph into the top drawer of my desk and locked it.

145

"I can look after that later – yes, thank you."

Alastair walked between us as we made our way to the park. The bright, dry weather had continued and there were lunchtime walkers, cyclists, joggers and sandwich eaters everywhere.

We walked up Chesterfield Avenue, Janine hanging on Alastair's arm, until we were opposite the Wellington Monument. We stepped over the low iron railing and walked across mown grass until Alastair found a suitable spot, where he spread out the tartan rug.

I eased myself to the ground, careful to sit on the rug so as not to get grass stains on my skirt. Janine emptied out the contents of the cooler box, praising each item as she carefully placed it on the rug. It seemed to be the called-for response, so I murmured my approval as well.

The food was straight from Marks and Spencer – a selection of overpriced cheeses and relish, oaten crackers in a tartan box, strawberries and double Devon cream. There were napkins too and some plastic cutlery and plates, along with disposable champagne flutes and a bottle of Prosecco.

Janine clapped her hands as Alastair popped the cork and let the bubbles flood into the first glass.

"Lovely, darling!" Janine poured appreciation into her words.

I declined the alcohol and took a bottle of water from my handbag.

"Your case is done, isn't it? And there's nothing much left in O'Farrell. You should take the afternoon off," I told Janine.

She didn't put up a fight, nodding and draining her glass quickly before putting it out for a refill. One of the great attractions of stenography was being self-employed. As long as the work was covered between us, we didn't have to explain anything to anybody.

"So what are we celebrating?" I asked.

"Good fortune," Alastair said, and knocked his plastic glass against Janine's.

He went on to talk about how psychiatry was an excellent career and how he enjoyed being able to really help people while simultaneously being well paid.

"But, of course, the secret to making real money is to get involved in the business end of things," he said.

Janine munched on a cracker, the crumbs sprinkling down on the tartan. Alastair looked down at them and, for an instant, there was a shadow of irritation across his face, until she flicked the crumbs away.

"And are you, getting involved?" I asked.

"Let's just say a plan is coming to fruition and when it does, well, I'll be in another league financially speaking."

I finished my strawberries. "You have your eye on private practice? Your own offices perhaps?"

He laughed.

"I'm sorry to say Janine that your friend has a somewhat limited vision. Believe it or not, Bea, I don't own any property at all."

Janine smiled benignly, as though every word from him was a nugget of wisdom.

I only just stopped myself from asking why he was so happy to live in Janine's property for free then, with the mortgage hanging like a dead weight on her.

"Of course, you like property, don't you Bea? You have that little house on the coast road, Janine tells me."

Maybe this was why he'd asked me to join them, he wanted to make sure I was going back to my own home soon. He wanted to drop a massive hint in the guise of a picnic in the park.

"Yes, and I miss it terribly. I'll be glad to get back."

"Have you had word?" Janine asked.

"They've said two more days to be absolutely sure my visitors are gone." I wondered if Alastair was good at detecting lies. But if he was, he didn't say anything, and he seemed to be satisfied with the promise of my departure.

He nodded and emptied the remainder of the champagne into Janine's glass.

"So tell me, where did you train?" I asked him.

He was happy to talk about himself. Though he'd qualified as a doctor in Edinburgh, he'd specialised in a psychiatric hospital in the north of England.

"Meadowwood Park taught me everything," he said.

He gazed into the distance and I thought I saw a curious, vulnerable expression, cross his face. It was gone in an instant, but I wondered if it might be the side of himself he showed to Janine, that made her so adore him. Perhaps that was the real Alastair and the rest was a facade he wore for other people. Vulnerable men did that, I knew, to protect themselves from the world. Maybe his pomposity served that purpose, though it made him hard to like.

I checked the time – quarter to two, 15 minutes to court.

"I better go back. Enjoy the rest of your afternoon."

Alastair got to his feet and put out his hand to help me up. I was grateful to be able to stand with a bit of decorum and I thanked him.

They were sitting close together, when I glanced back before leaving the park. Alastair had his arm around Janine and she had her head on his chest. They did make a fine-looking couple.

Back in court, the jury looked wary when the judge said he wouldn't keep them long. He began by telling them what he was going to tell them, then he told them, and then he told them that he had told them. It was a quarter to four when he finished.

"Please retire now and consider your verdict," he said.

The courtroom gradually emptied. There was nothing for it but to wait. It is a strange time, the minutes and hours spent waiting for a jury to return its verdict. Leona thought it was like the hours before a birth or a death – with no knowing when it will happen, only that it must happen.

Time itself behaves differently in that interlude. It has a kind of weight that slows it down and elongates it. There is chatter among the watchers, attempts to read the jury, best guesses of the time they'll return and what a lengthy deliberation might mean – all tea-leaf gazing, without an ounce of science to it, just a way of helping to pass the time.

I busied myself with typing up my notes and at five o'clock the judge called back the jury. When they confirmed they had not reached a verdict on any of the counts against O'Farrell, he sent them home for the night.

"It's been a long enough day," he told them.

When I checked my phone, I had missed a call from Bessie at the Companies Office. She'd left a voicemail saying I could call by and collect the data I'd requested. Gabriel had left a message too and, when I left the CCJ, he was sitting outside on a low wall waiting for me.

"I've lots to tell you, but there's someone wants to meet us, so we better get going," he said.

I followed him to his car and we both got in.

"I've tracked down an old friend of mine, Graham O'Donoghue, used to work in Store Street."

He pulled out into the traffic.

"Graham had more than a passing interest in some of the drug busts, if you know what I mean. Stuff would disappear, and he'd go missing for days. They retired him early, but before that they tried to straighten him out. Sent him to St Lucian's."

"Interesting."

"I'd forgotten all about him 'til one of the lads reminded

me," he said. "Gave him a call and he said we could come down to see him."

"Where?"

"Wicklow."

I sat back in my seat – the trip would take an hour if we were lucky.

"Behind the seat there – I thought you might be hungry."

I put my hand behind me and found a carrier bag containing a packet of chicken-and-stuffing sandwiches, along with an orange juice and a packet of crisps.

"That was decent," I said.

He mumbled something about not wanting me to starve.

"The other thing is, I've made a few calls– all the men on that list you gave me are still in prison."

I swallowed some sandwich and waited for him to continue.

"There's one appeal coming up," he said. "Terence Mills – got life for murder."

"I remember him."

I had a picture in my head of a tough nut, jaw set throughout the trial. He'd been a drug dealer who killed his girlfriend in a jealous rage. The level of violence had been shocking even to those of us in court used to hearing about violent crime. There'd been fists and boots, an iron, and then an ironing board.

"He shouted 'Filthy bitch!' at Leona – when they took him away, after the verdict," I told Gabriel. "Didn't bother her, of course, she was as relieved as everyone else at the verdict." The media had praised her closing speech about violence against women and how society needed to hold perpetrators to account. They'd said it'd looked like the jury would opt for manslaughter, but Leona had convinced them it was murder. He was given life and an appeal was inevitable.

"He has friends on the outside," Gabriel said.

"But isn't it all a bit subtle – getting a trial stopped? Isn't he more likely to have someone chase her down a dark alley some night and give her a beating?"

"These fellas aren't stupid. They know there's more than one way to ruin a person. A high-profile defeat, then a whiff of jury-tampering after, that could put Leona back in the Law Library, twiddling her thumbs for years."

Gabriel said he'd maybe have a word with a prison warden he knew and see who Mills' friends were.

While I was eating the sandwiches, I thought about Rachel Deere's file and began going through it in my head again. Her specialist was Dr Niall Forester. I knew the name from somewhere.

"I think he's been on the telly a few times," Gabriel said.

I remembered him then on a chat show, speaking about the addictive personality, a tall, thin man, benign and congenial, red-headed, with a beard of red and silver-grey. I made a mental note to check the Internet in case the programme was still available.

As we passed through the Glen of the Downs on the N11, we began talking about who might have killed Rachel Deere.

"The boyfriend's out, so who would you put on the list? O'Farrell of course, and this fella, 'Doc' Forester," Gabriel said.

"And 'Doc' Whittaker, don't forget, she'd only just met her."

"Yes, and the bald man, he might have."

I reckoned he was capable of murder. I felt he'd murdered Precious Alexander, by chasing her onto the Luas tracks.

"We need to find out more about them. See if we can get an idea where they were when she died."

I said I couldn't imagine how.

"We'll see," was Gabriel's response.

We reached Wicklow Town shortly after seven. Gabriel

drove left at the Grand Hotel and onto Church Hill.

He turned in at an ill-kept, double-fronted house, its gravel drive crunching beneath our tyres. Before we had time to knock on the door, it swung inwards. A wisp of a man, in brown cords and an orange T-shirt bearing the likeness of Che Guevara, signalled for us to enter.

"Graham," Gabriel said, extending his hand.

His former colleague didn't shake it immediately, but ushered us into the hall, stepped outside, looked up and down, came in again and shut the door.

"This is Beatrice."

We shook hands and the bones of his knuckles were visible through his skin. There was a yellowness about his pallor and the skin seemed stretched almost to breaking point across a hawk nose.

He led us both into a reception room where three armchairs had been arranged around a fireplace, the logs within it burning brightly.

"Sit, sit."

He insisted on making tea and brought in a tray, setting it down on a worn, pink footstool that he'd placed between us. The light in the bay window was evening-soft, though dusk had not yet arrived.

"Oh yes," he said, when he saw me looking out the window and hurried to close the pink damask curtains. He moved around switching on lamps – they gave off only a weak light, hardly lifting the gloom of the room.

Gabriel caught my eye with a look that was a mixture of pity and apprehension. I worried about the wisdom of our visit, given Graham's obvious vulnerability. We sipped our tea.

"You wanted to know about St Lucian's?" The light from the flames played on Graham's face when he sat down.

I nodded, and he began to describe the place, a converted

Victorian mansion, redbrick, on thirty acres with twenty private bedrooms, men in one wing, women in the other.

"Plush," he said. "Marble in the entrance hall, polished wood in the bedrooms, at least in mine. I didn't see inside the others, but I imagine they were all the same."

"Were there a lot of staff?" I asked.

"I only ever had dealings with two psychiatrists, but there was at least one other. Dr Niall Forester was the top man. I saw him most of the time. The other one was a woman, didn't see much of her. Dorothy something, White, I think, or – no, can't remember."

He put his tea back on the tray then and scratched at the back of his right hand and then his left.

"Dorothy Whittaker?"

"That's her – cold fish. Anyway, they did other stuff as well, you know, not just addictions, took in a few of those priests. Kept it quiet though."

I remembered another snip from the doctor's TV interview, about sexual addictions and how they could be controlled. He'd said he believed they could all be controlled with the right help.

"You don't happen to remember a big, bald man by any chance? Wide," I spread my hands to demonstrate, "hard eyes and nicotine-stained teeth."

I described him as best I could. It seemed like a long time ago, instead of just five days since I'd first seen him.

Graham shook his head.

"Means nothing to me, but that's not saying much – awful big that place was, impossible to have seen everyone there.

"Did it help? The treatment, I mean."

Gabriel winced, as Graham scratched his hands again.

"For a while I think, maybe." He began rubbing his hands then, one over the other, in a gesture that mimicked washing without soap or water.

"We should leave you in peace," Gabriel said.

Graham shook his head.

"I always had this feeling there was something more to that place. One night, I remember, there was a lot of noise. I heard a woman shouting for help, just down the corridor. Then there was running and a door banging and muffled voices. I asked one of the nurses about it in the morning – she said she didn't know what I was talking about, I must have imagined it."

He looked at us, as though trying to gauge if we believed him.

"Do you think you could have imagined it?" I asked.

"I suppose I could have – withdrawals do funny things to you – but no, not really, no."

Gabriel and I nodded, and he seemed pleased by that response.

"You said 'something more', what did you mean?" I asked.

"Just a feeling, I suppose, like there was something not quite right. I don't know how else to explain it." He talked for a while about the treatment at St Lucian's and said he remembered Stephen O'Farrell breezing through the lobby one day with Dr Forester behind him.

"Grinning the two of them, like they owned the place."

"He's on the board," I said.

Gabriel asked if he remembered meeting any women there and described Rachel Deere to him. Graham couldn't place her, though their dates overlapped by four weeks.

"You wouldn't see many people. Some of them never came out of their rooms."

He got up then and took a packet of thin cigars from the mantelpiece.

"Do you mind?"

We said we didn't and he lit one. We were silent as we watched him draw on it and blow the smoke toward the fireplace to mingle with the logs' fumes and escape through the chimney. He absorbed himself with this activity until the cigar was half smoked, then he pinched it off at the lit end and put the remainder back into its box.

When he turned back to us, his face seemed filled with suspicion.

"You weren't followed here were you?"

"Not at all, Graham," Gabriel smiled. "Nobody knows we're here."

"Good, because they don't know I'm here. They only have my Dublin address."

Gabriel looked worried for his old colleague.

"If Forester saw me he'd know I need to go back. He could always tell by looking at you, what trouble you were in," Graham said.

"But if you need to, would you not be better off?" I asked.

"No, I'm better off here. There's badness in that place, I told you, were you not listening to me at all?" He began picking, with his left hand, at the cord of his trousers.

"Is there anything I can do for you Graham?" Gabriel asked.

"I think you'd better go," he said.

He ushered us out into the hall. When he held the hall door open, he hid behind it, so he couldn't be seen from the road.

"I'll be in touch," Gabriel said.

"Not on that phone." Graham indicated the mobile, a block in Gabriel's jacket pocket. "You never know who's listening."

As soon as we'd stepped over the threshold, he closed the door behind us.

We sat into the car and, as we backed away from the house, I could just make Graham out, peering from behind the pink curtains.

"Poor devil," I said.

"I hate leaving him in that state. I didn't realise . . . "

He looked over his shoulder as he reversed, and then back at me as he straightened the car up.

"What would you feel about staying here tonight? I could check on him in the morning early and then drive you up to Dublin in time for court."

I gave him a look that barely concealed my suspicion.

"Really? Is that what you think of me, Bea? Well here's some news for you, I'm well over you."

I blushed. "Sorry, I didn't mean . . . I was just thinking about work and not having a change of clothes."

"I'll get you back early enough to change. Okay?"

I agreed to stay though I wasn't happy about it. I hadn't even a toothbrush with me. Gabriel must have read my mind because he pulled up at a supermarket saying we'd need some supplies.

The Grand Hotel had space available when we called in, two single rooms on separate floors. Gabriel suggested we get something to eat up town and we went to our rooms to freshen up.

We met again in the hotel lobby half an hour later.

"A friend told me that a restaurant up at the end of the town is good."

We walked through the narrow main street, past the hardware, the newsagent, the shoe shop and the clothes shop, provincial stalwarts that had managed to survive the lure of the glass shopping cathedrals.

At the centre of Market Square was a statue of a man with a pike.

"Billy Byrne, the 1798 rebel," Gabriel said. He pointed at an old stone building. "Wicklow Gaol where they hanged him – twenty-four he was."

A boy, I thought, the age of Laurence, though at his passing I'd thought him a big man.

"He looks like an older, mature fellow."

"Middle-aged by their standards," Gabriel said.

We found the recommended steakhouse nearby and Gabriel was pleased with his bloodied T-bone. He suggested we share a bottle of red wine and I agreed to take a half-glass, a rare indulgence for me. The brief melancholy, brought on by thinking of Laurence, lifted from me. I felt relaxed, content almost, to sit and enjoy the food and the company.

"If you'd told me a week ago I'd be down here sharing a meal with you I'd never have believed you," Gabriel said.

"There's a lot I wouldn't have believed this time last week," he said with a smile.

"To good friends."

They'd lit the candles on the tables and when we clinked our glasses, they glowed ruby. 'The Pearl Fishers' began to play. I put down my knife and fork to listen to it. Gabriel said nothing for a while and then asked if I thought they might have some Johnny Cash.

"Don't you dare," I said.

He laughed and smiled. There was a kind of affection in it. I looked away from him feeling suddenly wary. The atmosphere between us shifted.

"Do you think it's too late for me to go to the guards and tell them everything?"

Gabriel put down his own knife and fork and folded his arms across his chest.

"Honestly now Bea, do you not think it's gone too far for that?" He swallowed some wine. "Look at it from their perspective. You work for the courts, you see something suspicious but you say nothing. Then Rachel Deere dies, could be murder – you say nothing. You get a package with information about her and you still say nothing."

"But if I explained – "

"No Bea. We'll have to tough it out for now."

"I appreciate the 'we', you know that, don't you Gabriel? You're a true friend."

"Friend, yes, I know."

He finished the bottle of wine and I declined dessert. We both had coffees.

I wanted to pay the bill, but Gabriel said he'd be insulted if I didn't let him. I made a mental note to pay for our rooms in the morning.

Back at the hotel, we said a polite goodnight at the lift, arranging to meet for breakfast at half seven.

My room was on the third floor, with a view over the town. The bed was clothed with a standard white duvet and red scatter cushions. I moved them onto a chair.

In the bathroom I brushed my teeth and took my make-up off with the wipes I'd bought, not a product I would normally use. I read somewhere, cleansing wipes bring on wrinkles. I did not feel I needed additional assistance in that department – there were already generous crow's feet spreading from the corners of both eyes and at either side of my mouth I'd developed permanent lines. I find aging is much like growing as a child, it happens in spurts. And a person has just got used to the slightly more wrinkled visage when another spurt brings further slippage.

In the harshness of the bathroom light I was unhappy with this latest version of Beatrice. I looked overtired too, with dark circles beneath my eyes; the recent poor quality of my sleep was taking its toll. I mumbled at my reflection "Must do better" and got into bed. I tried to clear my mind, in the hope of a more restful night, but again I dreamed of Laurence.

I could see him at the water's edge, but the river was the Vartry, that passes through Wicklow Town. He was in his bell-bottom jeans and cheesecloth shirt and I was on a height running toward him. I was running and calling to him and, though he couldn't hear me, I could hear him singing – 'Perfect Day' it was, in his lovely, clear voice. Though I was anxious to get to him, the sound of that voice lifted me, it'd been so long since I heard it. I could see him then, wading out, and I was trying to run faster, but I was getting no further. And when at last I got into the river, Laurence had disappeared, and Rachel Deere was floating, face up, eyes open, her hair spread like pond weed on the surface of the water.

Chapter 15

Tuesday, 22ⁿᵈ September 1981

When I woke up I was still holding Leo's pillow. There was a grey light in my bedroom and steady raindrops rattled my window. I opened the curtain and looked at the street below. There wasn't much traffic and only a few men, with upturned collars and black umbrellas, walked quickly by, on their way to early mass at St Andrew's.

I checked the bedside clock – 7.00 a.m. – much earlier than when I usually woke up. It must have been because Leo wasn't there. I wondered about time differences and whether he'd ring while I was at work.

There was a small, sickening feeling in my stomach, which I tried to settle with toast and marmalade, and tea. As I dressed for work and put on my make-up, I wished I'd got the name of his hotel or that I'd an answerphone or that I'd asked him to take me with him on the trip. If I'd known how anxious I'd feel, I would have asked him.

Every time the phone rang in the office, I held my breath. And when it was not Leo, I began to worry again about why he hadn't called. He knew, of course, that Mrs Carmichael wouldn't approve of his calling the office; I'd given out to him enough for doing just that. I realised that was exactly why he wouldn't call – he'd wait until I was home again this evening. I felt reassured when I thought of that, but still, I struggled all day to concentrate on my work and was reprimanded more than once for not paying attention. Mrs Carmichael seemed to enjoy pointing out the errors in the document I'd been typing, a thesis for some professor of linguistics, that I found impossible to understand. She put the pages down in front of me and rapped the point of her fingernail at an offending word – "d-e-r-i-v-a-t-i-v-e Miss Barrington". I could sense the girls around me cringing in sympathy.

I ran all the way back to the flat after work, clipping along the still wet streets in my heels. I rang Mother and asked her to call me back to test the line. When it rang I didn't know whether to be happy or sad. I paused before picking it up, allowing myself to imagine for a moment that, by some amazing coincidence, Leo had chosen that exact time to call and when I lifted the receiver I'd hear his voice.

"Is everything all right?" Mother asked.

"Yes, it's fine. I'd a bit of trouble with the phone earlier so I was just checking it."

"How was work today, dear?"

She was ready, I could tell, for a chat. But I didn't want to delay; Leo might be calling at that very moment, and if the chance was lost he mightn't try again that night.

"Work was fine. Do you mind if I call you later? I've something on the stove."

She hung up and I replaced the receiver carefully in its cradle. I forced myself to eat some pasta and kept the TV on low, in case I missed the phone ringing. I couldn't concentrate on *Juliet Bravo* and the exploits of Inspector Jean Darblay anyhow.

What could have happened to him? I thought about that film with Cary Grant and Deborah Kerr. If he'd had an accident, how would anyone know to contact me? He could be lying in a hospital bed, he could be hurt and I'd never know. Or had he been assaulted? Paris was such a big city and in every big city there is danger. Leo was so self-assured, but it only takes one man with a sharp blade to rip that out of a person.

Three more days went by. The weekend came and I'd heard nothing. I spoke to no one about my worries and shut down any questions about Leo from my family with a brief explanation about time difference and the pressures of business. I allowed myself one hour on Saturday morning away from the phone. I got my winter boots heeled, bought some food and some magazines so that I could assess the fashions for the season ahead. I'd have to improve my dress-sense, I decided, when I was Leo's wife.

By Sunday, I'd read every magazine cover to cover and made a list of the kinds of outfits I'd like to buy. But though I'd thrown myself into the task, I began to feel like I was playing a game or rehearsing for a role in some play in which I'd never perform. With Leo away and silent, the prospect of a life with him began to seem like a dream. I couldn't sleep that night. I'd visions of Leo lying in some dark laneway in a pool of blood or mangled under the fender of a Citroën.

When it came close to morning, I dozed briefly and awoke to my Monday alarm, exhausted and feeling sick. I'd told no one how worried I was. I was afraid that telling would make it real, but, when I found myself talking to my pale and creased reflection, I realised if I didn't do something, I'd go mad.

I phoned the office and told them I was sick. It wasn't a lie. Then I searched the phone book and found the number for the nearest Garda Station, Pearse Street. I told my story to the desk sergeant who listened in silence and then explained gently that a week was not very long to be out of contact for a man on business in another country.

"He's probably just up to his tonsils, love."

I felt simultaneously comforted and patronised.

"I know my own fiancé. He wouldn't not ring."

"All the same, it's much too soon for us to be ringing the *gendarmerie*." He made it sound as though I'd be putting him in an embarrassing situation.

I cried and said I'd a feeling Leo might have had an accident. The guard, who seemed anxious to get me off the phone, suggested I ring the Department of Foreign Affairs for the number of the Irish embassy in Paris.

"If an Irishman is in a hospital somewhere there, they'll know about it."

I'd a vision of him putting the phone down, shaking his head and filing my concern under 'hysteria'. I tried to calm down before making any more phone calls. I wanted to sound reasonable and mature. I wondered if I should exaggerate how long he'd been out of touch, but decided that might backfire.

When I rang the embassy, it was mid-morning. I explained to the secretary of the consul that I was very concerned about my fiancé.

"He told me he'd contact me as soon as he arrived and I haven't heard a thing." I took a deep breath to slow down my speech. "That was seven days ago and I'm wondering now if something has happened to him, an accident or something."

"We've had no notifications," the secretary said, her voice a Kerry lilt, salted with Parisian.

"But he promised to phone." I knew my voice sounded childish and I heard her sigh.

"I'll ring around the hospitals. Leave your details with me and I'll phone you later."

I hung up the phone and felt at least I'd done something and I'd know for sure if Leo had been hurt.

The waiting seemed endless and I was feverish with worry and wild imaginings. Shortly after four o'clock the flat filled with the telephone bell. I ran from the couch where I'd been folded, fitfully dozing and sweating like an invalid. The secretary asked for Miss Barrington.

"Yes, that's me."

"There's no hospital in Paris with an Irishman as a patient."

"What about an unknown, a John Doe?"

"There are none, and no Englishmen either."

She paused for a moment before continuing.

"There's been only one murder in the last week, an Albanian, and two car crash deaths, both women."

"Well, thank you."

"If I hear of anything, I'll let you know."

I thanked her and tried unsuccessfully to disguise the sobs that were beginning. She didn't hang up.

"Men can be . . . I don't wish to seem unkind, but, perhaps he's left you?"

"But we've only just got engaged."

I slammed the receiver into its cradle, before picking it up again to check I hadn't done any damage. Then I sat on the couch and let the tears of tiredness, worry and anger flow out of me.

I knew then it was time I spoke to Mother and Father and to Laurence about it. The fear I'd been carrying that Leo might be dead or in trouble had been replaced by a terrible dread. What if he'd left me and taken all their money with him?

I phoned home and told them I'd be around for tea. I kept my voice as steady and light as I could so that they wouldn't worry too soon.

When I arrived at the house, Mother opened the door and looked past me down the drive.

"I thought Leo would be with you."

I shook my head and tried to keep from pouring all my fears out to her while we were still standing in the hall. I waited instead until we were seated around the kitchen table. Father and Laurence were discussing a programme they'd watched about Berlin and Mother said how much she'd like to see the Brandenburg Gate.

"Maybe we will when we get our bit of money," Father said.

I cut a triangle from the sliced ham on my plate, but I couldn't bring the fork to my mouth.

"How's Leo getting on? When are you expecting him back?" Laurence asked.

He was smiling at me and I thought if I say nothing he'll keep smiling, but if I tell them my fears, it might be gone for a long time.

"I don't know."

All three of them raised their gazes from their plates and looked at me.

"He didn't say?" Mother asked.

"I haven't heard from him since he left."

"I hope he's all right." Mother's mind was already beginning to follow the path I'd gone down.

"I rang the embassy and the hospitals have been checked." Mother looked at Father and he shook his head.

"A man like Leo gets caught up in business," he said. "He probably won't call until he's on his way home."

"I'm sure you're right, but he did promise to phone once he got to Paris." I couldn't hold anything back now.

"Did he pack much, Bea?" Laurence asked. His tone was level but his eyes betrayed the beginning of fear.

"His three best suits and his overcoat."

The tears began then, running between my fingers and plopping onto my salad plate. Mother began to cry too. Father's face turned from red to white and back to red again.

"We'll give him another 24 hours, then I'm calling the gardaí."

"I've tried that already – they wouldn't listen."

"I'll make them listen," Father said.

Mother suggested that I stay the night in my old bed, but I refused.

"He might call."

Laurence decided it'd be best if he went back to the flat with me. Mother hugged me tight on the way out and I did my best to reassure her, though now that I'd aired my fears, they were more real to me.

Laurence was blunt on the bus into town.

"I'm fucked if he doesn't come back, Bea."

I breathed in. I knew he was. He'd risked everything he had on the promise of enough money to escape his job and Ireland. And worse, he'd convinced our parents to invest too.

"I wish I hadn't come over. I should have given Leo more time before worrying everyone. He'll probably show up tomorrow or he might even be in the flat now."

Laurence put his hand out and tucked a strand of my hair, that had fallen forward, back into place.

"He'll be sitting on your couch wondering where you are," he said, looking out of the bus window and back at me. "Anyway, if you can't worry your family, who can you worry?"

"I feel like I'm in the middle of a bad dream and I don't know how to wake up."

"It'll be all right."

He was trying to make me feel better, but he looked like he needed consoling himself. His face had gone white and his eyes had the look of a trapped animal. I couldn't think of a single thing to say that would help him.

As I turned the key in the flat door, I imagined that Leo was inside, already sitting on the couch. My heart leapt in my chest with excitement, but when I opened the door wide on the empty room, it dropped again. As I'd done every day since he left, I picked up the phone, listened and replaced it.

"Do you mind if I . . . " Laurence signalled toward the bedroom and I nodded.

He went inside and began opening drawers and the wardrobe. I saw then how old the shoes looked that Leo had left behind, and how most of the shirts were ready to be thrown away.

"Did you have a joint account?" Laurence asked me.

I nodded and swallowed hard. "There wasn't much in it, only he said he needed it – for cash flow until after the deal. I said it'd be okay."

"Is his name on any of the bills here?"

"No."

He stared at me for a few minutes, his body shaking. "I think we should just stop talking about it now. Have you anything to drink?"

I opened a bottle of wine and we sat on the couch until late.

To pass the time, we dredged up memories of our childhood, of rain-soaked holidays in draughty caravans. We laughed about one sunny day when he'd brought me out to Leixlip on the bus to teach me how to fish on the Liffey.

"I thought I was so cool being brought along by my older brother. I still remember the landmarks you pointed out to me from the top deck of the bus."

I must have been thirteen or fourteen and he was seventeen, in denim bellbottoms and a cheesecloth shirt.

"Didn't I bring you into Rory's Fish and Tackle in town and you were throwing up at the pint of maggots."

I remembered the squirming bait then and how he'd showed me how to put one on a hook and how he picked out the lead weights for our line. We'd one fishing rod between us and a keep net. We sat on the left bank of the Liffey, just beyond the bridge, and he taught me how to cast a line. He'd brought a transistor radio and sandwiches and a bottle of lemonade. The sun shone – and I'd felt that life couldn't get much better.

"You always looked after me," I said.

We didn't talk about Leo or about Laurence's travel dreams. They were both taboos. He hugged me when I said it was time for bed and told me not to worry. He said he'd watch TV for a while before making use of the pillow and blankets I'd given him for the couch.

I remember feeling safe as I drifted off to sleep and closer to him than I'd ever been.

I didn't hear the front door close.

Chapter 16

Thursday, 1st May 2014

In the breakfast room at half seven, there was no sign of
Gabriel. I contemplated asking for a call to be put through to
his bedroom, but I decided to give him a little time. He
hadn't needed an early start in a long time and it was
probably hard for him to get out of bed.

I got some orange juice and a bowl of fresh fruit from the
buffet and secured a table by a rain-splattered window. A
waiter brought me the morning paper and I scanned it while I
ate. A short article with the headline 'Investigation into Death
of Juror Continues' caught my attention. It quoted garda
sources as saying the file on Rachel Deere had been re-opened
because there were questions about the cause of death.

I was eating a ham omelette when Gabriel finally
appeared, shaking the rain from his jacket.

"Oh, you've been out!" I couldn't disguise my surprise
that he'd been awake before me. He grinned.

"Sorry, wanted to drop in on Graham – took longer than
expected." He sat down and signalled to a waitress, ordering
the full Irish without black pudding.

"When I look at black pudding I see the congealed blood of corpses," he said.

"You didn't seem to mind your steak last night."

"Not the same at all – you'd know if you'd seen it."

I thought of Precious Alexander and the pool around her head, but that was fresh blood, still running. I shook my head, trying to erase the image.

"Was he any better?" I asked.

"He cursed me from a height for waking him so early, so yes he did seem better, less paranoid. Also, he said he was given a new drug while he was at St Lucian's and he was going to contact the doctor – start taking it again."

"I hope he does."

I read the newspaper article aloud for Gabriel while he ate his breakfast. He said he hadn't heard any more from Bob.

"Surprised the hacks got wind of it though, thought they were being extra careful." He drained his coffee and leaned forward in his chair. "I was wondering, Bea, do you absolutely have to go to work?"

I raised my eyebrows at him.

"Could you spare a couple of hours this morning? St Lucian's is on our way back to Dublin."

"What?"

"I'd like to take a look at the place, get a feel for it."

I wasn't sure what we could achieve and hated to be away from the court in case the jury returned a verdict.

"How would we get in anyway?"

"We'll figure something out. Will you see if you can manage it?"

I left the breakfast room and stood out in the hotel lobby to make the call. I asked Janine to attend the Signal trial in my place for a couple of hours.

"I went to a hotel in Wicklow with Gabriel and got a bit delayed."

"Delayed, right!" she said.

"I'll be back by lunchtime for definite. There probably won't be a verdict before that anyway."

"Where did you get the crystal ball from?" she scoffed. "He'd better be worth it."

I was glad I was well out of Gabriel's earshot.

From Wicklow Town we took the old road through Ashford, Newcastle and Kilcoole, to Priestsnewtown. There were no signposts for St Lucian's, but Graham had given Gabriel directions. After a few wrong turns, we drove up a country lane and found its wrought-iron entrance gates before us.

The most surprising thing was they were open. In my mind I'd imagined high, locked gates, with some class of intercom into which we would have had to speak to convince the voice at the other end to let us enter.

There was a sign '*By appointment only*' on a large brass plate discouraging unsolicited visits, with the name of the institution written above it, all in an exclusive hotel-style script. We parked for a few moments and got out of the car to look around. We couldn't see the building itself, only the curve of the entrance drive lined with poplars. On either side of St Lucian's grounds was farmland, furrowed fields greening with early summer growth and hedgerows filled with the twitter-song of fledglings.

We stood for a few moments, taking in deep breaths of sweet air.

"I love the promise at this time of year," I sighed.

"It's not a bad spot for an upmarket funny farm," Gabriel said.

"Ah now, they're just people – could be you or me next week."

"I don't think either of us could afford this place. And what's wrong with 'funny farm'? Why do you have to be so bloody politically correct all the time?"

He suddenly sounded impatient and I felt like calling off the visit, but I didn't respond. We sat back into the car and Gabriel drove through the gates.

The trees on either side of us whispered as we passed them, and the morning light, filtering through them, was green-tinged. Five hundred metres on, the driveway wound to the left and we could see St Lucian's clinic, set on an elevated site commanding the surrounding countryside. The redbrick, nineteenth-century building had an arched entrance like an open mouth. Twenty windows looked toward us and four rows of chimneys sat on its grey, slate roof.

We pulled into a gravelled car park, sparsely populated, mostly with expensive and highly polished cars.

"What now?" I asked, as Gabriel drew up close to a navy-blue 2014 Mercedes.

"We'll say we have a friend in trouble and we'll see what happens."

We walked under the stone arch to the glass double doors, set back from it like teeth behind lips. Before we could press the intercom, we were buzzed in by a man who could see us from the reception desk inside.

The first thing I noticed was the lack of something – I had expected the antiseptic smell of a hospital. Instead, the interior smelled of freshly polished wood and honeysuckle. An oak staircase dominated the space, rising straight from the centre of the lobby, before splitting into two flights, left and right. The reception desk, to the left of the stairs, was tucked in discreetly as though to disguise the purpose of the building. Graham hadn't been wrong about the sense of luxury.

The receptionist smiled broadly as we approached.

"Good morning, how can I help?"

"We want to enquire about the clinic," Gabriel said. "We have a friend in trouble."

The man continued to smile.

"It's usual to make an appointment, sir."

"I apologise for that, but it's an emergency. We really are very worried," Gabriel said in his firmest tone.

The man stopped smiling and nodded.

"I'll see what I can do. Take a seat, please."

He gestured to the seating area, where two wine-coloured cube sofas were placed either side of a glass table bearing a vase of freesias. The modernity of the furniture seemed to jar with its surroundings.

We sat and waited for 10 minutes before I approached the reception desk again. The man had his head down and was talking into the microphone on his headset.

"Putting you through now," he told a caller.

I waited until he seemed finished, though he hadn't raised his head.

"Excuse me, but it's been a long drive, is there somewhere I can powder my nose?"

A flash of disapproval on the receptionist's face was rapidly replaced with the same mechanical smile. He walked from behind his desk and used an electronic identity tag, clipped to his jacket pocket, to buzz me through a door.

"Just down that corridor and third door on your left. Mind you don't get lost on the way back." His hand-gestures and tone of voice reminded me of a flight attendant.

"Thank you."

There were doors either side of the corridor, each with nameplates, then a door with a brass plaque and the outline of a woman. The toilets were empty and, after I'd washed my hands and combed my hair, I took a moment to check my phone for messages. There was just one from Janine, sent at 10.30 a.m., telling me the jury was still out. I texted back my thanks.

In the corridor, I noticed the door to one room was open.

The name plaque said Dr Niall Forester. I looked inside, preparing to say I was searching for the ladies' toilet, but it was empty, so I stepped over the threshold.

In the centre of the room, was a large, leather-topped desk. A high-backed leather chair and a smaller, armless chair were either side of it. I had no doubts about where the doctor sat. In the corner, was a large filing cabinet and two walls were taken up with bookcases, filled with important-looking volumes. A large window looked out on the lawns and I wondered why anyone would want to sit with their back to such a view.

I wasn't sure what I was doing, but I started searching the desk. There was some blank writing paper, a silver fountain pen, and a silver-framed photo of a woman and a little girl. The desk drawers were not locked. They were filled with stationery, all neatly organised. One drawer contained only coloured paperclips, in clear plastic boxes, each colour separated and the boxes arranged in order of the spectrum.

"Physician heal thyself," I muttered.

The filing cabinet was locked, but its key was in the top desk drawer. I opened it easily and with as little noise as I could manage.

Inside there were patient files, sorted by year.

Rachel Deere's file was there. I lifted it out and a quick glance confirmed it was the original of the copy I'd been sent. I searched on, looking for familiar names and then I found one – Stephen O'Farrell. I took it out and used my phone to photograph each page. The click of the camera seemed amplified in the empty office. My hands shook as I took the pictures. I was careful to replace the pages in their original order, before putting the file back into the cabinet.

There were other names there that I recognised – an assistant garda commissioner, a high-profile hospital consultant and a Catholic bishop. At the back of the cabinet, out of place, were the files beginning with B. There was a Bailey and a Baron, then a Barrington.

I quickly lifted out the file folder. It was empty, except for a photograph held in place with a paperclip. The name on the folder was 'Beatrice Barrington' and the photo was of me.

I could hear the blood thumping in my ears and feel my cheeks burning. What was this? Beads of sweat began forming on my forehead. I put it back, closed the cabinet, locked it and replaced the key. As I made my way to the door I heard voices approaching – two men. They seemed to be standing outside the door.

"You're sure?" one man said.

"Certain. She's in reception now and she has a man with her."

The second voice was familiar, but I couldn't place it.

The doorknob began to turn and the door opened an inch.

My heart thumped louder. I stood flat against the wall on one side of the door, so that when it was opened wide, I'd be hidden behind it. I hadn't decided what would happen if the two men stepped inside and closed the door behind them. Maybe if I was quick, I could get out before they turned around and saw me. Maybe.

"What do you want me to do?"

I recognised the voice now, it was the bald man.

"Nothing yet. I'll go and get one of the nurses. You stay out of sight."

The door was closed again and their voices became fainter. I could hear them moving further down the corridor. Then there was the sound of a door firmly shutting. I allowed myself to breathe and counted to ten before opening the door a chink. I listened and, hearing nothing, opened it a little wider. I stepped out into the corridor and hurried back to Gabriel.

When I got to reception, he had a sheaf of brochures and forms in his hand.

"There you are. They've said we can't look around today. We'll have to call and make an appointment, or we could talk to a nurse."

I gave him my best 'let's go' look and I hurried to the door. The shock of what I'd seen was sinking in and I felt panicky. I heard him telling the receptionist we'd be back and thanking him for his help.

"What happened?" he asked, when he joined me at the car.

"Just drive."

I had trouble controlling my breathing and my cheeks felt like they were alight. Gabriel was silent, waiting for me to regain my composure. It wasn't until we were back on the N11 that I felt safe enough to speak.

"They have a file on me."

"What? Wait, what were you doing in there? "

It took me a while to tell him about going into Forester's office and finding the file, with the sole picture in it of me walking out of the courts. Though it had only just happened, my visit to the doctor's office seemed ridiculously improbable already. And them having a file on me seemed absurd.

"I was in my lavender suit, so it's recent," I said. "And O'Farrell was a patient there – I found a file on him, along with a few other notables."

"Bloody hell, Bea, what possessed you?" Gabriel was angry with me, for taking such a chance, but at the same time, below his anger, I thought I detected a hint of admiration.

"I photographed O'Farrell's file."

"You didn't?" he glanced across at me, before looking back at the road ahead. "Bloody hell."

When we got near the city it was almost one. I asked Gabriel to take me back to Janine's flat so that I could change my blouse before going to court.

He made tea while I changed. The radio news reported

that the jury in the Signal Investments trial had been sent out for lunch.

"Judge Reginald Brown reminded them to return at two o'clock sharp," the reporter, desperate to fill airtime, remarked.

I felt a little better after I'd changed.

Gabriel dropped me at the courts shortly before two and I made my way straight to Court 19. Janine left the stenograph, and as she passed me, told me I looked remarkably fresh considering.

I took my seat and the court filled up. Judge Brown appeared and we all awaited the customary recall of the jury, so they could be formally sent away again to continue afternoon deliberations. But when the door to the jury box opened, only the minder came out. He handed a note to the registrar before disappearing.

The note was passed to Judge Brown, who sighed deeply when he read it.

"It seems that two of our jurors have taken ill. A doctor has been called and has diagnosed a vomiting bug. He said it should clear in 24 hours." He looked down at both legal teams: "Suggestions?"

Raymond Rafferty looked like he was about to launch into his mistrial speech but thought better of it.

"Judge they can't continue their deliberations with only nine jurors," he said.

The judge made a 'stating the obvious' expression, almost rolling his eyes.

Leona suggested a 24-hour adjournment and reassessment at that stage.

"If it's viral of course, they might all catch it."

"Thank you for that, Ms O'Brien," the judge said. "That takes us to Friday afternoon, perilously close to the weekend. So be it."

He called the nine jurors in.

"Ladies and gentlemen, we'll see you all back here at two o'clock tomorrow, all well, hopefully. The usual warnings apply – keep your discussions about this case for the jury room. Thank you."

In my office, I emailed the O'Farrell file photos from my phone to my computer and then printed them out and hastily hid them in my handbag. It occurred to me then that I'd broken the law. Of course I had. I could be arrested and charged with trespass, and theft, or breaking and entering even. The evidence was there in my own possession.

I saw myself all at once in the dock trying to explain what I'd done. I thought of all the nervous, tongue-tied defendants I'd seen in that position. A barrister would demolish me with a few quick questions. It would be impossible to explain my motivation or justify the reasoning that had brought me to the point of being where I should not have been and spying on the file of a defendant whose trial I was actually covering.

For the first time in my working career I felt a modicum of pity for those found on the wrong side of the law. My pity did not, of course, extend to O'Farrell. I decided, speaking firmly to myself, that if copying his file compromised me, but helped to tie him to Rachel Deere's murder, then it would be worth it.

Janine was at home alone when I got to her place at half three. The case she was assigned to had opened and then quickly adjourned until Friday to give the defence time to examine additional evidence from the prosecution. She made a pot of tea and we sat on the couch and chatted.

"I'm sorry the jurors are ill, but I have to admit I'm grateful for the afternoon off," I said, sipping my tea.

"I bet you are – you must be exhausted." She laughed and I mustered a look of disapproval, but I didn't deny what she was suggesting – it was safer than telling her the truth.

Janine spoke then at length about the wonders of Alastair

and how he was always there for his patients when they needed him.

"Your turn now, tell me how great Gabriel is," she teased.

I changed the subject as quickly as I could to her old flames, listing them and pointing out their charms.

"Remember Barry? He was attractive in a soft kind of way and very self-contained."

"I know, too self-contained." She shifted on her seat, as though weighing up whether or not to say more. She leaned forward. "He didn't need me. he liked me, I know, he was very fond of me," she said, and paused to drink her tea. "But he didn't need me Bea, and I need to be needed."

"So you ditched him, then?"

"No, I was just honest with him. I told him how I felt and he said he suspected as much and he was sorry we couldn't make a go of it. Then he went into the bathroom, took his toothbrush and left."

Janine looked bewildered when she said that.

"What were you expecting?"

"I don't know – maybe I thought he might fight for me a bit."

"You can't have it both ways."

"At least I know Alastair needs me."

I must have looked sceptical.

"I know he comes across as this successful, confident man, but when he really opens up, Bea, he's like a child. You know what I mean? Like after we've rowed, and I say I'm sorry, he's like a boy with his gratitude – his face lights up. I'm not explaining it right."

"No, I think I know what you mean." I did my best imitation then of a little-boy-lost face, tilting my head to one side and batting my eyelashes.

We both laughed, but Janine stopped when she heard footsteps in the hall.

"What's the joke?" Alastair was standing in the doorway.

"We were just discussing – " I was about to say "Barry" when I saw Janine was suddenly looking tense and wary. "– a judge we both worked with. He loved his wine with lunch and slept so soundly one afternoon his snores were recorded on the digital audio recording."

Janine laughed again. Alastair sat down, smiling indulgently.

"You're early," Janine said, getting up and going into the kitchen.

"I could say the same about you," he replied. He turned to me. "I'm sure the defendant wasn't happy."

"He was delighted – his barrister moved for a mistrial the next day. I don't think they managed a second trial."

Alastair looked puzzled.

"They must have sacked the judge though?"

"Not at all. He found a doctor to diagnose him with sleep apnoea and then took early retirement."

"This country," Alastair said, shaking his head in disapproval.

Janine returned and stood before him, proffering tea. He took it and put it on the table.

"Ireland isn't all bad, you know – it has me for one thing," she said.

"So it does." Alastair took her hand and pulled her down onto the couch beside him and kissed her on the forehead.

I got to my feet.

"I've work to do – I'll leave you to it."

"Are you not hungry?" Janine asked. She looked relieved when I said I wasn't.

As I retreated to my room I could hear her ask Alastair what he might like her to cook.

I kicked off my shoes, sat on the bed and took out the printouts of the O'Farrell's file. Dr Forester had looked after him too, though alcohol was not his problem. Squinting at the handwritten medical notes, I could make out the word *ludomania*. Google told me it was an addiction to gambling. He'd checked himself into the clinic straight after the garda investigation into Signal Investments began. He wasn't the first defendant to seek refuge in a clinic of some sort or other, in an attempt to find a medical label to explain a crime.

In the handwritten notes Dr Forester had recorded the details of O'Farrell's problems. They'd begun with high-stakes poker games and glamorous outings to international race courses. He was part of the high-flying set who attended racing festivals abroad and at home, in the days when businessmen flew into the Galway Festival by private helicopters and threw thousands of euro at bookmakers and politicians. He told the doctor he knew he was in difficulty when he spent 36 hours straight on an online gambling site. I found it hard to believe, that O'Farrell would part with his money so easily. The evidence in court had shown his deep attachment to it.

The phone rang before I'd finished reading. Gabriel said he'd arranged a visit for us to Wheatfield Prison. Terence Mills had agreed to meet us when he'd heard we wanted to talk about Leona O'Brien. I had to admit I was apprehensive about meeting him, even if it helped resolve my worries about Leona.

"Will I pick you up?" Gabriel asked.

"I'll meet you at six in the prison car park."

I'd remembered I had to collect information from the Companies Office. I put the phone down, put my shoes back on and said goodbye to the lovebirds, sitting close together on the couch. I longed to be able to go back to my own home.

It was almost half four when I reached Dublin Castle. I walked under the ancient arch and into the cobbled courtyard. The modern office block, within the castle's curtilage, looked out of place beside the medieval tower and the Chapel Royal.

Inside the Companies Office, I asked for Bessie.

"I got a phone call to say she had documents for me. My name is Beatrice Barrington."

"Could you just hold on a moment? I'll ask her," the woman at the desk said.

Bessie appeared five minutes later with an envelope. I handed her the money, put the envelope in my bag and left.

In the courtyard, I paused to let a group of tourists walk by. They were dressed for the Irish weather and listening keenly to their guides. I could hear snippets of history about the castle and how it had played its role during Ireland's fight for independence. I thought of all the hobnailed boots that had marched over its cobblestones in assault and defence, each pair of feet attached to a soldier who thought he was on the side of right, when in reality he was only a pawn in someone else's game. I had always thought of myself as a person who would choose the right side, but now I began to wonder in whose game I was playing.

One American guide was louder than the others, as she described the events of Bloody Sunday, when British soldiers gunned down spectators at a football match in Croke Park. Though her facts were not all historically accurate, she held the crowd and when she began to move away toward the upper yard they followed her quickly, all except one. The single figure hung back and turned toward me. When I recognised the bald man, I made as swift a departure as I could. I hurried under the arch of the castle entrance and out onto Dame Street.

I flagged the first taxi I saw and threw myself into the back seat.

"Wheatfield Prison, please," I told the driver, when I had enough breath to speak.

Chapter 17

Tuesday, 29th September 1981

When I went into the living room on Tuesday morning, Laurence wasn't on the couch. I checked the time and it was just after eight. I felt refreshed and amazed that I'd slept through the night. I was grateful that Laurence had slipped out to work quietly and let me sleep on.

I put the kettle on and took the bedding he'd folded at the end of the couch into my bedroom. I made toast and tutted to myself because there was no sign that Laurence had fed himself before he left. I hoped he'd at least get something to eat on his way to work.

It wasn't until I sat at the kitchen table that I noticed the folded sheet of paper. It had 'Bea' written on it in Laurence's untidy scrawl.

'Dearest Bea,

Let's for once be truly honest with ourselves. We both know what's happened here. Leo is gone and we'll not see him again. I'm so sorry I'm not strong enough for this. Tell Mother and Father that I beg for their forgiveness. I should never have got them involved.

Please don't think too badly of me.
Your Laurence.'

The toast I'd bitten into stuck in the back of my throat. I felt as though I was choking and started coughing and spluttering. I read the note again – had he run away or something worse? It seemed to me there was only one message to take from what he'd written.

I grabbed my coat and bag and ran out onto the street. I stood absurdly on the footpath, where pedestrians all around me were hurrying to work, as though nothing was wrong. I wanted to shout at them to stop what they were doing, to help me find Laurence. I looked up at the train station – maybe he'd gone in there. He might have got on a train to escape the city. Or perhaps he'd gone in the other direction, toward Nassau Street and on to O'Connell Bridge and the Liffey. Where would he have gone? How would I start looking for him?

I couldn't do it on my own. I went back inside and phoned Father and then I phoned the gardaí. I paced the flat while I waited for them to come, moving from the window to the phone, checking for a dial tone, looking out the window again to see if Laurence was walking back down the street.

"Come back, come back!" I chanted like a mantra, conscious that yesterday my mantra would've been for Leo, but today, I felt only hatred for my 'fiancé'. I knew from the moment I read Laurence's note that it was true – Leo wasn't coming back. He'd taken all of Laurence's money and my parents' as well. I knew that he'd used me and never really loved me and that I was nothing to him.

All I wanted now was to find Laurence, to take him in my arms and tell him I was sorry and that it'd be all right.

Father and the gardaí arrived at my door at the same time. I wanted to go out with them straight away, but a female garda guided me to the kitchen table and insisted I tell her first everything that had happened. I showed them the note. Father breathed in sharply through his nose when he read it, as though he'd felt a sudden, sharp pain. He looked grey and exhausted. I imagined the night he'd spent, worrying about his savings, tossing beside Mother and trying not to infect her with his fear.

When I'd finished explaining everything, from beginning to end, the female garda told me I needed to think clearly and give her the best description I could of Laurence. When she said that for an instant I thought I could see him standing at Father's shoulder, a smile as sweet as ever on his face. I'd no photo of him in the flat so I described how he looked and she took notes. Her colleague rang the station and read out the description. When he'd finished he said people sometimes left notes but didn't actually follow through on them.

"I need you to tell me the details of your conversation with him last night. It might help us to figure out where he's gone," the female garda said.

She asked again what time I'd last spoken to him and if I thought he'd left long before I awoke. I felt angry with myself for having slept so well while Laurence was in turmoil.

"Is there anywhere you think he might have gone?" she asked.

Father looked puzzled when I suggested Leixlip, but the garda said it was a good place to try because it had been on his mind.

"We've alerted officers all over the city and they'll be on the lookout for him – try not to worry," she said. "Best if you come with us to Leixlip, though. You'll know the spot where he liked to fish."

Father and I got into the back of the patrol car. I wondered, as we pulled away from the kerb, whether passers-by thought we'd been arrested. The traffic was dense along the quays, crawling past James's Gate and Heuston Station. I'd an urge to get out of the car and just run there – run all the way to the bridge where we'd fished together.

I couldn't look at Father as we drove. I didn't want to see the truth in his face. I knew he wouldn't be able to disguise it, no matter how he tried. This was all my fault – my misjudgement, my gullibility, my stupidity was the cause.

The short journey passed in silence, apart from an occasional crackle from the Garda radio and a muffled enquiry from some unknown officer about location.

When we got to Leixlip Bridge I asked them to stop the car. The garda pulled in at the side of the road and we got out. I closed my eyes for a moment and pictured Laurence and myself making our way to the left side of the bridge and down to the bank.

"This way," I said.

They followed me, down along a rough path to the water.

We'd only gone 100 metres when a woman came running from the river with her hand over her mouth. Without speaking, she grabbed the male garda by the sleeve and dragged him to the water's edge.

"There, there!" She pointed toward the bridge's arch of stone and the column nearest the shore, to where the reeds were overgrown in the water.

I saw Laurence then, caught among them, face down in the water. His arms and legs were splayed, and his hair was plastered against the curve of his skull.

The male garda turned away from the sight and vomited onto the grass. I saw then the youth in his face and the shock it was to him.

Father dropped to his knees beside me and pounded the ground with his fists. "No! No! No!"

The female garda knelt beside him and put an arm around his shoulders. There was a scream then, long and high-pitched, like a wounded animal. It took me a minute to realise I was making the noise. I tried to wade in to him, but they held me back. I had to wait until the ambulance and fire brigade came to take his body from the water before I could cradle him. His face was still and cold, and his lips were pressed together in a small smile.

"He can't have been there long," I heard one of the officers say.

Father's hand rested on my shoulder, but he said nothing until they'd put Laurence into a body bag.

"I have to get home to your mother," he said. "I hope they fix him up a bit – she'll want to say goodbye."

The female garda gave us a lift and I could see Mother knew, when she saw the garda car pull up, what it was we were going to tell her.

Chapter 18

Thursday, 1st May 2014

Gabriel had already arrived at Wheatfield Prison when I got there, shortly before six. He was leaning against his car, talking on his phone – probably getting some last-minute information on Terence Mills.

I shivered when I stepped out of the taxi. In the middle of suburban Dublin, the Clondalkin "place of detention", with its brownish, pebble-dashed walls, stretched before me. A cool breeze whistled round the prison. Though there were housing estates not far away, there was a sense of isolation about the place, desolation even.

As we walked from the car park toward visitor reception, a tired-looking woman pushing a buggy with a baby in it came towards us. One young child was holding the side of the buggy, while a scrawny, wiry boy, was running around, ahead and then behind it.

"Fuck sake, Jonathan," the woman said, trying unsuccessfully to catch the boy by the collar of his blue school shirt. "I'm not fucking bringing you here again."

We passed through thick glass doors and sat on brown

plastic chairs, welded together in four rows, and waited to be allowed into the visiting area. I told Gabriel about seeing the bald man.

"Why didn't you call me? You needn't have come out here."

"I wanted to."

The frown lines between his eyebrows deepened.

"He must be trying to frighten you."

"I know, I know." I felt rattled, but was trying hard to calm myself. It seemed ridiculous that I was about to sit face to face with a murderer, a man who might be trying to destroy Leona.

"You must have been followed from work – I think it might be time to get the lads involved."

"Not yet, I'm all right."

Gabriel was about to argue with me, when a prison officer approached and asked us to sign the visitors' book. He made brief eye contact with Gabriel as he spoke and winked at him.

"Is there anywhere you don't have friends?" I asked, as we were led down a corridor to security.

The area smelled of disinfectant and sweat.

They asked me to turn out my handbag and they frisked Gabriel when he set off the security alarm. They weren't satisfied until he took the belt off his trousers.

We sat at a table in the visitors' room and waited for Mills to arrive. There were a dozen tables spread around the room, each with two chairs either side. Prison officers stood at the doors at both ends of the room, and three officers leaned against a wall, chatting.

Gabriel put a couple of car magazines Mills had asked for, and a Liverpool FC poster, both checked by his prison officer friend, in front of us on the table. When Mills sat down he took them immediately. Then he crossed his arms and pushed his chair backwards a bit, so that he could stretch out his long legs. I remembered his face then – the high forehead, the tightly-cropped hair, those chilly eyes and the way he held his mouth, as though he was insulted by the world.

"Any chocolate?"

Gabriel said no, and Mills put his hand in his trouser pocket and took out a two-euro coin. He pushed it toward me.

"There's a vending machine in the waiting room, would you ever get us a Crunchie?" He looked at me, half mocking, half challenging.

"I tried it earlier," I said. It was out of order, but I have a bag of peanuts and some chewing gum, would you like those?"

I took them from my handbag and put them on the table. He snatched them and put them into his pocket.

"What do yis want?"

"We want to talk to you about Leona O'Brien."

"That tart?" He forced the word out from between clenched teeth. "What about her?"

"Have you heard any talk about her in here?" Gabriel was picking his words.

"The usual – what fellas would like to do to her if they got the chance, that sort of thing."

I tried not to flinch.

"You know what I'm saying do you?" he said in my direction.

"Anything specific?" Gabriel asked.

"Why? Is she in trouble?"

"Just a few threats," Gabriel said.

Mills smiled. "I hadn't heard but I'm not surprised. I'd do it meself if I was out, two bullets through her pretty ankles."

I thought of Leona, standing confident in the courtroom, oblivious to the enmity held for her. It was frightening that men like Mills could be so casual about hurting her.

"That's how you'd do it, is it?"

"Maybe, or maybe some other way. I hear she has a brat now."

I looked away from him. I didn't want him to see that I was shocked.

"Of course, you know what they say about barristers? The only place you can really hurt them is in their fuckin' pockets."

Gabriel cleared his throat.

"Cut the bullshit. Has anyone been saying anything realistic about getting to her?"

Mills shrugged and shook his head. "Right, that's enough info for yis."

On an impulse, I described the bald man to him as vividly as I could.

"What's it worth?" he asked.

"Do you know him?" I asked.

He nodded.

"I've only a twenty on me," Gabriel said. I said I'd nothing.

"Fuckin' cheapskates." Mills put his hand under the table for the money. "Here, quick." He snatched it from Gabriel and shoved it in his pocket. "Sounds like Bobby Loftus. Charmer isn't he?"

"You tell me."

"You must be in right shit if you're messin' around with him. No moral compass at all that fella, do you know what I mean? He'll work for anyone if the price is right, do anything, like an expensive whore." He stared at me.

I held his gaze.

"What's he up to now, do you know?" Gabriel asked.

"Haven't seen him in a long time."

Mills pushed back his chair.

"Bored now. I've enough of this." He sauntered toward

the prison officer at the exit. "Nice knowin' yis."

I was glad to get out of the prison. I hadn't expected the sound of keys turning in locks to hold any fear for me, but there was something visceral in my reaction to it, a desire to run. I wondered if there were jailbirds or asylum inmates in my ancestry.

"Well, what did you make of him?" Gabriel asked when we sat into his car.

"He's every bit as obnoxious as I remember. Not much use to us though. I believed him when he said he hadn't heard about any violent threats against Leona. And when he said he'd like to shoot her in the ankles."

"Nasty."

"Yes, but where does that leave us? There's no one left on that list of defendants is there?"

"No, but it wasn't an entirely wasted trip. Are you hungry?"

I said I was and Gabriel suggested a restaurant in the city centre.

"I'm too tired for that – what about a takeaway?"

We ate a meal of fresh cod and chips sitting on his couch, both of us with our shoes off and feet up on his coffee table, the pungent vinegar filling our nostrils. He asked me to describe once more what had happened earlier with the bald man – Bobby Loftus.

I tried to explain the sense of fear Loftus could invoke in me by merely looking in my direction. The more I thought of it, the more frightened I became.

"Why do you think he's doing it?' I said. Is it like Mills said and someone is paying him? I wish I understood what Loftus is up to."

"I know, but it's good that we have a name now. It means we can find out what we're dealing with."

He took out his mobile and walked into the kitchen to call one of his contacts.

"Interesting," I could hear him say.

When he returned I asked him what was so interesting.

"Loftus has a file as long as your arm, no convictions though, and hasn't crossed anyone's radar in the last 18 months. I'm told he's a mercenary and very professional. Whatever he's at, he's been paid for it, Bea."

"And who do you think might be in a position to do that?"

"There's O'Farrell, of course, or maybe someone from St Lucian's."

He sat down again, took up his plate and picked over the cold, crispy bits at the end of his chip bag.

"I know Janine is great and all that, but do you think maybe you'd best stay here tonight?"

I took my feet down off the coffee table and began to gather up the detritus from our meal. Gabriel put his hand on my arm.

"I'm not, I don't mean – I just think you'd be safer."

"I know. And, to be honest, it's a bit uncomfortable with Alastair around all the time. I'll go over and pick up a few things."

He insisted on driving me and sat outside in the car while I went in to pack a bag.

Janine and Alastair were watching TV when I arrived.

"I'm not stopping. I'm staying over at a friend's tonight."

They both looked relieved and I realised what an imposition it must have been for Janine to have me there once Alastair returned. She was trying so hard to please him and my presence couldn't have helped that.

"You've been so good to me – hopefully I'll be completely out of your way in the next couple of days."

"You've been no bother, Beatrice," Alastair said. "Sure, you've hardly been here. Where have you been?"

I thought his response cheeky. His proprietary reference to

Janine's apartment seemed very high-handed to me, though she didn't seem to mind. And his desire to know where I'd been, as though he was entitled to ask, as though we were friends, stepped over a line. I felt like ignoring him, but I knew Janine would be offended if I didn't reply.

"Just visiting friends," I said, waving my hand at the same time to bat away any follow-up enquiries. There were none, and I decided Alastair had just been making polite conversation in the best way he could.

I finished putting a few items into a bag and left them, promising to see Janine at work in the morning.

I got into my car and pulled away. Gabriel followed behind me.

Back in Oxmantown Road, I sipped a camomile tea and felt myself relax.

"I got that in just for you, you know," Gabriel said. I told him I appreciated that.

We talked about old court cases we'd both played our part in over the years, he dealing with defendants, me tapping away at the words – all the murderers, the rapists, the drug dealers, the thieves, the fraudsters, the swindlers, the madams and the pimps.

Gabriel raised his glass of stout.

"Here's to them – we'd have had no work if it wasn't for them."

We were all, in some way, connected to the misery criminals inflicted on other people because our livelihoods depended on it. If, by some miracle, tomorrow all crime and evil was sucked from the world, there would be no work for me or anyone else in the courts. I'd never thought of myself as sullied by it; I'd thought the defenders of the guilty were sullied, but now I realised we all were – we were all making money from the misery of others.

"I think I might be in the wrong business," I said.

"Or maybe you're just in it too long?"

"I would have made a lovely florist. Everyone smiles when they get flowers. Nobody smiles when I give them a transcript."

It was then I remembered the envelope from the Companies Office. I got my handbag and took it out, turning it over in my hand. There were no markings of any kind on it. I opened it and inside there were pages of close-printed accounts. Looking at the figures, I could feel the weight of the last few days come down on me like a lead blanket.

"I think I need to sleep. We can look at this in the morning."

I put the documents back in the envelope and left it on a bookshelf. Gabriel gave me some blankets and a pillow.

"I'll fix up the spare room tomorrow, and sleep here in the meantime. You can have my bed," he said.

I refused, and he reluctantly went to bed as I organised myself for a night on the couch.

Chapter 19

Friday, 2ⁿᵈ May 2014

When I awoke on the couch it was to the sound of Gabriel in the kitchen. My throat and the roof of my mouth were dry, and my lips felt like crumpled paper. I suspected I'd been snoring. He came in with a glass of orange juice and set it down on the table.

"I'll make you some tea and toast."

There was a small smile on his face, which told me my suspicions were true.

I swung my legs to the floor, but kept the blankets over me. I gulped back the orange juice, its sweet coldness softening my throat.

Gabriel brought in the tea and toast and sat on the armchair. He was quiet while I crunched through the honeyed bread and drank the scalding tea.

"I didn't sleep much – I did a lot of thinking," he said. "I'm afraid for you, Bea. There's a detective, Matt McCann, worked on the O'Farrell case – I think we should see him. "

The name was familiar. I remembered him from the witness box, a heavyset man with thick black curls and a Cavan accent that would churn butter.

"I'll think about it," I said. Nothing had changed – the consequences of telling anyone would be just the same as they were a week earlier.

"It's getting risky."

I knew it was.

"Let's wait and see if there's a verdict today," I sighed.

"All right, but we'll speak to him after, okay?"

His phone rang and he took it into his bedroom. When he emerged, his face was drained of colour.

"Graham's gone."

"What?"

"They found him this morning, hanging from a tree in his garden."

"But he . . . I thought he was getting help. That's terrible." I was shocked.

I thought of the glimpse I'd got of the garden behind the house in Wicklow – long, overgrown and muddy. I wondered why Graham would have ventured out into it.

"It doesn't make sense, why would he go out into the garden? He could hardly bear to go outside the door."

"You saw how he was Bea – would you expect sense? Poor man." He shook his head. "I'm going to go down there, see what I can find out."

I helped him find his car keys and the phone he'd had in his hand only minutes before. He put on his jacket and patted his pocket, searching for his wallet.

"Right," he said when he found it.

I opened the hall door for him and, as he passed through it, I reached out and touched him on his elbow. "I'm sorry about Graham," I said.

He nodded, and I closed the door behind him.

The court was a rumour mill when I walked in. Journalists were huddled in one corner, and as I passed, I could hear them talking about food poisoning. Leona O'Brien and Raymond Rafferty were standing close together whispering in urgent voices. Brian, the jury minder, was standing outside the door of the jury room, shifting his weight from one foot to the other as though his soles were on fire. I began to set up my machine.

"It's hardly worth the bother," the registrar remarked.

The judge's assistant arrived and everyone took their places. For the first time since the case began, Stephen O'Farrell looked directly at me. I glanced away, nauseated by the brazenness of his gaze and a little frightened by it.

"All rise."

Judge Brown looked weary.

"Well?" he addressed Leona.

"Judge, I'm happy to report our two ill jurors have recovered – unfortunately another one has taken ill."

"Same problem?"

"Yes Judge, the doctor believes so."

He looked from one barrister to the other.

"If we continue without the one ill juror, where does that leave us?"

"With a legal verdict, I think," Leona said.

"Judge!" Rafferty protested.

The judge held his hand palm out.

"Do not say it, Mr Rafferty, I do not want to hear it. I've made up my mind – bring in the jury."

I watched as they shuffled in – a couple of them pasty-faced and all of them looking tired.

"Ladies and gentlemen, I'm going to ask you to continue your deliberations this morning. Is that acceptable to everybody?"

The ten jurors nodded in unison.

"Off you go."

When they left, Leona told the judge that the doctor had

ruled out food poisoning.

"Just a nasty virus, apparently."

There were sighs of disappointment from the journalists.

"Right, well I'll see you all back here after lunch. We'll check in with the jury then," the judge said, already standing to leave.

Everyone in court stood and Stephen O'Farrell turned to leave, and as he did, he looked over his shoulder at me again.

When I got back to the office, Janine was on her way out on a coffee run and offered to bring me back a tea.

"Or have you time for a quick chat?"

I said I had, and she suggested we sit in the court canteen. The busy eatery, on the second floor, was filled as usual with witnesses and defendants on bail. They were all sitting in close proximity, filling themselves with the dish of the day or whatever wrap or sandwich that happened to be on offer. The space was divided by a glass partition and door that created a separate sitting area for barristers and solicitors, only accessible with a swipe card. The kitchen and serving area was contained in the space between the two worlds. The food was the same in both places, and the woman who worked the tills, one on either side of the partition, turned from one side to the other and back again to take the money proffered, without fear or favour.

We found an empty table at a glass wall that looked out over a patio frequented by smokers and onto the park. Janine brought the drinks over in paper cups. I had watched her moments before, fishing the teabags out with one of those awful wooden sticks that pass for spoons. Her hand had been shaking and I knew she was anxious about something.

We talked about the mildness of the weather for almost five minutes, before she felt brave enough to tackle what she wanted to discuss.

"Bea, we're a bit worried about you."

"We?" I was puzzled.

"Alastair and me – we're both concerned."

I wanted to say that Alastair hardly knew me, that he certainly didn't know me well enough to worry about me and that they should both mind their own business.

"There's no need, I'm fine."

"You're not though, you're not fine. You haven't been yourself." She furrowed her brow. "Three times in the last week you've asked me to cover for you. You? The most conscientious person I've ever met – the fussiest."

I thought 'fussy' was a bit harsh, particular maybe. "I'm sorry, I won't ask you again."

She shook her head and took a sip from her tea. "You know that's not what I meant. You came to work with a stain on your blouse yesterday. It's not you Bea. You asked to stay with me and now you're somewhere else. What's going on?"

What was I to tell her? Not the truth. I couldn't draw her into my mess.

"And another thing, you don't look well this morning."

"Please don't worry about me. I'm just a bit uneasy over the pest problem – it's still not solved and you know how much I love my own home. It unsettles me not to be in it."

She nodded. "Of course, I can understand that. With your personality type change is difficult to cope with."

I felt like kicking her very hard on the shins under the table. "Personality type?"

"Alastair's been telling me about it. He says you're a sensitive introvert, with a tendency toward perfectionism and passive aggression."

She blurted it out in one breath, like a child who'd learned a line from the Bible by heart.

"Does he indeed?" I tried to keep the irritation from my voice.

Janine had the good manners to blush, but she couldn't stop herself.

"He says I'm a natural extrovert, with an overdeveloped sense of altruism."

"And what does he say about himself?"

"He says he's working on it."

"I bet."

I was glad I'd agreed to stay in Gabriel's.

"Thanks for the tea and tell Alastair not to worry about me. I'll drop by later and collect the rest of my things."

I stood up to go.

"You don't have to do that . . . "

I smiled as widely as I could manage.

"I'll talk to you later."

I'd just returned to the office when Janine arrived, her face flushed pink with discomfort. She'd spoken out of kindness, I knew, and it had cost her a lot to bring up her concerns. I knew Janine was not the type of woman who enjoyed conflict or who would wish to hurt. And her parroting of Alastair was merely another symptom of her infatuation with him. The words she'd said were not her own.

It was hard to stay cross with her for long. I mustered a chirpy tone and asked if I could borrow her stapler. She was happy to oblige.

Just as I'd finished typing up my brief notes from the morning, Gabriel phoned and asked if we could meet for lunch.

"Can I get you something from outside?" I asked Janine.

She shook her head looking a little forlorn.

"You know, I didn't mean . . . I'm just worried about you."

"I know, but I'm fine, really."

Raymond Rafferty was in the lift when I stepped into it to go downstairs. His hands were behind his back and the pose pushed his generous stomach further forward than normal, stretching his black waistcoat.

"Ms Barrington, is it not?"

I looked at him and nodded, surprised at the greeting

"My client has asked me to pass on his best wishes."

I looked away. I didn't know how to respond. What was this?

He was about to speak again when the lift doors opened on the second floor and two gardaí stepped in. They were discussing what they planned to eat for lunch.

"Can't beat a Ploughman's," one of them said.

All four of us got out at the ground floor. Rafferty said nothing more to me and I did not delay in exiting the building.

Gabriel was sitting outside.

"That was quick," I said.

"Didn't feel like waiting around."

I told him I needed to buy food, but he indicated a bag from the nearby deli.

We walked up to the park and found a bench under a tree. Gabriel took out a hankie and wiped away water drops, collected on the green wood after a brief morning shower. We sat down and he shared out his purchases.

"How was it?" I broke the silence.

"He used a length of clothesline. I saw the marks." He held his fingers to his neck.

"God, that's awful."

"The Station's closed the book on it already."

"Was there anything you didn't expect?"

He thought for a while, looked at the half-eaten sandwich in his hand and then placed it back in its wrapper.

"Do you remember the footstool, the one in the living room?"

I nodded, recalling the faded pink.

"It was under his body – where he did it."

"What about it?"

"There was no mud on the top of it – the path was muddy so he must have taken his shoes off so he wouldn't get it dirty."

I imagined Graham walking down the garden, carrying the footstool, carefully removing his shoes, reaching up to a branch.

"God almighty."

"I just didn't think he was that bad on Thursday," Gabriel said.

I finished eating and he took the wrappings from me and shoved them back into the paper bag.

"Is there any other explanation?" I asked, as we walked back.

He shrugged, looking bewildered and weary of thinking about it.

"I'll collect you later," he said, when we parted at the steps.

I considered arguing, telling him not to bother himself, to go and get a pint, but thought better of it. I couldn't shake off the cold way Loftus had looked at me and the brazenness of O'Farrell's gaze.

After the jury returned from lunch, Judge Brown made a quick headcount and sent them away again. We all left the court not long after two.

As I made my way back to the office a hand on my elbow startled me.

"Apologies, Ms Barrington, a quiet word?"

Rafferty steered me to the large window opposite the courtroom door. We stood looking out over the park and the Wellington Monument, and above the patio area where the smokers gathered.

"My client is down there," he gestured to the patio. "He'd like to speak to you."

What could O'Farrell possibly want to say?

"I don't want to talk to him."

"You don't need to talk – just give him a hearing."

Was this more intimidation? Had he recognised me? Did he know I'd seen his meeting in the park?

Stephen O'Farrell was looking up now. There were lots of people standing around him, smoking and talking, nervous witnesses being soothed by friends and defendants being talked up. I stepped away from the glass.

"What harm can it do?" Rafferty asked.

I did not answer and I felt my stomach flipping over inside me. I turned to go and as I did, the barrister asked me very politely for my phone number. I wasn't sure why, but I gave it to him.

"You needn't pass that on to him," I said.

"Of course not." He pressed the digits into his phone and then a text popped up on mine with his contact details.

"In case you change your mind."

"I won't."

Chapter 20

Friday, 2nd October 1981

Mother and Father were bewildered ghosts at Laurence's funeral a few days later. They dragged themselves through the ceremony.

I'd stood beside them in the front row of the church at the removal the night before and held out my hand to be shaken by all the people who'd come to offer their condolences, as though I was every bit as entitled to their sympathy as my parents. Those trite, meaningless phrases were repeated, again and again, phrases meant to comfort –"Sorry for your troubles", "He was a lovely young man" and "He's in a better place". The last in particular made me want to cry out at their stupidity, at the stupidity of the whole business.

"What are you doing here?" I wanted to shout. "Laurence is fine. He's gone travelling."

Of course, I didn't. I just thanked them for their kindness and let them shuffle on. The line took a long time to pass. A lot of Laurence's work colleagues were there, some not much older than he was. They looked shaken and pale. His boss was there too and looked not at all the buffoon Laurence had painted him, more like a middle-aged uncle, who might even have indulged Laurence's moody impatience.

"He'll be missed," he said to me, clasping my hand in both of his.

"He will."

After we followed Laurence's coffin out of the church, I cried and hugged extended family members who gathered around us to offer support, but I felt like a fraud. I didn't deserve to be hugged. Nobody knew that his death was my fault, that I was the one who'd brought Leo into our lives and offered up my brother to him like a sacrifice.

A strong wind was blowing across the graves and leaves from the nearby trees were beginning to shed, when they lowered his coffin deep into the ground. Mother curled at the knees as the box went down and looked as though she might follow it. Father had one arm hooked around her to keep her from collapsing. I felt like jumping in too, in the hope of escaping the grief and guilt, like a poison in me.

At home, we served tea and sandwiches to the mourners and there were a few bottles of whiskey on Mother's sideboard. But despite the alcohol, people didn't stay long; there was so little that could be said. When they'd trailed out, with more hugs and entreaties to mind ourselves, Mother went for a lie-down, complaining of a terrible headache. It was a recurring pain that seemed to keep her from talking to me about what had happened.

"She'll be all right," Father said. "It's good the formalities are over, anyhow. I thought the priest did a fine job." He was standing at the sink, his arms in soapy water, washing Mother's best china. "You heard what he said? No one can ever know what Laurence was thinking or what happened – it could well have been a terrible accident."

I nodded, though I knew he didn't believe it. I suppose it was easier to pretend he did and forget the note we'd both seen in the kitchen.

"I want to say that I'm very, very – "

Father placed a suddy hand on my arm to stop me talking. He shook his head and raised his gaze to me and his look said he couldn't bear it if I uttered one more word.

I dried the china in silence and placed it back on its shelf, just as it was and as it had always been.

I made a statement to gardaí about Leo the day after the funeral, and told them that he was a swindler, a conman and a fraud. I saw myself through their eyes – the gullible girl, duped by romance, naively believing all that I was told in my eagerness to be loved by him. I didn't like what I saw.

Gardaí could find no trace of Leo's company and his bank accounts had been emptied. There was evidence that he'd taken the flight to Paris, but after that, nothing.

"Even if we do find him, the money's most likely gone," a kind garda told me.

"And what about what he did to Laurence?"

"I'm sorry, there's nothing can be done about that. But if he ever comes back to this country, we'll try to get him on the fraud."

Mother and Father never mentioned Leo again. I suppose they thought there was no point in discussing him. Father spoke only once about money. He said he was sorry he couldn't help me in life, in the way that he'd intended.

"The little bit of fat we'd gathered is gone."

I told him I was sorry, and he said it wasn't my fault.

"Wouldn't you think a man with my experience would know when something was too good to be true?"

We didn't talk about it again.

I gave up my flat in Westland Row. It took me all my strength to go back into it. When I turned the key in the door, I almost expected Leo to be sitting there, with that inquisitive look on his face, wondering where I'd been. But it was empty and cold, and I couldn't even imagine why I'd loved it so much. I packed my belongings into boxes and the clothes into suitcases. I left behind what had belonged to Leo, his old suits and a few odds and ends of furniture – the landlord could deal with them. I could see then that when my fiancé left, he'd taken everything that was important to him. I just hadn't realised it at the time.

With Father, because Mother couldn't bear it, I packed up most of Laurence's clothes and took them to a charity shop. I kept a cheesecloth shirt and a scarf that still smelled of him, and the atlas he'd owned. I put his LPs in a box and lifted it into the attic. Though I knew I couldn't bear to listen to them, it was impossible to give them away to anyone else.

I went back to work and stayed with my parents. Each of us wandered around the house, trying to behave as though life was normal, and only occasionally bumping into each other. We didn't speak about Laurence, and Mother and Father didn't cry in front of me, but at night I would hear Mother sobbing and Father saying "there, there" to her in the dark.

Christmas came and went. There was no snow. We didn't even pretend to mark it, except by going to midnight Mass to listen to 'O Holy Night', and to Laurence's grave to plant a poinsettia.

Mother reasoned that a turkey would be a waste, when there were only three of us.

I roasted a chicken instead and we ate it, though it was dry as meal. I could almost hear Laurence's voice, joking about my cooking.

We sat on the couch together and watched TV on New Year's Eve. I wanted to go to bed and cover my head with a blanket, for I knew we were welcoming a year that Laurence wouldn't be in. But I didn't want to leave the two of them to see it in alone.

When the bells rang out, Mother, with tears running down her face, hugged me tightly to her. Then she put her hand over mine and squeezed it.

"It'd be better for you if you were gone," she said.

I handed in my notice at Melmount Secretarial on the second of January. Mrs Carmichael looked relieved and agreed to pay me a week's holiday money. I'd been next to useless for months and she'd been, as it turned out, too kind to give out to me. She even gave me a decent reference and said a few diplomatic and encouraging words before I left. The girls in the office queued up to hug me and tell me how much they'd miss me, but I knew that my grief had gathered like a grey mist around me and they'd be glad to see it follow me out the door.

I packed one large suitcase, mainly with suitable work clothes, and nothing that reminded me of Leo. I took a photograph of Laurence in a frame, as well as his shirt and scarf. I visited his grave, one last time before I left, to make a promise to him.

Father and Mother went with me to Dun Laoghaire to catch the ferry. Mother gave me a piece of paper with an address in London for her cousin Julia.

"She won't mind putting you up for a few months, until you find your feet."

I thanked her, but knew I'd only call by Julia's to let her know I'd found digs somewhere else. I didn't want to live with someone who knew anything about me.

Father insisted on carrying my suitcase as far as the gangplank and, when we got there, pushed a few scrunched-up notes into my hand.

"I'm sorry it's not more," he said.

We hugged one last time before I boarded the ferry to Holyhead. I stood on the deck as the boat moved gradually out into the water.

I couldn't take my eyes off my parents on shore; they didn't raise a hand of farewell – just stood still, and stared, unsmiling.

Chapter 21

Friday, 2nd May 2014

I went back to my desk after the encounter with Rafferty, feeling a little shaken. I'd just started going through the short transcript of the day's proceedings when Gabriel rang.

"Are you sitting?"

"What?"

"I've just heard – it's officially confirmed, Rachel Deere was murdered."

I didn't know what to say.

"Beatrice?"

"Yes."

"They're notifying Rafferty and O'Brien now. It looks like it's over."

Damn it – it was so close. I thought of O'Farrell and Rafferty and their smug faces, trying to pretend they were unhappy while they were congratulating themselves.

"He'll get off. There'll never be another trial," I said.

"I know. Listen, have you still got that file in work?"

"Yes, it's here."

"Best to bring it home here I think."

"Okay. I better go, they'll be needing me in court."

I hung up without giving Gabriel a chance to say any more; his words would have been wasted anyway. I didn't wait for the judicial assistant to fetch me, but went straight to Court 19.

Inside there was a tense silence, like the moments before a thunderclap. Leona's face was white. Rafferty was wearing his gravitas mask but below it, a smirk was simmering.

When the judge emerged, he looked utterly defeated.

"You have something to say to me?" he asked Leona.

"Yes Judge. The pathologist has made a finding that has led gardaí to believe the forewoman of this jury, Rachel Deere, was murdered."

There were exclamations and flurries of typing from the journalists, who seemed not to have been tipped off in advance for once.

"And?"

"Under the circumstances, the Director of Public Prosecutions has advised that the jury should be discharged."

"I'll do that now," he said.

He signalled to Brian and when the jurors had assembled, the judge addressed them.

"Ladies and gentlemen, you have no idea how sorry I am to have to do this at this stage in the proceedings. For reasons that will emerge no doubt in due course, I am going to have to ask you to cease your work. I am declaring a mistrial."

There were gasps of shock and expletives from the jury.

"I am sorry also that I can put it no further than that. But I will say what has happened during this trial is now a matter for the gardaí. Thank you very much for your service. You are excused from duty for the next ten years."

Looking shell-shocked, the jury left the court for the last time.

Rafferty got to his feet but, before he could speak, the judge addressed him.

"Yes, Mr Rafferty, your client is free to go, unless – ?" he paused and turned toward Leona, who shook her head.

"Thank you, Judge," Rafferty said, before adding, "Might you consider costs?"

Judge Brown looked sharply at him.

"Not today."

"I'm in the court's hands."

I unplugged my stenograph and folded it into its case. I had that horrible sinking feeling, as though I was in a lift that had dropped too fast. I could see O'Farrell smiling widely and shaking hands with Rafferty.

As I was leaving court, I heard journalists speculating on how Rachel Deere had been killed. The media, I knew, would be full of it tomorrow.

In the office, I texted Leona 'So sorry' and she responded 'Thanks'. Then I wrote up my notes to complete the short transcript, put the Rachel Deere file in my bag and left.

Gabriel was waiting for me outside, sitting in his now usual spot on the low wall. We didn't speak until we got into his car.

"After all we went through to keep this trial going – we needn't have bothered," I said, failing to soften the bitter edge in my voice. I knew I'd put both of us in real danger, for what turned out to be nothing.

"This trial might be done, but it isn't over for us," Gabriel said firmly. "We know a lot of things the lads in Store Street don't know yet, Bea. What if we could link O'Farrell to the murder?"

"I just know he had something to do with it."

"We'll go home, we'll pull everything we have together and then we'll go and see Matt."

This time, I didn't argue with him.

At Gabriel's I remembered the envelope from the Companies Office. I opened it and pulled out the loose pages.

We leafed through them, trying to make sense of what we were looking at. There was basic paperwork for Signal Investments, with an address and the names of directors, nothing that hadn't come out in court.

There was also a series of accounts, dating back over five years, for companies called Rell Pharmaceuticals Ltd and Rell International Ltd. They looked like any other balance sheets, with outgoings, earnings and assets marked neatly, everything adding up perfectly.

"They must be O'Farrell companies, otherwise Bessie wouldn't have sent them to me."

"Look here."

Gabriel held his finger under a line of text, showing a payment of €250,000 to St Lucian the Evangelist Ltd in 2012. The 2013 accounts showed the same payment.

I opened Gabriel's laptop and searched the Internet for Rell Pharmaceuticals Ltd. Its website described it as a small, specialist company based in Killarney. Its main product appeared to be benzodiazepine, but it also carried out research and development.

'On the cutting edge of psychopharmacology medications,' the blurb said. There was little information except its address and phone number. There were no details of ownership or management. I couldn't find Rell listed on any business intelligence sites.

"Okay, what else have we got?"

Gabriel spread everything we had on the kitchen table.

There was the medical file on Rachel Deere with the photos, the printouts of the copies I'd made of Stephen O'Farrell's medical file, and Rachel's note of what looked like blackmail payments, along with the Rell documents from the CRO.

"What are we looking at here?" Gabriel asked.

"What's the connection?" I wasn't getting it.

"Think about the case for a minute," Gabriel said. "O'Farrell puts investors' money into Signal Investments, then he takes it out and moves it around. The lads were able to track it down to a series of other companies. Then he takes it out of those and spends it, but they weren't able to trace it all. No mention of Rell Pharmaceuticals in court?"

"No. I'd remember if there was."

Gabriel picked up Rachel's medical file from St Lucian's.

"Whoever sent you this wanted to tell you something – what?"

I took it from him and looked through it again. The photo of Rachel, taken when she was admitted, showed a woman worn down by alcohol, looking ten years older than her thirty-one years.

The handwritten notes were hard to decipher. I found some details of a difficult childhood, the private demons such experiences visit on a person and comments including 'clinically depressed' and 'compulsive dependence on alcohol'.

Then I found an entry I hadn't noticed before: 'Approval sought for acceptance to Rell trial', and below that 'Patient consent obtained'.

"Gabriel, Rell was working with St Lucian's."

I read on. There was a record of daily doses of something called Camtrexonal and beside each day an entry detailing mood and physical behaviours, as well as physiological tests. A red circle was marked around what looked like blood-pressure measurements and toward the end of the entries, the words 'nausea', 'auditory hallucination' and 'suicidal ideation' were underlined.

"The drug trial seems to have ended before her discharge date," I said, showing Gabriel the notes. "So, St Lucian was allowing Rell to trial a drug on patients there – could that be right?"

"It looks that way. Is there anything wrong with that?" Gabriel asked. "Drugs have to be tested somewhere."

"But they were being paid for it – is that how it works? Is that ethical?"

I wondered about the approval and what had happened to the drug. I googled Camtrexonal and it popped up in the British Medical Journal as a drug under consideration for licensing by the European Medicines Agency.

"It says the drug has proved effective in UK and US trials for co-treating alcohol addiction and clinical depression. It's licence-pending in the US. There's no mention of an Irish trial."

"So, what does that mean?" Gabriel asked.

"Could the Irish trial have been buried? And if it was, why?"

Gabriel began gathering up the documents. "Maybe it's just that Ireland and the UK were lumped together."

That seemed more than plausible. "I wonder if Rachel knew something about the drug. Is that why she was killed?"

"We need to bring all this to Matt."

I followed Gabriel reluctantly out to his car. I was nervous about speaking to Matt McCann; no matter how good a friend he was to Gabriel, he was still in the force and had to do his job.

He'd arranged to meet us in a pub opposite the back entrance to Pearse Street Garda Station, the Long Stone. He was already sitting in a dim corner, nursing an orange juice and, to my relief, not in uniform.

He put a hand out for me to shake when we approached the table.

"Detective."

"Matt, please. What can I get you?"

I asked for a pot of tea and Gabriel asked for a pint. When the drinks had arrived, we told him all we knew. He sat back in his seat looking from one to the other of us as we spoke, occasionally making noises of encouragement when we faltered, and taking no notes.

He sat in silence for a few minutes after we'd finished, his head pressed against the wall above his seat. Then he leaned forward and cupped his drink as though it were a hot whiskey.

"Okay, first I'm not here at all, not for the moment anyway."

"That's a given," Gabriel said.

"Second, I'm surprised at you letting this go on so long. You should have come to me ages ago."

"That's my fault – I was afraid of the trial collapsing," I said.

He looked at us like a teacher confronting two errant pupils.

"You have no idea what you are dealing with here. And you," he scowled at Gabriel, "taking evidence from a crime scene. I'm surprised at you – you could be done for that."

"In fairness, the lads had come and gone."

"I know they had – don't know how they missed that. Wouldn't mind but it's one of the lines we're chasing, all that money she had. And now those photos. I can only sit on this for so long, you know that?"

Gabriel and I exchanged glances and he nodded.

"We were aware of O'Farrell's links to St Lucian's, but we found no connection to the fraud money," McCann said. "The drugs trial sounds like a sideshow, doesn't it? Still, the photos are reason enough to take another look around down there." He took out his phone and typed a few words. "To-do list," he said, looking up from the screen. "Forget to get dressed in the morning otherwise."

I had a sudden vision of him wandering into Pearse Street Garda Station in flannel pyjamas; he struck me as a flannel pyjama kind of man. I'd known a few and found they tended to compare me to their mothers. I always came up short.

"And Bobby Loftus is involved too. Now he's a character you'd want to be steering well clear of. They call him Teflon Bob inside."

He gestured toward the station with a nod of his head.

"We have him linked to eleven murders, mostly doing the work for drugs gangs. He's a dangerous character."

He looked over my shoulder toward the bar and I looked around to see if someone was approaching, but there was no one there.

"If you were wanted dead he would have killed you – you needn't doubt that."

I didn't know whether to be reassured or more fearful.

"What's the latest on Deere?" Gabriel asked.

McCann leaned in towards us.

"I needn't tell you, the boys upstairs aren't too pleased. The Commissioner, no less, said she wanted a fine toothcomb over the whole thing. I want to know where she went to playschool, says she."

"Well, she trained in a hospital in Leeds," I said.

"We're aware of that – Meadowwood Park. As I say, fine toothcomb. I'll have to drip-feed those documents into the system, as carefully as I càn."

Gabriel nodded again. I couldn't imagine how he'd manage that, and I knew if he made any mistakes nothing we gave him could be used in evidence.

McCann drained his orange juice and grimaced, as though it were a foul medicine taken only for the good of his health.

"Do you think now that the trial's collapsed, they'll leave me alone?" I asked him.

"It's possible."

He neither looked nor sounded convinced.

"The best thing you can do now is lie low. Have you

somewhere you can go, well out of the city?"

I wondered about leaving Janine with all the work again.

"For how long?"

He looked as though I'd asked him about the length of a piece of string.

"For a while, anyway."

"I have a friend with a place in Wexford – I might be able to go there."

"Haven't we all?" McCann laughed. "Go there for a few days and I'll be in touch."

He exited the back way, through the beer garden of the pub, our documents under his arm.

I rang a friend, Georgina, who'd helped me set up my computer system when I came home from England, and I mentioned stress at work. She commiserated when I told her about the trial collapsing.

Gabriel went with me to pick up the keys for the house in Ballymoney.

"Do you think he did it, though?" Georgina asked in a conspiratorial tone.

I would normally have rebuffed questions about something I was working on, but I didn't feel like it right then.

"Yes, yes I do."

She asked me a few more questions and held forth on how white-collar criminals were under-prosecuted compared to, for example, misfortunates who were only slightly over the speed limit on the M11, but got three penalty points on their licence and a hefty fine. I didn't need to ask if she'd been speeding down to her weekend retreat – I could hear it in her sense of injustice.

Back in Gabriel's car, I phoned Janine and told her I was taking a break.

"Are you sure you're all right?" she said. "Where are you going?"

I explained about Georgina's place and how it was near the sea and that I felt the salt air would help me get my head straight. That seemed to make sense to her.

"Of course, Bea – you're missing your own little house by the sea. Take as long as you need."

I packed a few clothes when we got home and left for Wexford.

Gabriel made me promise I'd phone him when I arrived.

I got off the motorway just before Gorey and went into the town, stopping at a supermarket. Georgina said she hadn't been down in weeks and there was nothing in the fridge. I bought bread, cheese, eggs, some ham and coleslaw from the deli and a few other basics. Then I took the narrow road to the seaside village and found Seafield Cottage, a pretty stone-walled building with two bedrooms in the attic and dormer windows like surprised eyes.

The little house was no more than 500 metres from the beach, almost at the end of a lane. The nearest building was a beach-hut-come-tearoom, its windows shuttered. It looked peaceful and asleep, awaiting the children's school holidays.

It was almost dark when I let myself into the cottage. I put on the central heating as instructed by Georgina to "air out the place". I found the bed linen in the hot press and spread it on a radiator before putting it on the bed in the guest room.

I followed her instructions, moving from one little room to another like an explorer, expecting to hear, in the silence around me, the scratch of mice or the faint whispers of the souls that had lived in the cottage before Georgina, and who'd left a part of themselves in its butter-coloured stone. But all I could hear was the lap of waves on the nearby strand.

After a time, a rain shower, blown in from the sea, barraged the window panes, making the little cottage feel like a sanctuary in a storm. I prepared an omelette, put on the stereo and sat down on the chintz sofa. Stevie Nicks sang to me about weather. It was cosy, and I had to cut short a mental exploration of what it might be like to have someone sitting beside me on the couch. It was easier and safer to be alone.

I remembered Laurence playing Fleetwood Mac too loudly in his bedroom one time and Father shouting about hippies. There was heartache in the music, and a kind of freedom. I wondered if he thought of it when he was dying. I shook myself then to cast off my maudlin mood, switched off the music and put on the TV.

The late evening news was full of the collapse of O'Farrell's trial. The reporter, leaning intimately into the camera as though she was imparting a secret to a handful of close friends, said Rachel Deere had been murdered.

She recapped then on the forewoman's death, the discovery of her body, her reported alcohol addiction and the heartbroken boyfriend who wouldn't speak to the media.

"Gardaí have refused to comment for operational reasons."

There was a shot of Matt McCann in uniform, his curls protruding from the sides of his cap, staring into the microphones pushed under his chin, saying nothing.

Gabriel texted: 'Everything all right?'

I'd forgotten to call him when I arrived.

I pressed the dial key.

"Sorry, Gabriel, it just took me a while to get settled."

"No bother. Listen, I've found a newspaper report on suicides. 'St Lucian had the highest rate of suicides per resident in Irish psychiatric institutions in 2013.'"

His tone of voice told me he was reading.

"Dr Forester is quoted – describes it as a blip, says statistical studies frequently demonstrate anomalies and a longitudinal study due next year will show St Lucian has an excellent track record in keeping vulnerable patients safe. There were seven deaths, Bea."

"You're thinking about the drugs trial?"

He said he was.

"What's the date on that article?" I asked.

"March this year."

"So, it was published during O'Farrell's case."

I heard Gabriel swallow before he launched into what sounded like a rehearsed line.

"I was thinking, I could do with a bit of sea air myself. Maybe I'll take a run down to you in the morning?"

My instinct was to tell him not to, that I was fine and safe, but I hadn't been able to entirely shake off the fear that Loftus had induced in me, and the impact of O'Farrell's unsettling overtures.

"If you like."

"Right then," Gabriel said, and I could hear the smile in his voice, "I'll see you tomorrow."

Chapter 22

Saturday, 3rd May 2014

Thin curtains in the cottage's guest room meant the morning light spilled in before seven. I tossed for a while beneath the covers, then gave up and went down to the kitchen. Outside the cottage, I could hear the morning birds greeting the sun, and, in the distance, the sea slapping against the rocks at Ballymoney beach.

I'd finished a pot of tea, got dressed in jeans, runners and a white shirt and listened to most of the eight o'clock news on the radio when I heard a knock on the door. I thought Gabriel must have got out of bed very early, eager to get here as soon as he could. It made me smile to think of him, driving down the deserted M11, keen to take 'the sea air'.

My smile vanished when I opened the door and recognised the person standing there. Loftus loomed over me, grinning. I pushed against the door to try to keep him out, but he put a foot over the threshold, his full weight easily forcing me back. He stepped into the cottage hallway and banged the door shut behind him.

I turned away and ran for the kitchen, but with two

strides he had caught me. There was no time, even, to call out.

He restrained me with one hand and took a syringe from his pocket with the other. I felt a sharp jab in my thigh – the sting as a needle pierced my muscle – and then the smell of Loftus's breath close to my face. He called out to someone to help him and then I was being carried, arms and legs. I smelled car leather next to my face. After that nothing.

When I awoke, I was lying on a bed in a simply furnished room. Heavy curtains shielded the windows and the only light came from beneath a door, a few feet from the foot of my bed. I blinked and then blinked again. Where was I? I tried to think, but my head hurt. I couldn't recall what had happened.

My left thigh was throbbing and the rest of my body ached all over. I was sure there were bruises where I'd been roughly gripped. My eyes felt leaden and though I tried to keep them open they drooped and shut.

I dreamed of Laurence. We were sitting on a bench in St Stephen's Green, next to fountains and circles of ruby geraniums. It must have been summer. He was talking to me in a low voice, explaining how he felt trapped and suffocated by home and by Ireland, and by our parents. And I was trying to tell him that it was worth something, that our parents loved us, and he shouldn't try so hard to get away. And I cried and tried to explain to him why it'd be better if he didn't want to go and didn't I love him and if he stayed, wouldn't he find some lovely young woman who would love him too?

He put his arm around me and said I was right and of course he'd go back to work tomorrow and tell his boss he hadn't meant it when he told him to shove his job where the sun didn't shine. And he'd apologise and explain how grateful he was to have a job at all in Dublin, when thousands like him were in the Dole office and would fall over themselves for it. And he did know, of course, what a lucky young man he was. He'd take back the remarks about his boss's wife walking late at night on Leeson Street and say he realised how disrespectful that was and that he didn't deserve another chance, but this time he'd appreciate it.

Even in the dream, I knew he wouldn't say those things and that there was a hunger in him for something other than what he had and a yearning in him that he could not put a name on.

The dream drifted back to our home and Laurence bitter with drink, shouting at our father, cursing him. And I saw Mother, sobbing by the fire, bewildered, while Father put Laurence to bed.

When I awoke my cheeks were wet with tears and my throat hurt. The curtains were still closed, but daylight leaked from between them and I could make out the shape of a glass of water by my bedside. I heaved myself up on one elbow and gulped it down. My shoulders and neck ached, but the headache had gone.

I slipped my feet out from under the covers and saw someone had put me in a hospital gown, short-sleeved, white and to the knee. I got to my feet slowly and walked as quietly as I could across to the door, past a small, round table on which someone had placed a vase of sweet pea, as though to please a guest at some upmarket hotel. I tried the door handle, but though it turned, I couldn't open it. I looked through the keyhole and could see no key inside it.

I went to the window and partially drew back the curtains. The view of lawn, poplars and gravel drive was familiar – I was in St Lucian's. A retching sensation overcame me and just in time I found another door leading to a little bathroom.

There was a toothbrush there and after getting sick I brushed my teeth and washed my face. In the mirror over the sink, my skin looked grey and my eyes seemed out of focus, as though I was looking at them through somebody else's reading glasses. I thought whatever drugs they'd given me must still be in my system.

I searched the bedroom for my belongings and found my jeans and a blouse hanging in the wardrobe, my runners below them, with socks neatly tucked inside. My handbag was there too. I wondered why Loftus had taken it. Perhaps he wanted anyone searching the house to think I'd left of my own accord. I thought of Matt McCann's words, "if you were wanted dead he would have killed you", and took comfort from them. I emptied my bag onto the bed and its contents spread over the white duvet. Everything was there – my make-up, purse, work identity, umbrella, receipts from past lunches – all of it except my phone.

My watch, left on my bedside, said 6.30 a.m. I must have slept all day and all night into Sunday morning. If I was going to get out of here, this was a good time, when most people would still be sleeping. I refilled my handbag again and began clumsily to dress. Sitting on the edge of the bed, I struggled to co-ordinate my limbs. I felt more like myself when I had my clothes on.

I opened the curtains fully and examined the window. It was one of the old-fashioned, sash kind and it contained no bars or locks, but try as I might, I couldn't open it more than an inch. I saw then that two brass blocks had been attached to the frame at the top, preventing it from opening any further. Still, it was only single-glazed, and I wondered, if I had to, whether I could smash it with something, though it would make for a noisy exit. The lawn outside was empty and I felt I shouldn't delay too long before trying to get away.

I emptied the contents of the sweet-pea vase into the toilet, put on my shoes and was about to try breaking the window with the pottery, when I heard footsteps outside my door. I put the vase in the bathroom, closed the curtains and jumped into bed, pulling the covers up and closing my eyes, just as the door opened.

"She's still asleep," a woman's voice said. "How much did Loftus give her?"

"Wake her up, will you?" It was a man speaking.

The woman opened the curtains and began calling my name. When I didn't respond she came over to the bed and slapped my face gently.

"Beatrice, Beatrice."

Slap, slap.

I opened my eyes.

"Beatrice, you've been asleep a long time," the man said.

"Where am I?" I kept my arms covered, the blanket up to my chin.

"I think you know where you are. I'm Dr Niall Forester and this is Dr Dorothy Whittaker."

He gestured to the woman beside him who was smiling at me now, her hair pulled back in a dark ponytail. I recognised her as the woman who'd spoken to O'Farrell in the park and to Deere on the tram.

"How are you feeling?" she asked, reaching under the blanket to find my wrist. "Niall!"

She pulled back the blanket to reveal me fully clothed.

"Oh now, Beatrice you've only just arrived," Dr Forester said. He lifted a clipboard from the end of my bed, sat down on the edge of the mattress and wrote something. "What are we going to do with you?" His voice was all paternalistic concern. "We've been very worried about you for a while now, Beatrice. You've been getting yourself into all kinds of trouble."

"I don't know what you mean."

Dr Whittaker sat on the other side of the bed.

"You've been snooping, haven't you? I caught you snooping myself."

I swallowed hard, my mouth arid and, though I hoped I didn't show it, fear was rising from my stomach to my throat. Dr Forester passed me a glass of water.

"Don't distress yourself. What you need is a good rest. What we're proposing is that you stay with us for a while."

"I don't want to." My voice warbled, though I tried to keep it steady.

Dr Whittaker took a syringe and vial from her pocket.

"If you co-operate, stay in your room, watch TV and just relax, there'll be no need for this," she said.

"How long?"

"Ten days – two weeks at the most."

I couldn't disappear for two weeks unnoticed.

"People will come looking for me."

They both laughed.

"You mean your ex-garda friend? We've sent him a message from your phone already. You've made it very clear you don't want to see him. He won't be looking for you."

I wondered about Gabriel and how he would take a single dismissive text from me. He was so easily hurt he might simply accept it and walk away, bury himself in a Stoneybatter pub and forget the whole business – after all what did he have to lose?

"I have work commitments . . . "

Dr Whittaker patted my arm.

"We'll be emailing your colleague with a doctor's certificate. Anything else?"

I knew that Janine wouldn't query a sick cert if she got one. She'd made her concerns about my health clear – and Alastair would be delighted to be proved right.

"And after two weeks?"

"We'll just let you out the front door and you can tell everyone you've had a lovely rest."

"I'll go straight to the guards and tell them what happened."

They laughed again.

"Do you think they'd believe you? Our records show you checked yourself in and two doctors certified that you needed help."

I decided not to tell them I'd already spoken to gardaí and that they'd probably be getting a visit soon.

"Tell me what this is about."

"I think you know, Beatrice," Forester said. We can't have you jeopardising the success of Camtrexonal. It's only a week until it's approved in America by the FDA and the European Medicine Agency will follow."

"You were sent something, weren't you?" Whittaker came closer to me. "We know you were and we can't risk you telling anybody."

I didn't say that Matt McCann had seen what I'd been sent and so had Gabriel and it wouldn't take them long to figure out what it meant.

She picked up the syringe again.

"Now, do I need to use this?"

"It's all right – I'll stay, just leave me alone."

They both stood up and Whittaker told me I needed to change back into a nightgown.

"For the moment – it wouldn't look right to the nurses," she said.

They waited while I changed in the bathroom and got back into bed.

"The window is alarmed, by the way," Forester said over his shoulder as they left the room.

I heard the door close and then lock. I put on the television.

It was eight o'clock and the morning news was still dealing with the collapse of the trial. The Minister for Justice would make a statement in the Dáil, the reporter said. She also mentioned the tragic death of a former garda, named locally as Graham O'Donoghue, and said gardaí were not looking for anyone else in connection with it. I wondered if such euphemisms were particular to Ireland, and if other countries simply said the man took his own life.

My breakfast was delivered shortly afterwards. I sat passively in bed while a young man who looked Filipino brought fresh fruit, croissants and orange juice on a tray. I made appreciative comments, admiring the quality of the fruit and the glaze on the buttery croissants. He told me his name was John Paul, from which I put his age at thirty-five.

"Tea or coffee, Ms Barrington?"

I asked for tea, and a china pot and matching teacup were produced.

"I'm just here for a rest."

"Of course." His tone was that of a kind uncle to a child who's just told a story about seeing fairies.

"If there's anything else, just press your buzzer." He gestured to a red button on the bedside locker.

"Could I have access to a phone?"

He smiled and closed the door, gently locking it.

I wondered if there was a sign outside explaining I was to be confined to my room. I swallowed down the breakfast and took the chart from the end of my bed. There were a series of illegible words and figures, measurements that looked like blood pressure and temperature. I could just make out the words 'chronic depression' and 'paranoid delusions'. I wished all that had happened in the last ten days was a figment of my imagination.

It seemed to me that all of the events had been triggered by my sighting of Whittaker with O'Farrell, but I was no closer to understanding what that meeting had been about. I was sure now though, that the drugs trial was at the heart of it. It seemed to connect O'Farrell, Whittaker, Forester and Rachel Deere. But how exactly? I knew I wouldn't find out sitting in this room.

When John Paul returned to take my breakfast things, I asked him when he'd be back with lunch. He told me half twelve and then wrote something on my chart.

I pretended to cry.

"What's the matter?" He came to my side and gave me a tissue.

"I can't help thinking about a friend of mine. She was a patient here too and she died."

"I'm sorry."

I dabbed at my eyes.

"Rachel Deere, a lovely, sweet girl, a great friend."

"Ah yes, Rachel. They're saying she was murdered."

I began to cry again, louder. "Please, don't talk about that." I hid my eyes behind the tissue to disguise the lack of tears. "I only want to hear good things about her."

He recounted how Rachel had improved greatly after only a short time at the hospital and how he thought she'd be one of those who'd make it. He handed me more tissues and I eased off on the sound effects.

"She worked so hard while she was here and co-operated with the doctors, just like you must do, Ms Barrington."

I said that I knew that and would do my best.

"But I don't know if being in here all day will be good for me."

"Maybe you could manage lunch in the dining room? Would you like that?"

"I might."

He smiled, benignly.

"I'll speak to Dr Forester. Now, I'll take these things out

of your way and you can have a nice rest."

"Yes, thank you, John Paul."

When he left I tried to visualise my whereabouts. I was at the front of the building and on the ground floor, and judging by the position of the car park I was to the left of the main entrance, perhaps not too far from Dr Forester's office. I'd have a good look around, I decided, once they unlocked the door to let me go to the dining room.

John Paul came back an hour later and told me the doctor had given permission for me to eat in the dining room. But only if I was accompanied there and back.

I hid my disappointment and thanked him. He smiled when he shut the door on me again. There would be no chance to search. They'd be watching everything I did. How would I get away from the place? They'd said they'd let me out in two weeks, but would they? Things might change before then, there might be developments that would make them hold on to me or, worse, need to get rid of me entirely.

I didn't think I could stand the place for two days, much less two weeks. I didn't like being confined. I'd always been my own master, never a day in hospital, never trapped, never incarcerated, never under the control of someone else – well almost never.

I began to perspire and my heart rate quickened. My breath became shallow, my head dizzy. I lay under the covers and closed my eyes. I wanted to shout for help, but I knew it would be pointless, a waste of breath. And worse than that, it'd give them something, some sign of my desperation and fear. And I wasn't prepared to give them that. Still I felt as though I was sinking, being pulled under, weighed down with stones. I thought how easy it would be, incarcerated and with no control, to lose a grip on reality.

I must have fallen asleep, because it was John Paul's knock that awoke me, a polite signal before the turning of the key. I roused myself as he came through the door.

"Are you ready for your lunch, Ms Barrington? Oh, you look sleepy– would you rather I brought it here?"

"No, please, just give me a minute." I slipped out of bed, went into the bathroom, washed my face and brushed my hair. I put on a white fleece dressing gown that was hanging on the back of the door.

"Am I all right like this?"

"Here."

John Paul handed me a pair of white fleece slippers that had been left at the side of my bed. I put them on and felt like I was dressed for a treatment at an expensive hotel spa. They were the sort with no back to them, so that I had to shuffle slightly to keep them on my feet.

Outside my room we turned left. I didn't recognise the corridor. I felt we were moving away from the exit toward the extremity of the hospital's east wing. There were no signs on any of the doors. The corridor turned to the left and we followed it, me still shuffling on the polished parquet flooring, until we reached a pair of wooden double doors with 'Dining Room' written on them in elegant art deco script. I stopped, suddenly fearful.

"Don't worry, you'll fit in." John Paul cupped my elbow and guided me through.

Fitting in was what I was afraid of.

The dining room was hexagonal with large windows, framed by floor-length pale pink curtains. It held ten round tables, with white cloths, silver cutlery set for six and small glass vases with yellow and purple freesias. There were people seated in threes and twos. I made my way to an empty table at the back and chose a seat close to the wall, looking out on the room.

"The safe seat," John Paul said. "I'll be over there if you need me."

He gestured to a table where two other nurses were sitting.

"Okay."

He walked away.

I waited, and half watched the other inmates. They were dressed just as I was, twelve of them, seven men and five women. They didn't look in my direction, but talked quietly to each other. More people drifted in. I lowered my gaze and hoped that no one would join me. A heavy-set man paused near me and I held my breath. I could feel his eyes on me, but I didn't look up and he moved on.

Then a young woman arrived who was not put off by my obvious aversion to company. She pulled out the chair one place from mine and sat down.

"I'm Julie – are you new?"

I nodded.

"Hello," she said, and tapped the table with her index finger, once, twice and then three times. I looked at her hand and she put it in her lap.

"If it's soup or salad, take the salad."

"Okay, thanks."

Two waitresses came out of a swinging door, which I took to be the kitchen. One approached our table and told us what was on offer – vegetable soup or smoked cheese and black pudding salad, followed by lamb cutlet or lemon sole. I chose the salad and the sole. So did Julie.

When the salad arrived, and I saw the nuggets of black pudding, I thought of Gabriel. What was I doing here, playing along? This was madness.

My hand shook so much that the food fell from my fork.

"It's okay, it gets easier." Julie put her hand on my arm to steady me.

I looked into her face and she smiled. Her teeth were even and slightly yellow in places, like a smoker's. I smiled briefly back at her, calmed myself and began picking at my food.

"Have you been here long?"

"Too long, too often. I've been in and out five times over the past four years. Things get on top of me and this place is very calming."

I told her my friend Rachel Deere had been here and asked if she remembered her. She sat back in her chair while the waitress took our plates away and drummed a finger against her jaw – once, twice, three times.

"She's been on the TV, I do remember her. Poor Rachel, hard to believe she's gone. She was so full of life – do you know what I mean?"

I said that I did.

"Always up to mischief, she was, had a couple of the men in here on the go."

She stopped talking when the food arrived and we didn't speak until we'd almost finished eating. The lemon sole was buttery and the new potatoes tasted of the earth. I felt for a few moments like an ordinary diner in a high-quality restaurant. I was tentative about asking questions.

"Did she get on with the doctors all right, Rachel I mean?"

"Mostly, I think." Julie carefully speared baby peas with her fork.

"There was one though, she took a terrible dislike to, irrational, I'd say, because he was only new. We were both sitting in the garden one morning and he came over to talk to us and she just started screaming, 'Get away you!'."

"Strange."

"Not really, we're in here for a reason." She laughed then.

"Do you remember who he was?"

Julie shook her head.

"Some locum, I only saw him the once."

They brought out strawberry cheesecake to us then and tea. Julie stirred a spoonful of sugar into her cup and tapped the spoon on the rim – once, twice three times.

When we'd finished, John Paul came to take me back.

"Chin up," Julie said.

She waved as I left, and I waved back, feeling briefly like a child who'd made a friend on the first day at summer camp.

I walked as slowly as I could back to my room, counting in my head the numbers of steps I was taking. I could manage this, I decided. I would just have to 'chin up' and get out of here. How long would it take to run from my room to the dining room? I imagined the windows there would not open, but if I could get into the kitchen, I might find an exit.

When John Paul let me into my room, I said I was tired and would rather take my evening meal in my room.

"I understand, it can be overwhelming for the first few days."

I told him he was very kind.

"Try to get some rest."

When he left, I lay on the bed to think. I would have to be careful, and I would have to get out tonight.

John Paul arrived with my evening meal at seven.

"Out or in?"

"Out of bed please."

He pulled a small table out from the wall and placed a tray on it, carefully setting the knife and fork on a napkin.

"There now."

I thanked him and, when I was sure he was gone, I scraped the food into the toilet bowl and flushed it away. My stomach was sick with nerves and eating would have made me vomit. I reasoned too, that there might be something gentle and soporific in my meal to help induce a calm night. For the same reason, I didn't drink the tea.

I rooted around in my handbag and fished out my chewing gum. There were three sticks and I chewed them vigorously.

When John Paul returned to take away my tray I told him I still felt incredibly tired.

"That's perfectly natural."

"Do you think, if I went to bed now, I could be let sleep until the morning?"

"Of course. I'll hang the do not disturb sign on your door."

He opened the door to the room and put the tray on a trolley in the corridor. I made for the bathroom and let out a little scream when I stepped inside. John Paul came back, leaving the door open.

"There's an enormous spider in there," I said, screeching the words at him. "I can't go in there – take it away, please."

I backed away, shuddering.

"Where did you see it?"

"Near the cistern. It's black and hairy."

He went inside and began to hunt for it.

I took the wedge of gum from my cheek and quickly forced it into the hollow of the strike plate on the frame of the bedroom door, almost filling up the space meant for the door lock. I'd seen it done on a science programme that was testing theories on how to escape from a locked room.

"I can't find it," hc said. "Show me where you saw it."

I walked into the bathroom and pointed into the corner.

"I've looked everywhere – it must be gone."

"Please check again."

I sat on the bed while he hunted for a little longer.

"It must be gone down the plughole. I've put in the plug, so it won't be back."

"If you're sure."

I got back into bed and he added something else to my chart.

"Do you want me to wait until you're ready for bed?"

"No, thank you."

He left then, and I heard the lock make a dull sound as it hit the gum.

It was eight, so I reasoned that if I waited until ten the hospital would have settled down for the night and it'd be dark outside.

I waited until it was almost time to leave before getting dressed. Then I searched in my purse and picked out a supermarket loyalty card. The gum had prevented the door lock from fully inserting into the strike plate and I was able to work the card around the lock and force it back far enough to open the door. I stepped out into the quiet, dimly lit corridor. With my bag tucked under my arm, I closed the door behind me, leaving the 'do not disturb' sign on the handle.

I turned right towards where I thought the exit might be. I felt it was closer than the dining room though I couldn't be sure. I crept as far as the end of the corridor. At the corner, I looked quickly round and could see no one. I went through a set of double doors to a corridor that looked familiar. There was a sign for the ladies' toilet halfway down, and at the end, the doors into the foyer.

I hurried into the toilets, which smelled faintly of drains. I stepped into a cubicle until I was sure there was no one else there. When I stepped back out I examined the room – three cubicles against one wall, three wash-hand basins set into a sheet of black marble, with three small windows cut into the wall above. They were open, perhaps to dissipate the smell overnight, and they looked big enough to take me. I pulled myself up onto the marble, stood one foot either side of a wash-hand basin and peered out. I was looking at the car park.

It was now or never.

242

Chapter 23

Sunday, 4th May 2014

I wanted to go, but I couldn't move. My mind raced with adrenalin. What would happen next if I got clear of this place? The idea that I might get away but that there would be no consequences for Forester and Whittaker, and the production of Camtrexonal would go ahead, was abhorrent to me. And what were the chances of the guards tying O'Farrell to it? Though I couldn't grasp his involvement, I felt that he must be implicated somehow. And because of it, Rachel Deere had been murdered.

I told myself I should leave quickly, but I felt I deserved more than just to escape. There had to be something I could gain, some answers, some evidence, to make what had happened to me – and to Precious and Rachel – of some value. There had to be something in the building that would help, some paperwork incriminating O'Farrell.

Before I knew what I was doing, I'd inched out of the ladies, heart banging against my ribs, and found Dr Forester's office. There was no light coming from under the door. I put my ear against it – silence.

I turned the handle slowly. It wasn't locked. I stepped inside and closed the door.

Dr Forester's desk had a neat pile of files and letters on it, with a Dictaphone sitting on top. The papers rustled too loudly as I looked through them. There were patients' notes and letters ready to be signed – nothing useful. I moved to the filing cabinet that I'd explored on my last visit and was about to open it, when the phone on the desk began to ring. I ducked under the desk, fearing the incessant tone would summon someone to the room, but no one came. The phone stopped ringing and clicked into voice mail.

"Dr Forester is unable to take your call right now, please leave a message after the tone," a woman's voice said.

Then another familiar voice came on the line.

"Niall, the gardaí have been by, they're asking questions about Rachel Deere. Where the fuck are you? Ring me when you get this."

The voice was O'Farrell's. My first thought was that he must have been in a panic or he wouldn't have been so careless as to leave that message; my second was that it proved he and Forester were colluding and had something to hide. I was sorry I didn't have my mobile phone to make a recording.

Then I remembered the doctor's Dictaphone. I played the voicemail again, recorded it, and put the Dictaphone in my bag. That would do.

As I approached the door, I heard footsteps outside. I stood still and felt as though my breathing could be heard through walls, as though the sweat of my fear could be smelled in the corridor. The steps did not pause. I hoped whoever it was wasn't on the way to check on me. Perhaps they would enter my room and realise I was gone. They would begin searching for me. They'd move from room to room until they found me. At any moment they might burst into the office and see me standing there. There would be no choice then – the syringe Dr Whittaker had threatened me with would be deployed. I could feel dampness in my palms and sweat on my forehead. I imagined the beads forming along my hairline, trickling down. My breath began to come in gasps; I tried to control it, to make it quiet. I concentrated on the door handle – it didn't move. The footsteps faded and, when all was silent, I stepped carefully outside again.

I darted back to the ladies, and once inside, flipped the lock on the main door. It would hold them for a while if they began to search. I hooked the strap of my handbag diagonally across my body and hoisted myself back up onto the marble top. I stood again with my two feet either side of a wash-hand basin, so that I could see out the window. This was the same view as from my bedroom, except closer to the entrance. I could see a handful of parked cars now and the tree-lined entrance drive. If I could make it to the trees, I felt I might make it out.

I told myself I must not be spotted. The place was so remote that even if they only saw me as I exited the main gates, it'd take them no time at all to catch me. I was sorry I'd put on a white shirt in Seafield Cottage the morning before.

The window swung inwards and I opened it as far as I could. The aperture wasn't much bigger than the size of a carry-on suitcase. I stuck my head out and looked up and down. There was no one outside and, because the entrance doors were set back, I couldn't see if they were open. There was a camera perched over the stone arch, pointing outward. I would have to keep tight to the building, before dashing for cover behind the first car.

I gripped the window frame and hauled myself upwards and out. My arms shook with the effort and I regretted laughing at Janine when she'd tried to coax me to attend a gym. I managed to get into a kneeling position on the window frame. I straightened one leg out, and then the other. I was balanced on the frame then, bent forward and panting. Inside, someone was trying to open the ladies' door, pushing it, twisting the handle. I knew I would have to move. There was nothing I could do but make the six-foot jump. I landed steadily enough on both feet, straightened up and looked around.

The nearest car was a midnight-blue jaguar – I sprinted to it. It wouldn't take long for them to fetch a janitor to unlock the toilets and not much longer to realise someone had gone out the window. They would be looking for me very soon.

I worked my way along the backs of the cars – Mercedes, BMW, Audi, and furthest from the door, a blue Nissan Micra. I remained at the last one for a few seconds, trying to gauge the distance from it to the trees, was it 70 metres or was it 100? It didn't matter; I would still have to run it. I looked round the side of the car toward the entrance. There was no movement, no one was looking for me, not yet.

I put my head down and ran until I reached the first tree. I caught my breath and dashed across the road to the trees on the far side where I'd be less visible from the entrance. I ran without looking back, from one tree to the next, keeping on the grass side, so I could take cover if a car came up the drive. When I got to the gate, I turned right and kept going as quickly as I could, determined to put as much distance between myself and St Lucian's while I had the chance.

I ran for as long as I could along the top of a ditch at the side of the road, lungs burning, feet throbbing, stumbling until I'd almost reached the turn for the main road. It was then I saw the headlights of a car coming from the direction of Newprieststown. Instinctively, I stopped running and stepped into the ditch. There was a good chance a driver on this road was on the way to the hospital. I reckoned if I was already spotted, whoever it was would pick me up and immediately return me to St Lucian's. All my effort would be for nothing and I wouldn't get away again – I was sure of that. As the car came nearer, it began to slow down. It pulled up alongside me and stopped.

I prepared to run and was turning away when I heard a voice call "Beatrice". It was familiar. I looked back and, now that the headlights were no longer blinding me, I recognised the car and then the man at the wheel – Gabriel.

He opened the door and jumped out.

"Jesus, Beatrice!"

I could feel my knees giving way beneath me then and I slumped against him. He carried me into the passenger seat, buckling me in before getting into the driver's side.

"The state of you!"

I looked down at my filthy runners and muddy jeans. My fingernails were chipped and dirty from the climb. I could hardly imagine what state my hair was in.

"You came."

"'Course I came."

He started the engine and pulled away.

"They said you wouldn't – they said they sent you a message."

He laughed.

"They did all right. I was cursing you yesterday, then this evening I checked the message again. It said 'u' instead of 'you'. I said to meself, you feckin' eejit Gabriel, that's not her! One of the lads managed to get a rough location for the phone and I guessed St Lucian's!"

The soothing tones of the radio filled the car with normality.

After about 15 minutes, Gabriel pulled over at a garage, got out and came back with fizzy orange and chocolate. He handed them to me.

"When you're ready, you can tell me everything."

I wanted to tell him everything, but when I'd finished the food, I felt heavy with relief and fell asleep. I didn't wake up until we reached Oxmantown Road.

"I should have stayed in Dublin. I hope Georgina's place isn't destroyed."

I couldn't remember if they'd been long in the house. They must have been a while, to take my bag and make it look like I'd decided to leave. At least then, they would have closed the front door.

"Don't worry, one of the lads checked it out for me, said it was grand."

In Gabriel's, the first thing I wanted was a shower, to wash away the smell of St Lucian's linen from my skin. I noticed, in the bathroom mirror, the black-and-blue thumbprints on my wrist, where Loftus had first grabbed me, marks on my right shoulder where he'd twisted my arm behind my back, bruises on my shins. When I closed my eyes, I could see his face next to mine, I could smell his breath.

In the kitchen, Gabriel asked, "Do you think you should see a doctor? Will I bring you to A & E?"

"I don't want to see the inside of another hospital for a very long time."

Gabriel gave me painkillers and tea. I sat at the kitchen table, a dressing gown on me and my hair wrapped in a towel, and I told him what had happened. He grimaced in some places and called me a fool in others.

"One thing I don't get – how did Loftus know where I was?"

"Maybe he followed you."

"But then why did he wait until Saturday morning? He could have picked me up on Friday when I got to the house."

It didn't make sense, but I couldn't think straight enough to work it out.

"I'm more interested in why they'd let you go after two

weeks? What would be the point of that?"

"They don't know I've been to the gardaí, do they? They said if they held me for a few weeks, no one would believe anything I said when I got out."

I thought of how wary we'd been of what Graham O'Donoghue told us.

"It was all about protecting Camtrexonal – that was all they seemed to care about."

Gabriel said there'd been something about the drug on the news. "Two Ministers were raving about it. Your man from Enterprise went on about how many jobs it would create and the health fella said it was a breakthrough for depression."

How easy it was, I thought, to wave a few jobs under the noses of politicians, and ensure they stayed on side.

"I wouldn't mind, but they weren't even pushed about Rell Pharmaceuticals being headed by O'Farrell." Gabriel sounded indignant. "Innocent until proven guilty, the health fella said, and the reporter nearly apologised for asking."

"Did they say anything about the licence?"

"Said the US one was imminent and the EU one was a week away."

"So they managed to bury the side-effects then?"

It seemed the increase in suicides in the Irish trial had been hidden because they'd hidden the entire Irish trial.

"Once Camtrexonal is licensed, it'll be difficult getting it revoked, maybe years before the negative effects are scientifically proved. Health authorities hate to be wrong," I said, recalling the battle the State had put up in court against women who'd been given contaminated blood products.

"I don't think we can sit on this," Gabriel said.

He made a phone call in the hall and said Matt would be dropping by unless I wasn't able. I shrugged off the question.

"Did you tell me you made a recording?" Gabriel asked, sitting down again.

"It's a voice message."

I found my bag and took out the Dictaphone.

"Hopefully Forester won't notice it's missing for a while."

I rewound it by a couple of minutes and played the message left by O'Farrell.

"What do you think?"

"Matt should hear it. Only, not that I'm paranoid, but I think we should make a copy. Things go missing sometimes."

He slid a button on the side of the device and a USB connector emerged.

"This will only take a minute."

He attached the Dictaphone to his laptop, downloaded the entire contents to a file, detached it again and put it in his pocket.

"There's 90 minutes of recordings here."

He began to play them from the beginning. The sound of Forester's voice made me nauseous.

"Can we do it later?"

He pressed stop.

"I'll give Matt this when he gets here." He patted his pocket and then checked his watch. It was after midnight. "Do you want to rest until he comes?"

I hesitated.

"It's okay Bea, I won't go out while you're asleep."

He'd read my mind before I even knew what I was thinking. His tone was so gentle, I feared I would cry. I went straight up to his bedroom, closed the door behind me and unwound the towel around my head. I was too tired to dry my hair, but I rubbed it to take away the heavy wet, brushed it and then stretched out on Gabriel's bed.

I wondered how long it had taken them at St Lucian's to discover I was missing and whether Forester would notice his Dictaphone was gone in the morning. If he did, would he assume I had it? Would he send Loftus after me again?

I could not afford another encounter with that man. Like it or not, Gabriel would have to keep me company until the whole mess was sorted out.

Though I would have liked to sleep, I couldn't switch off my mind. I thought of the two women who had died, Rachel and Precious. Their faces appeared when I closed my eyes. They were both so young. An old familiar ache at the injustice of it tugged at my insides. I tried to piece together logically everything that had happened. I couldn't make sense of it.

Eventually, despite the over-workings of my brain, I must have fallen asleep, because there were suddenly two voices downstairs. I was frightened for a moment, not sure where I was, until I recognised Gabriel's voice and then the Cavan accent of Matt McCann.

"Here she is," he said, when I joined them in the living room. They were either end of the couch, with amber-filled glasses in their hands.

I sat on the armchair by the fire Gabriel had lit, despite the mildness, and stretched my legs out toward the flames. Gabriel tilted the bottle toward me.

"If ever it was called for?"

I shook my head.

"Tea so." He got up and went to the kitchen.

The comfort of the fire lapped over me like a wave.

"Gabriel has filled me in – you don't need me to tell you you're a lucky woman."

Matt looked at me intently, trying, I thought, to assess my emotional state. I was determined to be in control.

"Is it enough?"

"You mean the recording of O'Farrell?" He rubbed the back of his neck with his left hand. "It's certainly something to question him about. But we have to pick our time. We don't want to be missing the bite, if you know what I mean.

Best to talk to the doctors first, I think."

I tried to hide my disappointment. Gabriel returned and put a mug into my hands. I sipped at the tea, as he turned on the television.

A repeat of a late news bulletin featured an item about economic growth and another about a rally against water charges. The crime correspondent's face appeared next, talking about the death of a retired garda. I was surprised the story was still being carried, given they'd written it off as a suicide.

"The man was named as Graham O'Donoghue who retired early from the force on health grounds. A source said tonight gardaí are now treating the death as suspicious and are calling on anyone in the area of Mr O'Donoghue's home at Church Hill on Friday, who may have seen anything unusual in the vicinity, to contact them."

The clip switched to a garda talking into a collection of microphones. The name Superintendent Adrian Humphreys was tagged under the speaker.

"Mr O'Donoghue was a hardworking officer who had fallen on unfortunate times. Anyone in the vicinity of Church Hill in the last few days who saw anyone coming or going from his home should contact us immediately at Wicklow Garda Station. Any small piece of information could be of value."

He looked straight down the camera lens before he turned and walked into the station. I felt he was looking right into Gabriel's sitting room. There was a shot then of Wicklow Garda Station with a contact number on the screen.

"Gardaí are ruling nothing in or out at this stage," the reporter said.

"Poor Graham, maybe he was right to be paranoid," Gabriel said.

"Do you think it's connected?"

"They must have found something to make them suspicious, but a link to the Deere murder might be a bit of a leap," McCann said. He turned his attention to me again. "Now, Beatrice, I want you to know that early tomorrow morning, officers will be picking up Forester, Whittaker and Loftus and taking them in for questioning, see if we can't get something out of them on Rachel Deere for starters. I'll be joining them, and we'll get to the bottom of all of this."

He drained his glass and stood.

"Sit tight now, all right?"

I nodded.

When he left, I told Gabriel I didn't have much belief in him.

"He seems to be sceptical about everything."

"Of course he is – doesn't mean he isn't thinking it through though. Give him a bit of time."

I yawned loudly.

"I can't believe I'm tired. I only just woke up."

"I'd say it's those drugs working their way out of your system. By rights I should have brought you to hospital."

I imagined sitting in the emergency unit, vying for a trolley with some really ill person.

"You've had a rough few days and I never got round to fixing up the spare room. Go on to bed and I'll take the couch tonight."

A strange sensation came over me, of being, the only word I could think of was, cosseted. I couldn't decide whether or not I liked it. He was looking out for me, I knew, but I didn't like being told what to do. I wanted to tell him I was fine and would sleep on the couch, and, at the same time, I wanted him to hug me. I shook my head.

"What?" he asked.

"Nothing, nothing. I'll go to bed then. I want to be all right for Precious Alexander's inquest in the morning."

He raised his eyebrows.

"Let's see how you feel." Again, he was trying to protect me.

"I'll be fine," I said a little too sharply.

He turned away.

"Gabriel?"

He turned back and looked at me, all concern.

"Thanks for, you know . . . "

"Night Beatrice."

Chapter 24

Monday, 5th May 2014

Gabriel and I sat on a bench against the back wall of the Dublin Coroner's Court. The wooden-panelled Victorian courtroom, with its elevated plaster ceiling and high windows, had the atmosphere of a church. This had the effect of silencing all those who entered. The only sound came from the tram that clicked on its tracks outside the court's door and from a driver occasionally ringing the warning bell as passengers crossed in front of it.

A garda shook hands with a man who was wearing the uniform of a tram driver, indicating where he should sit. Other people entered and nodded to the garda, taking up their places on what looked like pews.

There was one solicitor present and I presumed she was representing the tram company when I saw her approach the driver and pat him on the shoulder.

Then a tall, thin man, with the same cheekbones and dark polished skin as Precious, entered. The garda sat beside him and the coroner came in.

The tall man was the first to give evidence. As her brother

and only next-of-kin in Ireland, Max Alexander told the coroner he'd identified Precious in the mortuary. He listened while his garda statement was read out to the court and he swore it was true.

"I was very sorry to hear what happened to Ms Alexander," the coroner said.

"Thank you," Max responded, his voice low and steady.

"If you wish to ask any questions of the witnesses, just raise your hand."

The garda gave evidence about being called to the scene, then some eye-witnesses took the stand.

One woman clenched a handkerchief as she spoke.

"I heard the tram bell ring and I waited at the edge of the road – there were a few of us standing there. Then the woman, Ms Alexander, just ran out from behind me and in front of the tram. It all happened so quickly."

Other witnesses gave their own versions of what they'd seen, from inside the tram or on the opposite side of the road. There was little difference between their statements.

A man said Precious had been looking behind her when she stepped out. Max Alexander asked him if he'd seen what she was looking at.

"I'm sorry, no. It was just before the impact, so I didn't look."

The tram driver swore that the road ahead of him was clear when the woman appeared from nowhere.

"I just couldn't stop it in time." His voice echoed with bewilderment.

A pathologist's report, read out by the coroner, gave details of a catastrophic head injury.

"Death was instantaneous," he said.

When evidence was complete, the coroner addressed the jury telling them it seemed something had distracted Precious before she stepped onto the road.

"We may never know what," he said. "But it is clear Precious Alexander hadn't meant to injure herself. It is also clear, I believe, that the driver did all he could to stop the tram before impact."

The jury retired for 10 minutes and then returned a verdict of accidental death.

Outside, I told Gabriel I'd try to talk to Max Alexander. He agreed to keep his distance, so as not to frighten him off. I waited on the street until Alexander emerged. He stopped and stared as a tram slid by him.

"Hello, I'm so sorry for your trouble," I said.

He nodded and took the hand I'd extended, shaking it distractedly.

"Would you come for a coffee?"

He focused on me then.

"I met your sister just before it happened – I wanted to tell you about it."

He followed me into Robert Reade's. I was conscious of Gabriel walking at a distance from us. I led Max to a round table just inside the door. After we'd sat down I realised we could still hear the trams and wished I'd chosen somewhere else.

When the barman had left us with our hot drinks, I told him about Precious's warning.

"I knew she was in some kind of trouble," he said, when I'd finished. "She phoned me the morning she died. She was scared. I asked her to come over, but she said she had something to do first. I never heard from her again."

I wondered what it was that had frightened her.

"Did you tell the gardaí?" I asked.

"They weren't interested. They said her death was an accident and whatever happened before didn't matter."

"And have you been through her belongings? Was there anything . . .?"

"I haven't had a chance. She has an apartment in Bray. I was going to go out to it today."

I took a deep breath.

"I know this is a big ask, but, do you think, I could come along?"

He looked at me suspiciously.

"What is it you want?"

"I want to know what she died for, why they were after her."

He looked like he might refuse me, if he had the strength. I felt cruel pushing him, but I had to know.

"What harm can it do? I'm an extra pair of eyes and I'll leave the moment you tell me to."

He gave in, and I signalled a discreet goodbye to Gabriel and walked to Connolly Station with Max. We hardly spoke on our way out to Bray. We took the Dart and he sat opposite me, his head resting against the cool glass of the window, his eyes half closed, as the grey-blue waters of Dublin Bay slipped by.

We got out at the station on Florence Road and walked for five minutes to the apartment. It was over a bookshop on Main Street in Bray.

Max struggled with the lock for a few moments, and then opened the door. A narrow staircase was brightened with a chain of flowers painted on the white walls. Max ran his fingers over the artwork.

"She only finished this last week."

"It's lovely."

He unlocked the door at the top of the stairs and we both went into the apartment.

The front window in the living area looked down onto the town's traffic while the rear, a galley kitchen, looked into a laneway where a metallic-blue compact was parked. There was about twelve metres of space from front to back. It was a bedsit really, I thought, but Precious had made the most of it. Scandinavian self-assembly furniture was softened with hand-painted decorations. A bedside lamp had a winding ivy pattern, while plain kitchen presses were stencilled with daisies. The cushions on the couch were the same ruby-red as the flowers on the throw, neatly covering the double bed in the corner.

Max sat on the edge of it, loosened his tie, undid the top button of his shirt, and ran his finger around the collar. From the bedside locker, he picked up a photo of himself and his sister with three younger siblings and their parents.

"She looks so lovely, you look like a close family." I rested my fingers on the edge of the photo.

Max put it back in place.

"She sent money home to them every month."

"They'll miss that."

"They'll miss her."

I indicated the locker and a pine chest of drawers under the window.

"Do you think I could . . .?"

He nodded, and I began looking through them. The locker held cosmetics, nail polish in various shades, moisturiser and Vaseline. On top of the locker, next to the lamp, a directory of medicines rested, its pages softened with use. I flicked through the pages and saw some drugs were underlined and comments were written in biro in the margins beside them. Side-effects were highlighted and in one or two places, there were question marks.

"Look at her bedtime reading, she must have been very dedicated."

Max said she was and took the book from me.

I looked through the chest of drawers. It held her clothes, neatly folded, even nylons were carefully separated and organised by shade. I pushed my hand to the back of every drawer; there was nothing tucked away for safe keeping. A small wardrobe was the same – tidy and unsurprising.

The bathroom was pristine.

"Did Precious have a boyfriend?" I called over my shoulder to Max, who then followed me into the en suite.

"What? Absolutely no, she would have told me."

I pointed to a second toothbrush and a man's razor.

"You stayed with her?"

"No, not for a long time." He looked hurt, confused.

"Maybe she was keeping them for you."

"Maybe."

Back in the main room, I examined the contents of a half-height bookcase – titles in English and French, scholarly publications on biology, some poetry and lighter reading.

I cast around for other possible storage and found two drawers in the side of a paint-faded coffee table that rested between the sofa and the window. A vase of wilted flowers sat on the table. I perched on the sofa and began to look through the two drawers. Max took the vase away, and I could hear the click of a bin lid and the slosh of water as he emptied it out and rinsed it.

He came back with a card and handed it to me. It said: 'Love always, N'.

"I don't know who this is."

He sat beside me on the sofa to help search through the drawers. There were bills inside and menus from local takeaways, some unused greetings cards, writing paper and then an envelope addressed to Max. He caught his breath when he saw it and held it in his hands for a time, running his fingers over the ink, tracing the movements of her pen, before opening it.

I turned away to give him some privacy, but he read it aloud.

'Dear Max, if you are reading this it is because something

bad has happened to me. I want you to know that I have done nothing wrong, whatever they tell you. I have left my job at St Lucian's. Everything is not right there, though I have not yet figured out exactly why. I was seeing one of the doctors, Niall Forester. Do you remember him? He came to my housewarming? "I remember that guy – smug," Max said, before continuing. '*I walked into his office on Saturday and I heard him talking to another man on the phone. They were planning something, to get a woman or hurt her, I think. I heard him name her. Niall got cross when he saw me and asked me what I'd heard. I told him nothing, but I don't think he believed me. We had a terrible row and I said I couldn't work for him any more. I went back into his office when he'd left and found the woman's address. There is no point in going to the police, they would not believe me. I'm going to try to warn the woman, I don't know what else to do. Please tell Mamma and Papa and the girls how much I love and miss them and tell the police will you, if I'm not around? Love, Precious.*'

Max dropped the letter and hid his face in his hands. Big, fat tears dropped through his fingers and onto the page. I fetched him a glass of water and some kitchen towel. After a few moments, he wiped his face with the back of his hands and dried his hands on the towel. He drank the water back in one swallow.

"She's talking about you, isn't she?"

"I think so." I had a vision of her again, the blood from her head pouring into the groove of the tram rail, filling it up. "I'm so sorry."

"She was always too brave; always thought more about other people than herself."

And she worked at St Lucian's?" I knew that couldn't be a coincidence and it sickened me.

"She did, yes." He turned the envelope over in his hand and again began to trace the lettering.

"Why didn't she just tell me?" he whispered.

"You'll have to go to the gardaí with this."

"I hope they'll listen to me this time."

I thought of Matt McCann.

"There's someone I know. He's already investigating Forester, he'll listen."

He looked at me with suspicion again.

"Some friend of yours is it?"

"No, not exactly, but he's a good man, honest I think."

Max waved the letter. "I'll tell him she was talking about you."

"Of course."

"Okay, but I'm going to the garda who handled the inquest too."

"You should."

I called Matt McCann from the apartment and gave him Max's phone number.

"He'll phone you later and says he can meet you tonight, if you like?"

"Fine."

He sat back into the couch, turned the letter over in his hand and began talking about Precious and their childhood together in Mauritius.

"She was the eldest – bossy, single-minded, generous. She always wanted to be a nurse and when she qualified and moved to Ireland our parents were so relieved. They thought she'd be safe here."

"She should have been."

He said she'd been at St Lucian's for two years.

"She started off living there, but it got too much. She said it felt like she'd no other life, so she got this apartment. Precious really liked Bray. She loved walking along the prom."

I couldn't motivate myself to pry any further among the

belongings of this woman, this stranger who'd tried to help me.

"Is there anything I can do here? Do you want to tackle anything now?" I could have helped him bag up her belongings, that loathed and necessary post-death ritual. It would have been the least I could do.

"I'm not ready for that yet," he said.

I wrote my phone number on a piece of paper and gave it to him. He placed it on the coffee table without comment.

"If there's anything at all I can do, call me," I said, as I left.

Chapter 25

Monday, 5th May 2014

Gabriel was standing across the road when I emerged from Precious Alexander's apartment.

"You're good — I didn't realise you'd followed us all the way. It's St Lucian's again, Gabriel, Precious worked at St Lucian's."

"Okay. Another connection to that place."

On the Dart back into Dublin I told him about the letter and what had happened on the day Precious Alexander died.

"She must have followed me from home."

"That's what it sounds like. She must have known she'd be seen if she called to your house, so she waited until you were somewhere Loftus couldn't go."

"If she hadn't been trying to help me, she'd still be alive."

The reality of that was horrifying to me – protecting me had cost that young woman her life. How could my life be worth the life of Precious Alexander? It couldn't, it wasn't. I thought of Laurence and the pain after his death, and felt for Max.

"What happened wasn't your fault, Bea. You did nothing wrong."

The grey-blue water of Dublin Bay disappeared and suburban back gardens replaced it as the train rushed toward Sydney Parade Station.

"If I'd responded better or something, she might have stayed longer in the changing room."

"She didn't give you a chance to say anything, remember?"

I remembered her brown eyes looking into mine and the speed of her exit, fuelled by her own fear. I could have caught her and pulled her back. A few seconds' delay would have made a difference.

My phone rang then, its bell tone filling the carriage before I could find it. It was Janine. Her voice faded in and out as the train moved past Sandymount and I struggled to hear her. All I could decipher was that she was upset about Alastair, she was at home and wanted me to call out to her. I said I'd get there as soon as I could.

"I'm going to go back to Janine's," I told Gabriel. "I'll see you back at your house later."

We got out at Pearse Street Station and Gabriel insisted on putting me into a taxi, scrutinising the face and number of the driver before allowing him to pull away.

When I got to Janine's she was sitting on the sofa with a cushion held to her chest. Her eyes were red and sore looking from crying. For the first few minutes all she would say was "Fucker, the fucker" over and over.

I sat beside her and waited for a pause in her mantra.

"I couldn't hear you on the phone. Do you want to tell me what happened?"

"He just lost it." Janine spoke in a small voice, like a frightened child.

I noticed then the shards of glass on the hearth. She saw me looking.

"He threw a tumbler at me."

There was a mark on the wall above the mantelpiece, a

yellow stain where the glass had given up its contents. I struggled to imagine Alastair in a rage. He'd always seemed so controlled.

"Was he drunk?"

"No, I gave him one drink when he came in the door and he seemed fine. Maybe a bit tense but, you know, he works hard."

She waited for me to agree. I thought of the women I'd seen in court, reluctant witnesses to their partners' violence, desperate, even after broken bones, to explain in their own minds what had happened to them, to rationalise their partners' actions. Their stories often began with broken glass, broken glass and temper, and then later, broken bones.

"Go on."

"He was sitting having his drink and his phone went off. I could hear it in the pocket of his coat, hanging in the hall."

I nodded.

"I thought I'd get it for him but as I took it out of his pocket I must have pressed something, the call stopped, and I'd opened his photo file. A picture of a woman came up, blowing a kiss."

She took a deep breath and squeezed the cushion closer.

"So, I handed it to him, who's she I said – and he looked at me, and then at the drink in his hand and just threw it." Janine was shaking as she spoke, still shocked by it. "Then he got to his feet and started shouting into my face, telling me to mind my own fucking business. I backed away and he grabbed the phone off me and just walked out."

She shivered.

"It all happened so fast, and I kept thinking if only I hadn't gone near his phone."

"This is not your fault."

I fixed her a gin and tonic, placing it into her hand.

"He went straight out the door – slammed it. I could feel the whole place shake."

"Does he have a key?"

"'Yes."

I was shocked and angry that Alastair had treated Janine like that. All she'd ever done was adore him since the moment they'd met. My initial wariness about him had been correct.

I called a locksmith.

Janine looked dubious.

"Nothing says 'think again' like changing the locks," I said.

She shrugged agreement, though she didn't look too convinced.

"There's something else as well." She looked at me from beneath her lashes, as though trying to decide whether to tell me or not. There was a pause.

I looked away, to signify it was up to her to decide if she wanted to speak.

"I bumped into Liz in town yesterday, remember her? We were in school together. I think I introduced you at that drinks thing last summer?"

I'd met many of Janine's friends at that drinks party and couldn't recall any of them. All I could remember was my exit strategy, a trip to the country to visit an elderly relative I didn't have, in a nursing home that didn't exist.

"She has bushy brown hair, round glasses and is a bit plump?"

I shook my head.

"Never mind. She works with Alastair at St Jerome's, right?"

"Right."

"So, I said something about how hard everyone works there and how it's tricky to plan your life and she said yes, she'd been called in last Saturday and ended up working all day when she should have been at a barbecue."

"Okay."

"So, I said we'd had our Saturday spoilt as well when Alastair was called in. And she said no, he wasn't. Then, when she saw my face, she said maybe he had been and she just didn't see him, and she'd probably made a mistake."

"Oh."

"Then she hurried off, as quick as she could."

I didn't wish to jump to conclusions for her.

"So, now, after this," she gestured at the wall, "all because of that photo . . . I think he must be cheating on me. I think he was seeing that woman, Bea." Janine's voice was mournful. "What does that make me?"

I didn't want to defend Alastair, but it was hard to see Janine so upset.

"You don't know that – it might have been work stuff. She could have been a relative."

"Relatives don't blow kisses like that."

She began to cry. I put my arm around her and let her sob into my shoulder.

"Let her have him, whoever she is," I couldn't help saying, when the tears came to an end. I wanted to tell her then about everything that had happened to me in the last week. I wanted to transact that exchange of secrets, that currency of friendship, that evens out the balance. But I was afraid of what she might think and, more importantly, what danger I might be putting her in if I told her everything.

I made her something to eat and stayed until the locksmith came. He said he'd changed six locks that day, none of them broken.

I wanted to call Janine's sister before I left, but she made me swear I wouldn't, and that I wouldn't call Alastair either.

"I'm a big girl, I'll deal with it."

I thought of asking Gabriel to rustle up a few friends and give Alastair a fright.

"A temper like that only goes one way, you know? Pack up his stuff and tell him he can collect it from one of your neighbours."

Janine nodded, without much conviction.

"I'm just going to get into bed with a glass of wine and watch TV."

"Promise you'll call me if he tries to get back in."

She said she would.

I hugged her quickly and when I closed the door behind me, I thought I could hear her already on the phone. I feared the next time we spoke, she would be explaining away his actions. I resolved to talk to Gabriel about how I might help her to get out of the relationship.

Gabriel's place was empty when I got back around seven. I sat in the silence of his living room and thought about Precious, Rachel and Graham. They'd all spent time in Lucian's, they'd all met Forester – Precious had worked for him, Rachel and Graham were patients. Did they all know Stephen O'Farrell? Did they all know about Camtrexonal? Rachel had been on it and perhaps Precious had found out about the trials.

When Gabriel walked in I was still thinking of those dead people and it must have shown on my face. He sat down beside me and placed his hand over mine. The touch was meant to comfort, but it felt intrusive, as though he'd pushed his way into my thoughts. I stood up, went over to the fire, dropped on my knees and began raking the ashes of yesterday's blaze.

I knew my reaction to Gabriel's touch wasn't quite right, it wasn't how other women would react. Most people would accept such a gesture. But there was too much hardness in me. Everyone has some hardness in them, I think, but if they have a soft life, a life filled only with kindness and love, the

270

hardness never grows. If life is tough and unfair, though, in some people the hard pebble gathers grit to itself until there is only a sort of density. The person is who he or she is – immovable, contained, incapable of being hurt, unable to accept a gentle touch. I considered it the price I paid for self-protection and, most of the time, only a small regret.

"Matt said he'd call shortly," Gabriel interrupted my thoughts. "How's Janine?"

"Very upset. Alastair threw a glass at her and stormed off. I made her change the locks but I don't know if that's going to stick."

"That's outrageous – good enough for him."

I emptied the ashes into yesterday's newspaper and folded the pages around them. He took them from me.

"You don't need to do that, Bea."

"Where's your kindling?"

He sighed and gestured to a basket, tucked out of sight beside an armchair. I arranged pieces of wood in the grate, firelighters and coal and set a match to them.

"I don't know what it is with you, Bea, I'm not trying to . . . I just want to be a good friend, that's all."

"Isn't the smokeless fuel great? Do you remember the smog on winter nights?"

"I remember." He turned his back on me and left the room, returning only after the doorbell rang.

"Jaysus, that's a right puss you have on you," McCann said to Gabriel.

The detective was in uniform and I wondered if it meant he was on an official visit. He took off his jacket and placed it carefully across the arm of a chair, before sitting down on the couch, legs open and one elbow on each knee. He declined an offer of whiskey.

"Well I met your Mr Alexander. The boys will have a few more questions to ask at St Lucian's."

"Did nobody ask questions at the time?" I asked.

"Course not – it was a run-of-the-mill road traffic accident as far as Store Street was concerned. They'd their witnesses sorted. Do you know how many people get hit by trams?"

I said I didn't, and I didn't much care. It sounded to me as though the gardaí hadn't done their job right.

"Surely after what Max said, they would have made some enquiries?"

"Relatives say a lot of things. The boys wouldn't have paid much attention. The last thing they need is more work."

I felt outraged for Precious. McCann could see it in my face and didn't like it.

"Lookit anyway, as I say, I'm going down there tomorrow. I'll let you know how I get on."

"What about the arrests?" Gabriel asked.

"Early days. We thought we'd tackle them on Rachel Deere first, then hit them with kidnapping and the drugs trial stuff. Bad news is Loftus has an alibi for the Saturday she died, a real one. He was in for some medical procedure in St James's."

"Oh." I'd been sure it would have been Loftus they sent – their hired thug.

He stood up then and put back on his jacket, which was clean and well-pressed.

"Anyway, pathologist said whoever injected her, had to know what he was doing – sounds like a medic, doesn't it?"

"Or a junky?" Gabriel suggested.

McCann gave him a sideways glance.

"Your mind always works that little bit different, doesn't it, Gabriel?"

"What about the other two? What are they saying?" I asked.

"Whittaker claims she was away with some friends at one

of them, you know, spa things women do." He waved his hand in the air and furrowed his brow, as though trying to explain an impossible concept. "Says her friends can vouch for her."

"Where?"

"Powerscourt, she said. Of course, that doesn't make it impossible. She could have driven from there to Glasnevin, in what, an hour or so? She and her friends can't have been together all the time. And you saw her talking to Rachel on the Luas, didn't you? So, Rachel would most likely have let her in if she came to the door."

I went to the kitchen and poured myself a glass of water from the sink to get rid of the sour taste in my mouth.

"That's a two-hour round trip though, hard to be away for that long without her friends noticing," Gabriel said.

"As I say, early days – the lads will be checking out her alibi."

I came back to see Matt checking his watch and backing toward the door.

"What about Forester, what's he saying?"

"Got quite a fright when murder was mentioned, went really pale. Then when he realised I was talking about Rachel Deere, he relaxed."

I remembered what Precious had said about being in a relationship with him and told Matt. "Good, I can use that," he said. "Maybe that's what had him on edge – he felt guilty about how Precious died."

"So where was he when Rachel died?" Gabriel asked.

"He was on duty, roster confirms it. Though again, he could possibly have slipped off without being noticed or got a last-minute swap."

He spoke as though he were thinking aloud.

"When we get their phone records there'll be GPS co-ordinates, so if either of them travelled to Dublin and took their phones, we'll know."

"What about the blackmail, did they say anything about her blackmailing them? It must be one of them, I mean 'Doc', who else could it be?" Gabriel asked.

McCann said they'd both pleaded ignorance when they were asked.

"Forester said we could look at his bank accounts, no direct debits."

"That doesn't mean anything, he'd have given her cash," Gabriel said.

"Have you thought about who 'Dick' is?" I asked, and without waiting for him to reply said, "It must be O'Farrell, who else could it be?"

"We'll see," McCann said, "I'll be back to you, and please you two, don't do anything stupid. Actually, don't do anything at all."

Gabriel saw him out the door.

I didn't say a word then, but he read the frustration on my face.

"He's a good man," he said.

"Okay."

We talked about other things, about when I might return to work.

I phoned Janine.

"Are you all right?" I asked.

"I'm fine now, thanks Bea."

"Okay, if you're sure . . . "

"I am really, thanks."

She hung up and she didn't have to tell me she'd let Alastair back in. I could hear Charlie Parker playing in the background.

"There's nothing you can do about it," Gabriel said when I told him.

"I know, it's just so hard to understand why she'd put up with it."

"Would you like tea or something?"

I suddenly realised how hungry I was and searched Gabriel's fridge for something to eat. I found two frozen beef dinners.

"God almighty, is this what you feed yourself?"

"Don't knock it 'til you've tried it."

I put them in the microwave and, despite my reluctance, managed to eat the meal.

"I keep wondering if it was Precious who sent me that file, though, she didn't seem like the type to spy on people."

"Didn't her letter say she heard them talking about you?"

"I know, but, did you ever track down who took those photos?"

"God, I forgot about that! I was supposed to ring a fella back."

He stepped out to the kitchen to make the call and came back in shortly after.

"He reckons it's a private detective called Declan Spring. Does a lot of that kind of dirty stuff."

I laughed.

"You mean sex shots?"

"No, no – spying for husbands and wives, adultery work. How would you feel about paying him a visit?"

I looked at my watch; it was almost half nine.

"Is it not a bit late?"

"No, that fecker lives in his office."

We drove over to Parnell Square and found Spring's office opposite the gates of the Rotunda Maternity Hospital. He answered his intercom and buzzed us up after a little persuasion from Gabriel.

He was on the third floor, up a narrow stair covered in linoleum, and smelling of damp and gas heating. His office was small, but well organised, and I could see, through a half-open door to the right, what looked like a bedsit. Spring closed that door and sat down behind a tidy desk, a computer before him. To one side, were a series of closed cabinets and a gas cylinder heater, its chalky panels glowing orange. Behind him, two windows looked out over the square and toward Croke Park.

Spring's pinched features arranged themselves into a smile and he put his hand out to shake mine. He did not extend the same courtesy to Gabriel.

"What is it you want?" he asked him.

Gabriel produced the photos.

"Your work?"

"You know it is or you wouldn't be here."

"Who did you take them for?"

He looked from Gabriel to me, and back again.

"Why would I tell you that?"

"Call it a professional favour. There's things I know about you that Store Street might be interested in."

"Oh please!"

He stood up, crossed to the window and turned his back on us. I could see the thinness of him. His cheap suit hung from his shoulders and looked as though he'd borrowed it from a broader man. I could picture him lurking in doorways and squinting in windows.

"There must be a few bob in this for you, Gabriel. Cut me in."

Gabriel laughed drily. "There's no money in this for anyone – let's just say I'll owe you one. Who commissioned them?"

"She did."

"Rachel Deere?"

"She came in here and said she wanted me to follow her and take pictures of her with a man."

He pulled open the window suddenly and leaned out.

"Hey you! You can't park there!"

He turned back.

"They think they can leave their cars anywhere just because their women are about to pop – I swear the number of times I've been hemmed in by them double parking."

"Did she say why she wanted them?" I asked, the cogs beginning to turn in my head.

"Not my job to interrogate customers – I just do what I'm asked."

"Yeah, right," Gabriel said.

Spring scowled at him. "I always keep the right side of the law."

"What did you do with the photos after?"

"I gave them to her – she paid me. That was the end of it."

"Did you do anything else for her?"

"Not a thing, never heard from her again."

Gabriel glanced around at the filing cabinets.

"There wouldn't be any more pictures in here would there, that you took of them?"

He shook his head.

"And what about on the computer?"

"Fuck off now, will you? I have work to do." He opened a drawer and took out a camera and a zoom attachment. From another drawer he took a soft cloth and began polishing the lens.

"That's expensive gear, you must be doing well for yourself," Gabriel said.

"Don't bang the door on the way out."

Outside Gabriel told me Spring had got himself in a lot of trouble after not only taking photos of an adulterous wife with her lover but making a video and selling it to a pornography website.

"Nasty man," I said. "But I believe him about Rachel."

Gabriel agreed. "She wanted the photos so she could blackmail O'Farrell."

"Could she have sent me the file then?"

"I'm guessing you were her insurance policy. She sent the stuff to you in case anything happened to her."

It made sense.

"But if she just wanted to blackmail him over their affair, why would she send the medical file too?"

"Belt and braces maybe – she wanted you to know they'd met under other circumstances too or maybe she'd suspicions about Camtrexonal."

We drove back to Gabriel's in silence, both of us puzzling over what we'd learned. In my own mind, I'd put Rachel and Precious in the same bracket, as victims, but they were such different women – Precious seemed only to want to help others and Rachel only wanted to help herself.

Gabriel drummed his fingers on the steering wheel while we waited at a red light on North King Street.

"Why you though, Bea, why did Rachel choose you?"

"Maybe she just saw me as an official of the court, someone who'd know what to do if anything happened to her."

"Why not Leona O'Brien though? Wouldn't she have been the more obvious choice?"

I supposed she would.

"Maybe she noticed I was watching her that day on the Luas when she was with Whittaker and she thought I'd understand if something went wrong." There were other possibilities too, but I didn't dwell on them. "She must have known she was in danger when she posted them, otherwise she was taking a big risk. I might have gone straight to the gardaí."

It was half ten when we got back to Oxmantown Road. The fire I'd lit earlier was dying in the grate and I went to try to revive it. Gabriel fixed himself a whiskey and put the kettle on for me.

I made some chamomile tea, slipped off my shoes and sat on the sofa. We were both silent contemplating the flames, beginning once again to spurt into life in the grate, until Gabriel's phone rang. He got to his feet and walked into the hall. He spoke in staccato for a few moments before hanging up.

"Graham's death is officially being classified as suicide."

"Are they sure this time?"

"They're sure. The toxicology is back though – seems he had Camtrexonal in his system."

"No!"

"Apparently the neighbours saw a doctor go into Graham's place a few hours before he died, and they found a jar of the stuff in his kitchen," Gabriel said.

"Was it empty? I mean had he overdosed on it?"

"No – pathologist said he'd taken a standard dose."

Gabriel's face was pale. He sat down on the sofa and put his head in his hands.

"I encouraged him to call the doctor. What if it was Camtrexonal that triggered the suicide? He'd have been better off if I'd left him alone."

I put my hand on his shoulder and patted him a couple of times.

"You were being a good friend, that's all."

Then I thought of something. It couldn't have been a GP who saw Graham.

"It's not released yet though is it?"

"Camtrexonal? No, it hasn't been licensed yet."

His face changed – it was dawning on him.

"It must have been one of St Lucian's doctors that visited him. Why would he contact one of them? He was frightened of them."

"Maybe he didn't."

"I'll have to let Matt know."

279

He jumped up and found his phone, punching in the digits, and waited for the ring tone. He let it ring for a minute before giving up. Then he texted 'call me asap'. It was after midnight when McCann finally did call. He said he'd drop over to the house in the morning.

Chapter 26

Tuesday, 6th May 2014

I made rashers and eggs, and Matt and Gabriel slurped from their mugs of tea like farmers after a milking.

"I spoke to them in St Lucian's about Precious Alexander. No one had a bad word to say about the woman – very popular nurse. And her HR file was clean."

Matt paused to dip toast into the yolk of his egg.

"So, then I went back to the station, questioned Forester about her. He seemed genuinely upset about what happened to her and completely baffled when I told him about her note. Didn't know what I was talking about."

I could picture him, turning on the compassion tap.

"I asked him about O'Farrell. He agreed he'd been a patient. Looked uncomfortable when I mentioned Rell Pharmaceuticals, but made a quick recovery – said they were involved in a trial with them and it was finished."

"Did he say why?"

"Just that it came to a natural end."

"Or the patients did," Gabriel said.

He asked if they'd made a connection with Graham

O'Donoghue's death.

"I didn't ask Forester about him yet, but I will."

"What did he have to say about Rachel Deere?" I asked.

"He called her a vulnerable young woman. Insisted he knew nothing about her death and stuck to his story about working on Saturday. I'm still waiting on info from the phone company."

He paused again, this time to fork a mouthful of rasher into his mouth. He chewed it rapidly.

"I spoke to Whittaker too, she said nice things about Alexander. She repeated that bit about the spa. And she denied being involved in the treatment of Deere or O'Farrell – said she didn't know anything about either of them."

"Well that's not true," I said.

"No, we know that, but she doesn't know we know. We're taking our time with this one. I asked her about Graham O'Donoghue. She said she hadn't seen him since he checked out. And that some other doctor treated him a couple of times while he was in St Lucian's, a locum. She said she thinks he went back to the UK. I have someone looking into him."

I thought of Julie and what she'd told me about Rachel Deere being upset by a locum doctor. I mentioned it to them.

"It might be the same man," I said. "Did the neighbours say if it was a man or a woman who called to Graham?" I asked Gabriel.

He thought for a moment.

"A man, I think, I'm pretty sure I was told 'he' left after 20 minutes."

So, it wasn't Whittaker that visited him.

"Did you ask either of them about Loftus?" I asked.

"He's employed at St Lucian's as a porter. Forester and Whittaker both acted like they knew him only vaguely when I asked about him. We kept them both in the dark about picking him up as well. We have him at a different station."

I thought of the two doctors, whispering at my bedside

about the drug Loftus had given me.

Gabriel took the salt from the table and shook it over the last of his breakfast. McCann held out his mug for a top-up and I filled it up.

"Thanks – I told them we took copies of files, and copies of the hard drives on both their computers. Their solicitors screamed blue murder, I can tell you, but we had the warrant. Your statement was a help with that." He smiled, as though annoying solicitors gave him particular pleasure.

"I have officers going through them with a fine-tooth comb. I'm told there's signs of some deletions, but the lads can get round them."

"Is there nothing else on Rachel Deere?" I asked.

"Nothing useful, only whoever did it was very clean – not a stray print to be found anywhere, and only the boyfriend's were on the bottles, so alarm bells there straight away."

"You don't think he had anything to do with it?"

"Not at all. He was out all night sure with his friends, even caught him on CCTV around Lillie's Bordello. No, this was a professional, someone who knew how much to give her and how to give it."

"Stephen O'Farrell could never have done that himself. We need to be able to tie him to the others," I said.

I feared the chance to see him imprisoned was slipping away from me. I didn't care what he was imprisoned for now, as long as they got him for something, and if it was for murdering Rachel Deere, he'd be put away for a long time.

"He's involved somehow, I know he is."

The two men looked across the table at each other. I had an urge to bang their heads together – could they not see O'Farrell all over this? Then I remembered his request to meet me, made through Rafferty.

"You need more, and I can get it," I said. "Rafferty asked me to meet O'Farrell."

"Did he now?" McCann said. "What's that about, do you think?"

I hesitated. "He's involved in the whole business, isn't he? Maybe he thought he could put pressure on me, or something."

"Come on Bea, you can't be putting yourself in harm's way again for this," Gabriel said. "Do you think if he was involved in the murder he'd have any qualms about hurting you?"

"Have you any better ideas?" I remembered then that my mobile phone was still at St Lucian's.

"I'll have to contact Leona and get Rafferty's number from her. I'll do it now before I change my mind."

Gabriel scowled.

"Make it somewhere public," Matt said.

"Why on earth would you want Raymond Rafferty's number?" Leona asked when I phoned her.

"I promised I'd let him know when I had a copy of the last transcript."

"You'd wonder why he'd be bothered now." She sounded sceptical but found his number and read it out for me.

I thanked her. "How are you feeling?" I asked.

"Disappointed, frustrated – pretty damn angry actually."

"I can imagine."

I didn't need to imagine.

"Gardaí aren't telling me much," I said. "Have you heard anything?"

"Not a lot. You should try and forget about it for a few days, give your brain a rest."

I knew it was stupid advice, the trite kind of small talk that posed as comfort and usually made the recipient feel worse rather than better.

"Actually no, you should join a boxing club and go a few rounds with a punchbag."

"That might actually help!"

When she rang off, I dialled Rafferty's number and got through to his voicemail.

"Beatrice Barrington here, please call me on – on this number when you get a chance."

I handed Gabriel back his phone and thought of the contacts on my one, the friends Loftus might harass once they let him out.

It wasn't long before Gabriel's phone rang again.

"Who is this? Just a minute."

He handed the phone to me, mouthing: "Rafferty."

I told him I'd changed my mind about meeting Stephen O'Farrell.

"I think I want to hear what he has to say for himself."

He suggested the Saddle Room in the Shelbourne Hotel, for an early dinner.

"I'd prefer drinks in the Horseshoe Bar."

The last thing I wanted was to be trapped with O'Farrell for an evening, making polite conversation over a T-bone and learning nothing.

"Thank you, Ms Barrington, I'll let him know – drinks at seven." He rang off abruptly.

"I'll get you a buttonhole microphone," Matt said. "Try to get him into a quiet corner if you can and don't worry, he won't try anything in a public place."

He gulped down the rest of his tea and wiped his hand over his mouth.

"All right so, better get going. Need to get those custodies extended."

After he left, I called Janine to see how she was.

"We're fine, everything is fine," she told me.

"So, you let him back in?" I tried to keep the disapproval out of my voice.

"It was just a silly tiff, Bea," she spoke quietly. "Alastair's under so much pressure at work – I caught him at a bad moment."

Her excuses, so familiar from court, made me want to go around to Janine's and tell Alastair what I thought of his behaviour, but I knew I'd lose a friend if I did that.

"You know where I am if you need me, Janine – any time."

"Thanks."

I had other things to worry about – meeting O'Farrell would not be easy.

Gabriel said little to me about the meeting and I pretended not to notice his disapproval. At five I began my preparations.

I dressed in Gabriel's bedroom, choosing a pencil skirt and a pink silk blouse. It seemed ridiculous to me that I was going through with it at all, but since I was, I wanted to look my best – it would make me feel stronger.

I took my make-up into the bathroom and applied a delicate pink-gold eye shadow and mascara to my lashes. I outlined my lips with a pencil and filled them in carefully with blush lipstick. I sprayed perfume on my wrists.

"Careful now," I warned my reflection. "You're in control this time."

When I emerged from the bathroom, Matt had returned. He looked me up and down and I thought there was fleeting admiration in the glance, quickly smothered.

"You'll need a jacket, for the microphone."

"Of course."

I fetched a dove-grey blazer and he attached the tiniest of microphones to the lapel, putting a key chain with a button in my pocket.

"Just press the button when he arrives. We'll be able to hear everything."

I said I would.

"And build up to the big questions – don't frighten him off too early."

I nodded. They both brought me into town, dropping me off on Schoolhouse Lane, a couple of minutes' walk away from the hotel.

"Any funny vibes – just get out of there, okay, Bea?" Gabriel said.

"Of course," I reassured him, though I didn't feel as confident as I sounded.

It was quarter to seven when I arrived. I didn't want to have to walk into the bar with O'Farrell watching me. I found a corner table, sat with my back to the wall, and ordered a soda and lime.

At seven precisely he was there, standing for a moment in the middle of the room, his feet hip-wide apart – the man who had ruined my life.

He pushed his hair back from his forehead, scanned the room, then spotted me and crossed to the table. I pressed the button in my pocket.

"Hello Beatrice."

My name in his mouth was as smooth as I remembered. He took the chair at right angles to me and, worried about the sound, I uncrossed and re-crossed my legs in his direction so the microphone was turned toward him.

"You know you haven't changed a bit," he said. He signalled to the waiter and ordered a brandy for himself. "And yours?"

"Soda and lime."

"Really?" He ordered it with an air of disapproval.

"It must have been a relief for you, the trial I mean," I said.

My voice sounded strange. There was a scratchy, tightness in it.

He shrugged, the shoulders of his sharp navy suit rising

and falling again.

I couldn't help noticing he looked younger than he had in the courtroom – relief had taken the worry-creases from between his eyebrows and the colour had returned to his cheeks.

The drinks came and he sipped at his brandy. I added the end of my first drink into the second glass and stirred it with the blue plastic stick supplied.

"Why did you want to see me?"

"Believe it or not, I wanted to set the record straight with you, Bea, as simple as that."

I looked away from him at the barman in his waistcoat with its shiny brass buttons. Like there could be any other record than the one I knew to be true, the nerve of him. And calling me Bea, and using the velvet voice on me, like I was still that young girl he could so easily charm. I wanted to pour my drink over his head and leave.

"I meant to come back but everything went wrong, and I couldn't face you."

I hadn't wanted to get into this. His words were already making me nauseous, but I couldn't let him away with that – the 'business-gone-wrong' excuse. My legs beneath the table were shaking.

"You didn't just rob my family, you destroyed it."

"I was a coward."

I was conscious that Matt and Gabriel would be listening to this. I was supposed to stay in control and get him talking about Rachel Deere, but instead I'd plunged straight into the depths of my anger. I feared I would be overwhelmed.

"You were more than a coward, you were a murderer."

He blinked twice and sipped from his glass, shifting in his seat.

"You killed my brother."

"I was sorry to hear what happened to him."

"Laurence trusted you – we all did."

He lowered his voice so that I could barely hear him.

"I know that . . . I'm sorry, I really am."

I wondered if he'd cared for me at all, even a little, at any time or whether his courtship had been only an elaborate plan to part fools from their money.

"What did you do with the money?"

"I can't remember. I think I used most of it to pay off a friend."

He couldn't remember. And it was all the money my family had. My hands shook as I brought the glass to my lips.

"What am I supposed to call you anyway? Is it Stephen O'Farrell or Leo Hackett?"

"It's Stephen now . . . I changed it after . . . I wanted a fresh start."

"You wanted to be untraceable."

I had recognised 'O'Farrell' when I saw his face in the paper the first time he was charged in the District Court. The charges against him, the way he'd operated, were so familiar, and that defiant upturn of the chin for the camera, as he played the wronged businessman.

When I'd returned from England in the 1990s, I'd got legal advice about what he'd done to my family. "Historical," I was told, "too late, too little evidence."

I'd made sure then that when the Courts Service was seeking stenography services for his case, Janine and I got it, and I told Janine I would take it on. There was nothing I could do for Laurence, but I'd thought at least I could play a small part while his killer was punished.

"I really did regret what I did to you."

"That can't be true, or you wouldn't have done it again, to those people."

He held up a hand.

"Hold on now, I haven't been found guilty of anything. Those were business mistakes. If the property bubble hadn't burst, everyone would have been happy."

I thought I would vomit or scream. What had I expected from him? An act of contrition? I swallowed hard. I was supposed to be there to get information.

"I need to understand what's been happening."

He signalled for another brandy. I declined another soda and lime.

"You can do that much for me, can't you?"

He swirled the amber liquid in his glass.

"I've tasted more expensive brandies, but Hennessy has always been my favourite. It really warms you from the inside, Bea, you know? I think maybe you could do with a bit of that."

"Tell me about Rachel Deere."

"Rachel Deere?"

"The jury woman, the forewoman. Why was she killed?"

He shook his head.

"Oh no, Bea, I know nothing about that."

"Tell me about St Lucian's then."

"They saved me there."

He launched into a speech about his time at the clinic, how much he'd struggled with his gambling addiction before going in and the great help they'd given him. He emphasised the difficulties he'd been through, the turmoil of his addiction. As the words of self-pity dripped from him, all I could think of was Laurence, face down in the water.

"It sounds like you've been through a tough time."

"It was hell, Bea, it really was."

I wanted to scream, "Hell is where you ought to be."

"And when did you get involved with them business-wise?"

"That was after. One of the doctors there was so passionate about what he did, and I knew we'd this drug in development, Camtrexonal, it was a perfect match . . . I can be real with you, Bea, do you know that? That's a hard thing to find."

He reached his hand out as though he was going to touch mine, there on the table, and then changed his mind.

"You were never real with me. There wasn't even an Angie, was there?"

He shook his head.

Anger again, rising, making my pulse quicken.

"I was real with you most of the time, though. Aside from the money, the rest was real, we were great together."

"What is it you want from me, absolution?"

"Have another drink."

I shook my head and he ordered another brandy. That was good, I decided, it might make him slip.

"Tell me, did you stay in our little flat, Bea?" He smiled as though we were sharing reminiscences.

"Our little flat?" I laughed and knew I sounded bitter. "I went to England, worked there for a few years. Then I came back to Dublin and set up my stenography business here."

"Good for you. And how are your parents?"

I swallowed hard. How dare he speak about them so casually.

"They're dead a good while now. After Laurence died, they just . . . they withered away."

"I see," he said, without a hint of remorse.

I struggled to regain my focus.

"Did you ever meet her, Rachel Deere?" I asked.

"She was in the clinic. I met her at a group session a couple of times."

"What was she like?"

"Depressed mostly, lost soul type – alcoholic father, very vulnerable."

I could imagine him consoling her, offering a listening ear, guiding her to his bed.

"I think I only spoke to her a couple of times."

Should I challenge him? I kept my gaze steadily on him.

"I know you two had an affair and I know she was blackmailing you."

He looked away and quickly back again. I could almost see him calculating, trying to work out how much I knew and how much he should tell me.

"I have photos of you two, together. I think she sent them to me."

"I was wondering where those went." He sounded half amused. "It must have been a shock for you to see me like that after all these years." That smile again.

"Did you tell her we . . . did you say something about us?"

"I might have, pillow talk, you can imagine?"

I could, though I didn't want to. But at least I knew now why Rachel had sent the file to me. If he'd even told her half the truth about what had happened between us, she might have seen us as sort-of allies. I mustered my most confident tone.

"I think you had her killed."

He gulped back a mouthful of brandy.

"Now wait a minute, Bea, you're right about the affair and the blackmail, but I had nothing to do with her death."

"Am I supposed to believe that? I'm going to tell the guards."

"Wait – just let me explain."

He took another drink.

"We met at St Lucian's, at one of the group sessions. It could be boring there a lot of the time, and we hit it off well, so we, we amused ourselves." He arched an eyebrow and gave me a familiar grin, an echo of the younger man who'd taken my hand and led me to bed.

"We hooked up after we left a few times, and it came to a natural end, with no hard feelings." "Tell me something, why didn't Rafferty object when Rachel took the oath to serve on the jury – you must have recognised her?"

He shrugged.

"I thought she might be useful, friendly ears in the jury room, that's all."

I wondered about Rafferty. He read my mind.

"Rafferty knew nothing about it. When we met he told me not to tell him what he didn't need to know."

"Rachel turned out to be more troublesome than useful though, isn't that right?"

He didn't respond for a while and the hum of the room intruded briefly on our silence. The waiter came and offered us another drink. I asked for another soda water, lots of ice. My mouth was dry.

"We hooked up for one last time, and then she called me the next evening. She said she had photos and I had to pay up."

I was glad someone was getting money out of him for a change.

"What could I do? I figured if I didn't pay, that would be my marriage over and I didn't want that – Roxanne is a wonderful woman, you know?"

Ha! I found it hard to believe he'd care that much about anyone other than himself and thought Roxanne must be independently wealthy to make him so fond of her.

"So?"

"I paid up and hoped she might be a bit loyal in the jury room. I said I could give her something extra if things went my way. I suggested a once-off lump sum. The last thing I wanted was to get rid of her before the trial ended."

Our drinks arrived.

"Why did you meet Dorothy Whittaker in the park the day before Rachel died?"

It seemed like a long time ago now, the first day with some spring warmth, when the path ahead seemed clear.

"I had some information for her about the company's investments, why?"

Could it have been as simple as that?

"Strange place to do business."

"I was a little preoccupied at the time," he smirked. "I didn't know you'd been spying on me, Bea."

"I wasn't, I was having lunch." I blushed, his playful tone making me uncomfortable. I changed the subject. "Tell me about Camtrexonal."

He drummed the table with the fingers of his left hand. I remembered the gesture – a sign of growing impatience.

"We're hoping to launch it soon. It could be really big for us. It's a breakthrough, they tell me."

He paused then, making no attempt to hide his self-satisfaction, and paid the waiter, giving him an ostentatious tip.

"All we're waiting for is the licensing, and there's nothing holding that back now."

"What was holding it back before?"

"Sorry?"

"You said there's nothing holding it back now."

"I just meant it's been through all the legal hoops."

Was that what he'd meant?

"Was Rachel Deere holding it back?"

"What? Of course not."

"Why was Dr Whittaker talking to her on the tram?"

He looked confused and then suspicious.

"What are you up to, Bea?"

"On the day you met her in the park, I saw them talking on the tram."

"For God's sake . . . all right, I'd asked Whittaker to ask Rachel how the jury was taking the evidence, so we'd have a better idea how to steer it. She was my go-between."

He was getting irritated. I had a flashback to an evening

with him when he'd gone from calm to volcanic in half a minute. I remembered being a little frightened of him and withdrawing to the bedroom. A temper like that could make a person do anything, but no, Rachel's death was carefully staged. It was too calculated for a temper tantrum.

"Where were you when she died?"

"Seriously, Bea? When was that, a Saturday was it? I was down at the Royal Dublin all day for a tournament. Came in two under – that was a good round for me."

"Who with?"

"Raymond Rafferty and a couple of his colleagues. Nice meal and a few drinks after."

I thought of him swaggering on the golf course with his barrister. This country. Then I thought of Whittaker, a medic who was doing his bidding. "You could have sent Dr Whittaker?"

"What? No, I did not!" He was exasperated. "Why would I hurt Rachel in the middle of the trial, when she was still useful to me?"

That made unfortunate sense to me. It would have been more to his advantage to wait until afterwards to have her killed, when he'd got all he could from her.

"Ever meet a man called Bobby Loftus?"

He shook his head. I described Loftus, keeping my voice as even as I could, though conjuring up his image filled me with fear.

"No. Why?"

I didn't answer. I was sure he knew about the kidnapping, but talking to him about it would be too much to bear.

"What about Graham O'Donoghue? He was a patient in St Lucian's too."

"Graham? No, I don't remember anyone called Graham. We didn't see all that much of the other patients, only in group session."

"Except Rachel, of course."

He smirked again and looked at his watch.

"I'm going to have to go now, Bea. I hope our chat has been of some comfort to you. "

I looked directly into those blue eyes that I remembered so well and tried to ascertain whether he actually believed the words he was saying. There was only coldness there.

"Why?" I asked.

"I have to meet somebody."

"No. Why did you do it Leo?"

He pressed his lips together and shrugged those shoulders again.

"I needed the money. That was all. But I was sorry, I am sorry, about Laurence."

We said our goodbyes and I picked up my bag and left the bar, but did not exit the hotel. I stayed in the foyer, kept out of sight and waited for him to leave.

He crossed the foyer, nodded in the direction of the concierge and left without seeing me. I followed him. He went out onto St Stephen's Green, turned right and then right again onto Kildare Street. I kept my distance, stopping once to look at a restaurant menu when he paused and patted down his pockets.

On Molesworth Street, he stopped outside Buswell's Hotel. I lingered at the corner, waiting to see if he'd go in.

He took out his phone and spoke to someone. Then a man approached him, and they shook hands and went inside. From where I stood, I could not make out who it was. I walked quickly past the hotel and glanced in the window. O'Farrell was sitting facing out and the other man, in a grey suit, had his back to me. I hoped he didn't see me.

Further on, I put my hand out for a taxi and asked the driver to take me to Oxmantown Road. I texted Gabriel to let him know I was on my way.

My shoulders ached with tension. I'd done it – I had looked Leo in the eye and called him a murderer. But what had I gained? Nothing, as far as I could tell, that would help to put him behind bars. My efforts had been wasted.

Chapter 27

Tuesday, 6ᵗʰ May 2014

When Gabriel opened the door of 9 Oxmantown Road to me, the smile on his face was born of pure relief.

He pulled back a chair for me at the kitchen table and held it until I sat down. Matt McCann was sitting opposite and there was an opened bottle of whiskey and two glasses on the table.

"There yeh' are," Matt said.

Gabriel fixed a tea for me. I wrapped my hands around its warmth for comfort and took a deep breath before speaking.

"I couldn't get anything out of him on the murder, not one useful thing, nothing. He has a strong alibi and good witnesses – all from the Bar."

"I never thought he did it himself," Matt said.

The two men exchanged glances. Their disappointment was obvious. I had failed to deliver. I'd got too caught up in my own past and hadn't been clever enough to trap O'Farrell. I began to feel perversely angry at them both. They'd been listening in while I'd revisited the most difficult time in my life, and though I knew Gabriel would have already filled Matt in on the details, I felt exposed.

"I know what you're thinking – I wasn't up to the job."

"That's not true, Bea, you got him to say plenty, even about Rachel Deere blackmailing him," Gabriel said.

"Very useful," Matt agreed. "It's just, with your history, you mightn't see things as clearly as you think."

"Is that right?" I put the mug down on the table with a little too much force. "Do you think I'm stupid, is that it?"

"Ah no Bea, we're not thinking that, it's just . . . " Gabriel's tone was gentle, as though he was humouring me.

They exchanged glances again and Matt put a hand up, a gesture aimed at holding off my now all too visible anger. It was wasted. I gulped down the last contents of my drink.

"Do you think because he fooled me once he could fool me again? For God's sake!"

"Ah now, you know that's not what we mean." Gabriel stood and took the mug from me, gesturing toward the kettle.

"I don't need more tea." My voice vibrated with emotion. "You weren't there. If you had been, you'd understand."

I wasn't sure whether I was talking about my meeting with O'Farrell or about the past. All I could think of was that men were all the same – they stuck together and made me feel like I was on the outside. Even Gabriel did it, with his "lads" and his contacts and his friends of friends' network.

"What about you, Gabriel, always taking your phone calls in the hall so I can't hear you? What's that about?" I knew as the words left my mouth, they didn't sound wholly rational.

Gabriel looked flummoxed.

"That – that's just good manners."

When I looked down at my hands, I saw they were clenched and I noticed the bite of my fingernails in my palms. I tried to drop my shoulders and relax.

"Lookit, you got details from O'Farrell tonight that'll be

useful when we question him again," Matt said. "There's all sorts we'll be able to get him on – I can add interfering with a jury to that list now."

I nodded, he was trying to placate me, and I feared, all of a sudden, that I might actually cry.

"Okay, I think I'll just . . . "

I went into Gabriel's bedroom, lay down on his bed and waited for my pulse to calm. The meeting, I realised, had almost overwhelmed me. All of that hurt and anger I'd pushed down for so long had rushed to the surface. I had willingly exposed myself to that man again and I had failed. He had an alibi for Rachel's murder and if he ordered it, there was no proof. There was nothing O'Farrell had said that would help link him to anything.

The meeting had left me sickened, yet there wasn't one word he'd said to me that I was going to be able to forget. The conversation would play on a loop in my mind for a long time and I would analyse every syllable he'd uttered. And after that, I knew I'd rewrite the conversation in my own head, substitute my own responses with cleverer answers, my questions with more insightful ones, the kinds of questions capable of tripping him up, catching him out, hurting him, not weak questions that he could bat away with ease. I wanted to use my advice to Leona and punch something, repeatedly, myself perhaps.

After some time, Gabriel knocked on the bedroom door.

"Bea?" He entered the room. "Beatrice?"

I sat up.

"Matt needs a word with you before he leaves."

I dragged myself reluctantly back into the kitchen. Matt waited until I sat down, then inhaled deeply. He looked wary and reluctant to speak.

"What is it?"

"I should let you know, I wanted to let you know, the lads

301

got around to asking our two doctors about you today." He looked very uncomfortable.

"Oh?"

"Forester said you showed up at St Lucian's in a state of panic and told him you needed a break from the world. He admitted you as a voluntary patient and said you were being treated for anxiety and depression. You checked yourself out on Sunday against his advice, he said, and he hasn't heard from you since."

"That's preposterous!"

"We know that," Matt said. "But what we don't have is proof. At the moment, it's your word against his and Whittaker is backing him up."

"Of course, she is!" I thought of Precious and understood her fear of speaking out. I ran through the whole incident again in my mind – where was the proof? "Gabriel found me out on the road, escaping from the place, isn't that enough?"

"It's useful, of course it is, but do you see, Gabriel only knows what you told him."

I looked at Gabriel for back up.

"What about the text message they sent from Bea's phone?"

"She could have sent it."

Gabriel dropped his gaze and Matt turned to me again.

"Don't be worrying about it. I just wanted to let you know what's being said. I didn't say I believed them."

I looked away from him. I could feel my temper rising again and I couldn't speak for fear I'd lose control of it. Only doing his job, only doing his job, I told myself.

Gabriel coughed.

"Well I better go," Matt said. "I've to catch an early flight in the morning. I'm going to Leeds to visit the hospital Rachel Deere trained in. We don't know enough about her at all."

"Could you not just call them?" I said.

"I find the best way to get information out of a hospital is to use the personal touch. I can't be doing with the bureaucratic hoops they'd rather we went through. I'll only be a few hours over there."

He stood up, stretched and yawned. I wondered, for the first time, about his private life. Had he a wife and children he ought to be getting home to?

"I'll talk to you both tomorrow. Try and get some rest and, for God's sake, Bea, you've been very lucky so far – will you stay here with Gabriel until you hear from me?"

I didn't answer him.

Gabriel walked him to the door and I heard him make reassuring noises about making me stay put.

"House arrest, lovely," I said, when Gabriel returned, though I wasn't really unhappy about it.

I was exhausted yet wired from seeing O'Farrell, and from having to face up to him after all the time that had passed. What had happened to Laurence had seemed almost like a story I told myself or something I'd read in a book that had happened to other people. But no, it had happened to my family. It made me shiver to think I'd once felt O'Farrell's hands on my skin. And now Forester and Whittaker were twisting the truth.

"I wouldn't mind all that," Gabriel said.

"I should have thought about proof. I should have known what they might say."

"How could you have known?"

There was no answer to that. We went into the living room and I sat heavily down on the couch.

"I feel like I'm forgetting something," I said. It was something Matt had said, it had triggered a memory, but what was it? I couldn't think.

"Maybe a night's sleep might help your memory."

It was just after half ten and we'd both had such a long day.

"Maybe, but . . . "

"What?"

"The Dictaphone I took from Forester's office on Sunday! We never listened back to all of it. The recording is on your laptop, isn't it?"

Gabriel started to suggest that we should leave it until the morning, but stopped mid-sentence. Tired as we were, we both knew the idea of sleep was ludicrous.

He took out his laptop and set it down on the coffee table between us. I got a pen and paper, so I could make a note of anything I thought might be important.

Gabriel opened the file into which he had copied the entire contents of Dr Forester's Dictaphone and pressed play. I took my shoes off and folded my feet under me on the couch, leaning my head back on the cushion behind me. Gabriel took his shoes off too and put his feet up on the coffee table, the heel of one sock had a hole beginning in it.

"Needs darning," he said, when he saw me looking.

I closed my eyes and listened.

The doctor seemed to be using the recorder as an aide memoir, for his own use rather than for a secretary.

We listened as Forester reminded himself to recheck one patient's medication and to sign off on treatment forms for another. His voice was a monotone for the most part with occasional expletives, like steam release valves, when he realised he'd done something wrong or forgotten to do something. I struggled to maintain my concentration, as snippets of O'Farrell's words intruded on my thoughts and his smug face appeared before me. I had to open my eyes again to banish him.

About 65 minutes into the tape, Forester had begun making a note on a young patient he'd diagnosed with something called oppositional defiant disorder when someone walked into his room.

Forester didn't turn off the recorder.

"What has you back so soon?" His tone was mock-casual, a tension beneath it. He directed the person to take a seat. There was a sound of a chair being moved and the sigh of upholstery as the visitor sat down.

"Well?" the visitor said.

"It's going to be fine – all we have to do is prevent the news from getting out before the FDA give their approval, then everything will be okay."

"What do you think I am, stupid?" The voice was louder now. "What are you doing about her?"

"Play that again," I told Gabriel.

He stopped and rewound the recording.

"What are you doing about her?"

"It's O'Farrell, isn't it?"

Gabriel agreed. "Who's 'her'?"

I knew we were both thinking the same thing – this could be evidence linking O'Farrell with Rachel Deere's murder. That would mean her death was a conspiracy and that O'Farrell and Forester were in on it.

Gabriel checked the date imprinted on the file.

"This was made Wednesday, 30th April, four days after she died."

"Oh."

Gabriel switched the recording back on. Dr Forester was talking.

"I've made arrangements. She'll be picked up from Ballymoney and brought here. She can sit it out as our guest for a few weeks. Then when the FDA approves, and we formally launch, we'll let her go. No one will believe her anyway."

"Who's doing it?" O'Farrell asked.

"It's better you don't know."

"Well, no rough stuff, okay?"

"Fantastic!" Gabriel said, swinging his feet off the coffee table and pausing the recording. "You know what this is? Evidence Forester was lying about you, and proof of the kidnapping."

He beamed at me with relief. I knew I should have been happy, but all I felt was revulsion at the thought of O'Farrell looking at me in court, knowing what Loftus had in store for me and letting it happen.

"How did they know I was in Ballymoney, Gabriel? I mean, only you, Georgina and Janine knew that?"

"He must have been following you the whole time."

I nodded. There could be no other explanation.

Gabriel restarted the file.

"Anyway, we've buried the data and there's no one else we need to worry about." Dr Forester's tone was casual now, as though they'd just discussed plans for a round of golf together.

"Right then." O'Farrell's tone had brightened.

"And once it's on the market, the share price will go through the roof." Forester sounded like he was smiling. "And you and your colleagues will have more money than you know what to do with."

Their goodbyes were considerably warmer than their greetings and then we heard the click of a button as Forester switched off the recorder. We listened through the remainder of the file. More medical notes followed and then the recording I'd made of the voicemail O'Farrell had left on Forester's answerphone.

"He must have decided to keep the recording of their meeting as an insurance policy," Gabriel said. "I'm going to ring Matt. This will be great ammunition for the lads, and you never know what Forester will say, once he knows they have this."

I thought of the Dictaphone Gabriel had handed over to Matt two days earlier.

"Wouldn't you think Matt's crowd would have found that on the Dictaphone themselves by now?"

"They've a lot on, probably haven't got around to it yet. We didn't and we're doing nothing else."

I wanted to say speak for yourself but resisted.

"Pity there was no mention of Rachel."

"At least they'll get them both on conspiracy to kidnap and hopefully on drugs fraud now. I'll call Matt."

He went out to the hall and I could hear him laughing down the phone.

I wondered what sentence O'Farrell might face. I pictured him standing in the dock with a new jury foreman or forewoman delivering the verdict.

All we needed now was to get him for ordering Rachel's murder, then they'd put him away for a very long time – for life hopefully – ordering a murder attracts the same penalty as carrying it out.

Gabriel clapped his hands together.

"Matt is delighted, says he'll get one of the lads assigned to the Dictaphone straight away. He'll call us tomorrow when he's back from Leeds."

I yawned widely and checked my watch. It was gone midnight.

"It's already tomorrow."

Gabriel sat down on the couch close to me. Our shoulders were just touching, and I could feel the warmth of his leg, the heat of the muscle, leaning against mine. We sat still like that for a few minutes, neither of us moving.

"You should go to bed," Gabriel said, after a while.

I got up and moved to the door. He stayed where he was.

"Goodnight," I said, without turning to him. I was not sure what I might do if I looked into his face.

Chapter 28

Wednesday, 7th May 2014

Something had made me restless during the night. It was a question, but I just didn't know what it was. I lay in bed, shortly after dawn and tried to figure it out. There was some information I knew I was aware of, and yet I couldn't consciously bring it to mind – it was just over the horizon of my thoughts but every time I reached for it, it moved away.

I tried not to focus on it, in the hope it would bubble to the surface unaided, but that didn't work. Then I tried distracting myself by singing the lyrics of 'Dreams' by Fleetwood Mac in my head. It was one of Laurence's favourites. I sang each perfect word, almost hearing the lilt of his voice, seeing the embarrassed grin he'd turn on me when he realised I was standing at his bedroom door listening.

I must have dozed then because when I woke up I was once again conscious of being in Gabriel's bedroom. It was after nine. I showered and dressed quickly, grateful for the en suite, before presenting myself for breakfast.

Gabriel was making a pot of tea and toast when I walked into the kitchen.

"Up long?" I asked him.

"About an hour, got a text from Matt – he's at Meadowwood Park already."

Something clicked in my brain.

"Say that again."

"About an hour –"

"No, no the hospital."

"Meadowwood Park."

Where had I heard it mentioned before?

Gabriel began to speak but I shushed him, closed my eyes and said the words to myself again.

"Meadowwood Park, Meadowwood Park." I had a picture in my head – green grass, and squares of colour, tartan, a tartan picnic rug.

"Meadowwood Park."

I could hear the words now in the voice of Dr Alastair McAuliffe. I opened my eyes.

"There was a locum at St Lucian's, remember, did we ever find out who that was?"

Gabriel said he didn't think so.

"Rachel met a locum and she didn't like him."

"And?"

"She trained at Meadowwood and so did Alastair McAuliffe – he told me that – what if she knew him from before?"

Gabriel looked perplexed – his mind on St Lucian's.

"Janine's boyfriend? The one with the temper." I tried not to sound impatient.

"That fecker?"

"Yes, and Alastair's a psychiatrist remember? He works at St Jerome's now, but he did a lot of locum work before that. And – " I bit into the toast. " – he told me he was going to make a lot of money soon, some scheme. What if Alastair was involved with O'Farrell's drug trials for Camtrexonal?"

"Possible, but – "

"They must have known each other." I was talking quickly now.

"God almighty . . . if you're right, it could have been him."

He grinned, and I couldn't help but smile back. Alastair had the medical knowledge, and if he was in on the drug trials he could have killed Rachel to get her out of the way, so the FDA approval could go through without anyone mentioning the Irish trial. Was he capable of it though? I didn't like Alastair – but murder?

"What about Janine? I should warn her."

"Warn her about what? We have suspicion, that's all. Better wait until we know more. I'm going to phone Matt first, he can check if Rachel and McAuliffe were there at the same time."

He nodded to himself, as though working through the implications in his own mind. He went out and came back with his laptop.

"In the meantime, see if you can find anything out about McAuliffe. He would have to be registered with the Irish Medical Council, wouldn't he?"

Gabriel went into the hall to phone Matt and I went onto the Medical Council website and searched the register of doctors. I found his entry under specialists. The registration date was 1st October 2011. That must have been when he came to work in Ireland. His primary degree was from Edinburgh University Medical School, with a conferral date of 1st January 1990. His speciality was listed as psychiatry. There was no information about where he'd trained.

I googled 'Dr Alastair McAuliffe' and his name came up under staff at St Jerome's Psychiatric Hospital. It listed his qualifications and said he'd trained at Midpark Hospital, Dumfries and other units, including Castle Craig and Gartloch, Glasgow.

"Including could mean anything," I said to myself. There was no mention of Meadowwood, but that didn't mean he wasn't there. If he hadn't worked there though, then he'd lied to me. I felt a jolt of electricity run through me as I read the next entry – St Lucian's.

I could be right.

I told Gabriel as soon as he got off the phone.

"Matt says he'll find out what he can. Says the lads got an extension on custody for Forester and Whittaker so he'll get one of them to drop McAuliffe's name, see if he can get a reaction."

So, this was how gardaí worked, the subtle nudge, the careful word, the softly-softly approach.

Gabriel sat beside me and I turned the laptop toward him to show him the entry for McAuliffe.

"Matt says Forester has his solicitor in and he's all ready to make a statement about the kidnapping. Whittaker will probably follow. Loftus is doing his usual act – saying nothing. They've picked up O'Farrell too. He's denying everything, but they haven't told him about the Dictaphone yet."

I felt satisfaction at the idea of O'Farrell being questioned by gardaí. I could picture him in some magnolia-painted room that smelled of antiseptic and dead air. He'd be drinking weak coffee from a Styrofoam cup and he'd find out that I had something to do with his being there. That gave me the most satisfaction of all.

Gabriel tapped the screen of his laptop with one finger.

"How old did you say McAuliffe was?"

"I think Janine told me he was forty-two."

"Must have been a boy genius," he said, pointing to the conferral date – 1990. "That would mean he was eighteen when he qualified in medicine."

He had either lied to Janine about his age or to the

312

Medical Council, so more lies – the question was why?

"Don't doctors have to provide certificates and all sorts when they come here to be registered?"

"It could just be a mistake. I think we should call over and ask to inspect the originals," Gabriel said.

"What about Janine? I really should warn her."

Gabriel shook his head. "Don't do that yet – there might be no need and, if there is, McAuliffe might get suspicious. Give her a call there and find out where she is now."

I took Gabriel's phone from him and dialled Janine's number. I was relieved when she chirped a hello after a couple of rings.

"Where are you?"

"Work of course – is everything all right?"

I checked my watch, just gone ten, and realised she would be preparing to go into court. I had almost forgotten that the CCJ was rolling on, hearing the next case and the next and the next.

"Could you meet me in Ryan's after work, say half five?"

She was hesitant. "Is everything all right?"

"I just need to talk to you. You won't be going out for lunch, will you?"

"I can't see how I'd manage that, when I'm doing the Giffney case on my own." Impatience, like a tight string twanged through her voice. Then she sighed. "Look okay, I'll meet you in Ryan's then, but not for long. I have plans with Alastair."

I thanked her and said goodbye. It was a relief to know she would be busy and safe for the day. I was glad too, that we could keep ourselves occupied going to the Medical Council. I did not relish the idea of sitting in until Matt returned from Leeds.

The Medical Council office was in a Georgian building at the end of a lane off Fitzwilliam Place. It had been extended with modern structures to the rear. The receptionist was initially helpful, then curt when we asked about registration records, then helpful again when Gabriel said he was a guard.

"You'll have to stop doing that," I muttered to him, as we waited in the cool, marbled reception area.

A young man in a dark blue suit approached us then and took us into an empty conference room. When we'd seated ourselves at the table, he presented us with a file.

"You may look at this, but you may not remove anything from the file and I'm afraid I can't make copies for you," he said.

"That's fine, we won't be long," Gabriel said.

We didn't open the file, but instead we both looked at the young man steadily until he began to reverse out of the room.

"I'll be back in five," he said.

The documents were not originals, but were certified copies, with an important looking stamp and signature on them. Before we examined them, Gabriel spread the pages out on the desk and took a photo of each one with his phone. Then he put them back in order and we began to look at them.

The first was a copy of a university degree from Edinburgh. We looked closely at the date of conferral and it did say 1990.

"Maybe he didn't want Janine to think he was older, might have frightened her off?" Gabriel suggested.

I supposed it was a possibility.

The second document seemed to be a training log of some sort, with a list of hospitals where Dr Alastair McAuliffe had worked as house officer and senior house officer and then a registrar. There was no mention of Meadowwood. His first Irish appointment was at St Canice's in Cork in March 2011.

"Maybe I misheard him," I said, beginning to doubt my memory. It looked like we'd come across the city for no good reason and I'd been ready to accuse Alastair of murder just because he had a temper. I was glad that I'd said nothing about my suspicions to Janine.

The other documents included a photocopy of a passport. I looked at a stern-faced Alastair with a serious beard, staring out from the page. The date of birth was 5th February 1972. Gabriel tapped it with his finger.

"Matt needs to see this." He took a photo of it again and attached it to a text message.

'Thanks' was the one-word response.

The young man reappeared at the door and coughed. We told him we were finished and thanked him for his time.

In the car, Gabriel suggested we get something to eat and then drop by Rachel's flat.

"We could talk to Dave and I could have another look around."

"It isn't possible that McAuliffe could have graduated as a doctor in 1990, is it?" I asked.

Gabriel shrugged. "There's something wrong all right, we just have to find out what."

Chapter 29

Wednesday, 7th May 2014

We ate sandwiches and tea at a coffee shop near the Botanic Gardens.

"When will Matt be back?"

"Said he'd be on the half three flight and he'll drop in when he gets the chance."

I took a mouthful of a roast chicken and stuffing sandwich so dry that I couldn't chew without a gulp of tea. I left it aside.

"Not hungry?" Gabriel took the plate from me when I shook my head and polished off the meal. "Have to keep up the energy," he said between mouthfuls.

We'd almost finished when Dave Wiseman came in and ordered a takeaway coffee.

"He's looking better," Gabriel said in a low voice.

He got up and went to the counter to pay.

"Dave, how are you keeping?"

He extended a hand and Dave shook it, looking bewildered. He squinted into Gabriel's face and shook his head.

"You mightn't remember, we spoke last week about Rachel. I was with the guards."

"Oh, oh yes, last week." Dave scratched his head. "I'm afraid it's a bit of a blur."

"Are you going back to the apartment now? There's something I want to talk to you about."

"Yeah, okay."

I followed the two of them out.

"This is my colleague, Beatrice." Gabriel waved in my direction and Dave nodded.

We walked the five minutes to the apartments on the Old Finglas Road, making small talk about the weather. Dave let us into an apartment on the third floor. We stepped into the narrow hallway and, when we passed the open bathroom door, I thought I saw Rachel slumped in the shower. I caught my breath and the image was gone.

The hallway opened into a light and airy space – a kitchen, living-cum-dining-room with a balcony beyond.

"It's lovely here," I said, admiring, through glass doors, the view of the Tolka River, the Botanic Gardens, Glasnevin Cemetery and the Dublin Mountains beyond.

"Can I?"

Dave turned a key and we both went onto the balcony and stood at the black railing that surrounded it.

"Is that Three Rock?" I asked, pointing at a distant shape on the mountain.

Dave shrugged. "I couldn't give a shit about this view any more – I hate the sight of it without Rachel. "

"What will you do with the place?"

"Go on living here. I can't afford to sell it at today's prices."

I felt for him, a young man tied to an apartment that he'd have been better off getting away from.

"You could rent it out and live somewhere else."

"It wouldn't cover the mortgage."

I sat down at a little patio table with my back to the view so that he'd sit on the opposite chair, looking out.

"I'm sorry about what happened to Rachel."

"Yeah, I've heard that a lot from people. And I know you mean well and all, but to be honest, your sympathy is fuck all use to me."

I decided it was better not to comment, but to hold his gaze as gently as I could.

"I was in bits when I thought she'd gone back on the drink – now I know she didn't and I'm in bits wondering why someone would want to kill her."

"What was she like?"

He looked into the distance, over my shoulder toward the mountains.

"Lovely, funny, exasperating, always kind, not a bit mean."

"How did she manage financially?"

"After she came out of St Lucian's she got a job as a carer – you know she was struck off the nursing register?"

I nodded.

"The carer job paid well enough, and she liked it, I think. She never complained, even when the hours were a bit funny."

"Did she ever mention Stephen O'Farrell at all?"

He hesitated.

"I know she wasn't supposed to talk about the court case, but she mentioned him once or twice, said he was a bit of a dick."

I thought of the page Gabriel had found with the payment schedules: 'Dick' and 'Doc'.

"Did she ever mention any of her doctors?"

"I think her main doctor was called Forester and I know she saw someone every week for a while after she got out. It could have been him, not sure. She did complain about another fella at the hospital, said he was a chancer." He looked over his own shoulder then and into the apartment. "Where's, what's his name? I told all this to the other guards."

"Yes, sorry, left hand doesn't know what the right hand's doing half the time."

He looked angry. "Jesus, I've great faith in you so."

He stood up and I coughed loudly. When we went inside, Gabriel was sitting on the couch.

"You said you'd something you wanted to talk about," Dave said.

"I was wondering if you found any other paperwork belonging to Rachel, anything from her time at Meadowwood? It might help."

Dave looked from Gabriel to me and back again.

"Just a sec . . . "

He went into the bedroom and came back with a small yellow notebook.

"Mechanic gave me this last night. I was going to drop it in to you."

He handed it to Gabriel.

"The mechanic?"

"He was doing a bit of work on our car – it was trapped down the side of the passenger seat."

"Okay, thanks," Gabriel said, and slipped it into his pocket.

"I couldn't bring myself to read it," Dave said to me.

We thanked him again and left.

"Make sure you give it to the right hand," he said after us.

In the car, Gabriel took the notebook out of his pocket and we examined it. It wasn't a diary, but it had some dated entries. The first was for 9th May 2013: 'Tired mostly, fed up, slept until lunchtime. Bitch of a nurse made me get dressed.'

"That's during her stay at St Lucian's," I said. I quickly scanned the dates that followed. Each entry seemed to refer to her mood on the day, with random incidents recorded.

On 25th May she'd written: 'Unbelievable! Ian Robertson is a locum here, wonder if they know what happened at Meadowwood.'

"Ian Robertson?" Gabriel repeated. "Who's he?"

Ian Robertson was who she'd complained of, not Alastair McAuliffe.

"But Alastair definitely named St Lucian's on his CV," I said, confused now. "Could it all just be a coincidence? Could I have got it all wrong?"

"No, there's something off here," Gabriel said.

My head was beginning to hurt. I should have forced myself to finish that sandwich. I checked my watch – quarter past three. What was I going to say to Janine now?

"Have we time to stop off at Phone4You? I really miss having a phone."

Gabriel looked sideways at me.

"Right so."

He switched on the radio. A current affairs show was discussing the arrest of two unnamed doctors from a private hospital. The presenter was speaking to a crime correspondent who, in an excited voice, told listeners that well-known businessman Stephen O'Farrell had also been arrested in connection with the same investigation.

"Sources say Mr O'Farrell was not very happy to find himself at the receiving end of Garda attention again, less than a week after the trial against him for fraud collapsed at the Criminal Courts of Justice."

"So, can you tell us, is this related to those charges?" the presenter asked.

"Sources are saying this is a completely separate investigation. We don't have much detail yet, but what we do know is it's related to his business, Rell Pharmaceuticals. There's also some suggestion that kidnapping might have been involved."

"Matt will be raging when he finds out there's a leak," Gabriel said.

"A fourth man, known to gardaí, has also been arrested in connection with this investigation," the reporter went on. "Sources say charges against them are imminent."

"Thanks for the update, Brian," the presenter said. "Now, did you know cabbage is good for your sex life? More after the break."

Gabriel switched off the radio and pulled in at the phone shop.

Inside, I managed to buy a smartphone, after browbeating a young shop assistant into accepting a supermarket delivery docket as proof of address – it was all I had in my handbag.

"Okay, but you'll have to drop a utility bill in tomorrow, otherwise my boss will be down my throat."

"I will," I promised.

I told her my old phone had been stolen and she said she could assign me my old number, but couldn't do anything about restoring my records.

"Was it not backed up?" she asked, aghast.

I felt as though I hadn't done my homework.

"I'll introduce you to the Cloud when I get a chance," Gabriel smiled when I told him.

We'd just pulled up outside his house when his phone rang. It was Matt.

"All right, sure, I understand." Gabriel switched off the engine. "He's a bit delayed, says we've to stay where we are until he gets here. He has things to tell us."

I checked the time.

"I'll give him an hour – I'm not going to be late for Janine."

My worry for her had been increasing. I sent a text to make sure she could still meet me.

'Fine, see you then,' was the brief response.

"What if Alastair is waiting for her outside the court and takes her away before I can get to her?" I asked Gabriel.

"Why would he? He doesn't know we're investigating him." He was being reasonable. "And Matt was pretty adamant."

He pushed his hall door firmly with his shoulder as he turned the key.

"Isn't it a pity he didn't just tell you on the phone then, instead of this waiting drama."

"I'm sure he has his reasons. Now, Ian Robertson, we should see what we can find out about him." Gabriel reached for his laptop.

"Why don't we go through the file again first?"

I took a banana from a bunch on the worktop in the kitchen.

"Do you mind?" I asked, before peeling it.

"Go ahead."

As I ate it, I found Rachel's medical file and began searching through her notes for dates.

"I can't see a Dr Ian Robertson anywhere here."

We both squinted at the pages and tried to decipher the names from the almost illegible scrawls.

"Hang on, I have a magnifying glass somewhere."

While Gabriel rummaged through drawers in the kitchen, I used my new phone to google Dr Ian Robertson.

His name popped up in a search result for the *Leeds Bugle*.

"Look at this!"

Gabriel sat beside me, magnifying glass in hand, waiting for the page to load.

'Meadowwood Drug-pushing Psychiatrist Struck Off,' the

headline read. I scrolled down and made the print larger.

'The General Medical Council has today announced that Dr Ian Robertson, formerly of Meadowwood Psychiatric Hospital, has been struck off the register of practitioners.

The move comes after last January's court case when Robertson was found guilty of selling prescription drugs. He was sentenced to 18 months in prison and, once released, he will no longer be allowed to practice medicine. Local MP Barry Staunton praised the swift action of the medical council.

"Of course, Robertson is not from this area. He moved down from Edinburgh in the last few years," Mr Staunton told the *Leeds Bugle*."'

The article finished with a recap of evidence against Robertson, including that £150,000 worth of benzodiazepines had gone missing from the hospital pharmacy over the course of his six-month tenure.

"Well that's interesting," Gabriel said.

"Rachel recognised him and then what? Do you think he's 'Doc'?"

"Makes sense. Let's check these notes again." Gabriel began scouring Rachel's medical notes for any sign of Robertson.

"Have a look at 31st May," I said.

Gabriel began reading.

"'Appears anxious, talked about checking herself out', and there's a signature after that, I can't make it out."

I took the magnifying glass from him and closed one eye.

"It's – it looks like Dr MA and then a squiggle."

Gabriel looked again.

"It's McA," he said.

"Dr McAuliffe?"

I checked my watch. It was nearing five o'clock and I was sure Janine wouldn't wait if she walked into Ryan's at half five and I wasn't there.

"I wish Matt had just told you what he knows over the phone."

Gabriel made a steeple with his fingers. His appearance of concentrated calm, so often a source of comfort, was annoying me.

"He's probably paranoid about saying anything over the phone now."

That was reasonable, I knew, but I couldn't admit it. "And he never said anything to me about bringing kidnapping charges. I had to hear that from the media."

Gabriel didn't rise to me. "Do you think maybe you should put off meeting Janine? Alastair might not be mixed up in this at all – just until we get more on Ian Robertson?"

"She's my friend, Gabriel. I have to do all I can to keep her safe."

I could hear the temper rising in my voice, but I was unable to stop it.

I took out my new phone and began punching the keys too vigorously, storing the few numbers I knew off by heart – Gabriel's, Janine's, the office, who else? Surely, I could remember more? Georgina? 085 677, no 085 657 . . . no, it wasn't there. When did my brain get so sluggish? I tossed the phone onto the couch.

"If the press knows about the kidnapping, it won't be long until they have my name," I said. Then they'll find out I worked on O'Farrell's trial. Matt should have warned me. I thought he'd warn me first."

"Sure, what choice had he got? He had to do his job sooner or later, you know that."

"You guards always stick together."

I could feel the colour rising from my chest to my cheeks.

"I didn't ask for any of this you know!" All of a sudden, I was shouting at him and, at the same time, wondering why I was shouting.

He stared at me, shocked. He moved from his own spot on the couch to sit beside me.

"It's been a tough few weeks." He used the calmest voice he could muster. It was infuriating.

"I'm not going to sit here any longer being patronised." I growled the words.

His face showed insult.

I ignored the urge to lean into him and let him put his arms around me, to draw comfort from the warmth of his body.

I checked my watch again.

"I'm going to meet Janine."

I didn't look at him as I spoke, but grabbed my phone and bag and walked out. He didn't try to stop me.

I attempted to bang the door, but its swollen wood caught on the frame and I could only manage a dull, dissatisfying thud. I sat into my car and banged that door instead.

I waited until my breathing settled before driving off.

My new phone pinged a text message.

'**Please be careful.**'

Chapter 30

Wednesday, 7th May 2014

In Ryan's I took a seat near the front against the wall, so I could see both doors. I ordered an orange juice and waited, trying to piece the entire picture together in my head.

Rachel Deere recognised Ian Robertson when he worked as a locum at St Lucian's. McAuliffe was working there on the same date – also as a locum. McAuliffe and Robertson had to be one and the same person. Instead of telling anyone about Robertson's past, Rachel had decided to blackmail him. 'Alastair' had paid for a while and then got tired of it, or perhaps she'd looked for more money to pay for her American trip. Maybe she'd got too greedy for him and he decided to get rid of her, so she couldn't ruin his new life. He'd called by her apartment, she'd let him in and he'd injected her with a fatal dose of alcohol. It would take a level of callousness that, even in my worst imaginings, I hadn't thought Alastair capable of. It made me shudder. I'd have to tell Janine everything as soon as she arrived.

If I was right, it looked like Rachel's death had nothing to do with the drugs trial at St Lucian's, nothing to do with

Camtrexonal or with Rell Pharmaceuticals and worst of all – nothing to do with Stephen O'Farrell. I felt ashamed at my own disappointment.

Janine was five minutes late, so I sent her a text. She responded: '**On my way**'.

I wondered if I should phone Gabriel and let him know what I thought had happened to Rachel, but I decided not to. If I'd worked it out, so had he.

It was hard to believe that Rachel's death was unrelated to the deaths of Graham O'Donoghue or Precious Alexander, but I had to accept that Graham's really was suicide, helped on by Camtrexonal, and Precious's was what it looked like, an accident. The fact that she'd probably been running away from Loftus at the time didn't make it any less so.

Ten minutes later there was still no sign of Janine. I wished I'd arrived earlier and gone to the court to meet her before she'd left the building. Gabriel and I could both have gone over there if I hadn't picked a fight with him. Instead I might have given Alastair time, and a chance, to get away or worse.

I tried her phone again. This time it rang out. I dialled Gabriel's number.

"She hasn't shown up, I'm going over to the flat. It was him, Gabriel, it was Alastair all along."

"I know – wait there will you? I'll pick you up and we'll go in my car. You can't go over there on your own."

I agreed to wait.

I nursed the orange juice and tried Janine again – no answer.

At five to six, I left my seat and stood on the street outside the bar. That way Gabriel wouldn't have to get out of the car when he arrived, and we'd save a little time. The traffic was heavy going down Conyngham Road, away from the city. Commuters were making their way home. It seemed absurd to me that Dublin was going on as normal, untouched by what was happening. The sensation echoed how I'd felt when Laurence disappeared from my flat all those years ago. I hoped this time I wouldn't be too late.

A car pulled up to the kerb, but it wasn't Gabriel's – it was Janine's.

"Thank God!" I said as I approached it.

Janine, sitting in the driver's seat, looked pale and tense. I could see the white of her knucklebones through her skin on the steering wheel.

I put my hand on the rear door handle.

"Don't," she said, in a voice so small she barely moved her lips.

I opened the door and saw Alastair. He was in the front seat footwell, crouched low and holding a hunting knife against Janine's ribs.

"Get in or I'll hurt her!"

I slid into the back seat.

"Drive!" he barked, sitting up.

Janine revved and tried to pull away, but the engine cut out. This is good I thought, the longer it takes to get away the better. Alastair pushed the knife closer to Janine's ribs.

"I said move!" he growled.

"You're putting me off," she said.

She started the engine again and began to move slowly out into the evening traffic.

"What do you want?" I asked.

"Shut up, you trouble-making bitch!" He was sitting almost side on to Janine, looking over his shoulder at me.

"I don't know what you mean."

"I found the memory stick this morning, the one you kept in the vase? Rachel's medical file was on it."

I was furious with myself. I'd forgotten I'd put it there for safekeeping.

"Then I got a call from the Medical Council, telling me someone was snooping in my records. I described you and that boyfriend of yours and they confirmed it."

"He's not my boyfriend," I said, before realising how irrelevant that was.

Alastair pulled his lips back in an angry, mocking smile, revealing perfect, sharp canines.

Janine drove us past Heuston Station – progress was slow in the heavy traffic. I looked out at the cars behind us and wondered if I could get someone's attention.

"Keep straight," McAuliffe said, when we reached the next junction. We were heading for the N4.

"Where are we going?" Janine asked.

"I've a lovely spot picked out in the Dublin Mountains for the two of you."

"Jesus!" Janine said, her voice at an impossibly high octave.

"You know you're going in the wrong direction?" I said.

"Shut up!"

He squinted out at the road ahead for a moment. The evening sun was partially covered with cloud and just beginning to sneak below the car's visor.

I put my hand into my bag as quietly as I could and tried to feel around for my phone. He saw what I was doing, quickly switched the blade from his right hand to his left, reached back and slapped me – one hard belt across the mouth. I wasn't fast enough to get out of his way.

"For fuck sake!" Janine shouted.

A metallic taste of blood filled my mouth. I found a tissue in my pocket and held it to my lip.

Alastair put his hand out. "Give me the phone."

I gave it to him. He opened the car window and threw it into the gutter. Two phones gone in less than a week – what a waste.

I looked out the back window. The Wellington Monument was receding as we left the city behind.

"I know all about you and so do the guards," I said.

"The guards know nothing – they're as soft here as they are in Leeds."

"I know you killed Rachel Deere."

"Fuck!" Janine said.

He didn't deny it and I wished I still had Matt McCann's microphone on me. I kept talking, aware I was antagonising him, and unsure of the consequences.

"I can understand why. You got sick of paying her and if she told, she would have ruined everything – you'd have lost St Jerome's and Janine too, probably."

He made a noise as though blowing fluff from a garment. Janine registered his disdain.

"Bastard!" she said.

He moved his hand as though he might hit her, but he thought better of it.

"Rachel Deere was a money-grabbing slut who deserved what she got," he said. "She would have bled me dry if I'd let her."

"How did you manage it, without her fighting back, I mean?"

His pleasure at being asked was frightening to see. It was as though someone had asked him how he cured a patient.

"I put a little something in her tea and waited until she was asleep. By the time she came round, it was too late."

"Toxicology didn't show anything."

"No, I timed it carefully. It was probably out of her system before she died."

I must have looked puzzled, because he obliged me by continuing.

"The shower? I gave the guards a story they could tell themselves, a dramatic distraction."

I thought of Rachel, how she'd been found with her knees bent up toward her chest, as though she'd collapsed like a rag doll. I imagined him carefully positioning her, the cold calculation of that hard to grasp. And here he was now, taking us both somewhere. I wondered if he had help.

Janine was making sobbing noises as she drove.

"Did Loftus help you?"

"Who? You mean that oaf who worked at St Lucian's? No. He called looking for you a few days ago when Janine was out. I told him you'd gone to that place in Ballymoney."

Janine had told Alastair. Why wouldn't she? I hadn't asked her to keep it a secret.

I wondered how well-worked-out Alastair's latest plan was and concluded it could only have been a rushed decision. I was wondering how to take advantage of that when Janine spoke.

"We're nearly out of petrol Alastair. I forgot to fill it up this morning."

"That's typical of you!" Alastair snapped, sounding more like a bitter husband in the throes of a marital spat than a kidnapper and murderer.

The Phoenix Park was well behind us now and we were on Tower Road. Traffic was moving at a steady speed.

"Next garage, pull in," he said.

Janine drove for half a mile until we came to a petrol station. When she pulled up at a pump, Alastair clamped his hand on her knee and held the blade of his knife against it. He turned to me.

"Get out, get petrol, pay for it. Don't say a word to anyone. If you're longer than five minutes, I'll start with the artery behind her knee and let her bleed to death."

"I've no money."

He looked like he might hit me again, but instead he reached into Janine's handbag, took out her purse and gave me a fifty-euro note.

I got out of the back seat and for a moment, considered running. I could go straight into the shop and tell them what was happening and call the gardaí. But what would Alastair do if I ran away? He would hurt Janine, kill her even – he'd have nothing to lose.

I opened the petrol cap and checked to see if he was watching before grabbing the diesel hose. It didn't quite fit, but I could get the fuel pumping and into the tank. I kept going until I'd spent the €50. I wasn't sure what the consequences would be, but it was all I could think of to do.

When I went inside to pay I spoke in a low voice to the cashier.

"Don't look out the window. I'm in the blue Peugeot, and my friend and I are in trouble. When I leave get our registration number and call the guards, okay?"

"What? What trouble?" The young man looked panicked. "Wait, will I come out with you? I'll come out with you." He began to move to the counter hatch.

I put up a hand to stop him.

"Please don't, he'll hurt my friend. I have to go. Just call the guards."

I walked back to the car and sat again into the back seat. Janine had tears running down her cheeks but was making no noise.

"Go!" Alastair nudged her with the blade.

She started the engine and pulled out into the traffic. It was then I thought I glimpsed Gabriel driving in the outside lane, six or seven vehicles behind. I resisted the urge to look back again, for fear of alerting Alastair.

We'd gone less than a mile when the car began to slow. Alastair let out a stream of expletives.

"I'll cut you right now if you don't speed up!"

"I'm trying!" She was leaning forward, pressing hard on the accelerator. "It's not me. There's no power."

The cars behind us began to overtake. Alastair started thumping the dashboard with his fist.

"Heap of shit! Heap of shit!"

Janine indicated and steered the car into the hard shoulder. It travelled on a few yards, before it spluttered and shuddered to a stop. Alastair's face was purple, his eyes bulged with rage and he shouted a string of unintelligible curses. He looked lost in a paroxysm of fury.

I quickly leaned forward, released Janine's seatbelt and pushed against her hip. She took the hint and opened her car door, as I released mine. Alastair lunged toward Janine as we both threw ourselves out onto the road. He managed to grab at her skirt with one hand and was trying to pull her back inside, waving the knife at her.

I landed on the gritty tarmac, hands and knees first. The traffic was a roar in my ears, and I could hear Janine screaming. I was struggling to stand and help her, when I felt two hands lifting me to my feet. I was upright just in time to see Matt opening Alastair's door and walloping him on the back of the head with a baton. He dropped his grip on Janine and his knife fell to the floor.

"I think he would have killed us both," I said to Gabriel.

He put his arms around me and I leaned against him. Matt helped Janine to her feet and led her to the barrier at the side of the hard shoulder.

Three garda cars pulled in then, one after another, sirens screeching, followed by an ambulance. Alastair still lay slumped across the front seats of Janine's car, like a dangerous animal temporarily subdued. A part of me hoped he'd never wake up.

Chapter 31

Tuesday, 28ᵗʰ April 2015

It was a strange experience, sitting in the body of Court 19, looking up at another stenographer in my usual seat, preparing to begin tapping away. It would have been impossible for me to work at this trial, much as I would have liked to – a witness cannot be involved in the operation of the court. Yet I felt I could have done a good job, I'd have enjoyed letting the words recording Stephen O'Farrell's conviction flow from my fingertips. I was pleased that at least Judge Reginald Brown was taking the case. It seemed fitting somehow that he should see this one through.

I watched as the defendants were led in – O'Farrell, Forester, Whittaker and Loftus. They stood in the dock as the registrar read out the charges against them. Listening to them charge Stephen O'Farrell, or Leo Hackett as he would always be to me, I felt that justice would be served.

"Stephen O'Farrell, it is alleged that between the dates of 5ᵗʰ March 2013 and 7ᵗʰ May 2014 you did conspire with Dorothy Whittaker and Niall Forester to commit a fraud contrary to the *Medicinal Products Regulations 2012*. How do you plead?"

There were other, related charges too and a standalone charge of conspiracy to kidnap that included Loftus. To each one, O'Farrell lifted his chin, looked straight at the jury and intoned "Not guilty". He seemed every bit the respected businessman he liked to project, but when the words had left his mouth, I thought I could see, for the first time, a little fear there.

I was not afraid. Leona, who was prosecuting, had shown me the book of evidence. They'd expert witnesses who would prove Camtrexonal had triggered the suicides in Ireland and there'd been investigations into the UK drug trials too, showing that medics had raised concerns and had been silenced. Camtrexonal was over. And once that became obvious from media reports, Rell Pharmaceuticals would be ruined. St Lucian's had been taken over and then shut down by the Health Service Executive. And the lovely Roxanne, who'd stood by O'Farrell so loyally during the first trial, had left him before the second.

I knew I would have to take the stand and not only answer questions about what had happened the previous year, but also be subjected to a grilling from Rafferty. He would try to insinuate my motives were not pure – and try to taint me because of my past relationship with O'Farrell. I knew he'd drag Laurence into the courtroom and try to use him. But I wouldn't let my brother be used again by Leo Hackett.

I was also going to have to give evidence at Alastair's murder trial, which I was not looking forward to. There had been constant publicity from the moment his arrest was announced. Janine had journalists at her door night and day for a while and had to move home to her mother in Kildare. We'd both taken a break from work for a couple of months, and when it was time to go back, we'd sought safe, dull cases at the commercial court. The sunny Janine, who only saw

336

good in people, hadn't yet been restored.

Alastair, or Ian as he really was, had been charged and pleaded not guilty. He'd sought bail, but gardaí had convinced the judge he was a flight risk and pointed out his proven skill at assuming someone else's identity. The case was expected to be heard in a few weeks' time. Matt had told me they'd got the location of Alastair's phone on the night Rachel died, and he was in Glasnevin, not in St Jerome's working, as he'd told Janine. They'd also searched his office and found a locket that Dave Wiseman had identified as Rachel's.

"Some sort of ghoulish memento," Matt had said.

The DPP was content to enter only the murder charge, leaving the other assault and kidnapping offences to one side for the moment. I was grateful – to be kidnapped once could be regarded as a misfortune, but twice made me seem careless.

We'd been rushed to hospital after Alastair was arrested and they'd forced us to stay for a few days.

On his visit that first evening Matt had filled me in on what he'd found in Meadowwood. He said he'd examined the exemplary record of Dr Alastair McAuliffe and was preparing to leave when the hospital administrator approached him. She'd asked why he needed to see the file and said how sad the staff had been when the great doctor died in a car crash in 2010.

Matt knew then that Ian Robertson had stolen Alastair McAuliffe's identity and his record so that he could practise in Ireland after he'd ruined his own career. There were only seven years between the ages of the two men and no one at the medical council had noticed that the dates didn't add up.

Gabriel, sitting beside me in Court 19, nudged me.

"You okay?" he asked.

"Yes, I am."

"Ladies and gentlemen of the jury, you have heard the

charges and the defendants' pleas. Please be here tomorrow morning at half ten, when Ms O'Brien will make her opening statement."

When we'd left the court, I told Gabriel that I didn't feel the need to return until I was called to give evidence. He seemed surprised.

"I don't think I need to waste any more time on Stephen O'Farrell," I said. "I'll be there for the verdict."

We took a drive out to the cemetery at Sutton and parked near the entrance.

"I won't be long," I told Gabriel.

I bought white lilies from the flower seller at the gate. He remarked that I was lucky to catch him. The side door of his van was open, and I saw then that more than half his stock of flower-filled buckets was in the back of it. He rubbed the base of his spine.

"Gettin' too old for this."

I thanked him and walked to Laurence's grave, six rows along, ten in. The headstone, like all the others there, lying flat.

'In loving memory of Laurence Barrington Died 5th June 1981, aged 25' was outlined in silver lettering on grey marble.

I lay the flowers down, their waxy petals curled back, revealing pollen-laden stamens. The fine orange powder was caught by the sea breeze and sprinkled on the stone. Above me, the melancholy sunshine of evening, laced the clouds with pink hems. There was a quality to the light particular to this time of day and this time of year – a kind of clarity.

"It's okay, it's over now," I told Laurence.

I said a short prayer for Rachel and Precious and Graham.

Sea salt on the air made my eyes sting.

I looked back toward the cemetery gate. I could see the car and Gabriel sitting at the wheel, waiting patiently for me.

The End

If you enjoyed this book from
Poolbeg why not visit our website

www.poolbeg.com

and get another book delivered straight
to your home or to a friend's home.

All books despatched within 24 hours.

Free postage on orders over €25*

Why not join our mailing list at
www.poolbeg.com and get some
fantastic offers, competitions,
book giveaways, author interviews, new releases
and much more?

 @PoolbegBooks

www.facebook.com/poolbegpress

poolbegbooks

*Free postage over €25 applies to Ireland only